THE SUMMER I LOVED YOU

J L LORA

Larimar

THE SUMMER I LOVED YOU

For information contact J.L. Lora at:
P. O. Box 47022
Windsor Mill, MD 21244
http://www.JLLora.com

Book and Cover design by Deranged Doctor Designs
Copyediting by Nina S. Gooden
Proofreading by Katie Testa

ISBN: 978-0-9994469-6-6 (eBook)
ISBN: 978-0-9994469-7-3 (Trade Paperback)
First Edition: July 2018

❀ Created with Vellum

the Summer I Loved You

A LOVE FOR ALL SEASONS #1

J.L. LORA

FROM MY HEART

This book is dedicated to all the moms, especially single moms. May you always have a love that fills your heart and consumes your soul. You deserve it!

PROLOGUE

Acacia Falls, MD
August 2007

She was about to shit on her own parade.

Adrianna Hayes forced her arms through the sleeve of her shirt and shook her wet hair. Her body still tingled from Cam's kisses and bites. She wanted nothing more than to cling to this moment. She stole another glance at the big rock and her face heated with memories of his fingers trailing her skin, the rough texture digging at her back. His wet mouth explored every nook, every crevice, inciting successive moans.

"What did you want to tell me?"

His gaze settled on her face, sending more heat to ripple over her chest and into her cheeks. For so long she'd dismissed him and those eyes, green like grass after the rain. Now she lived for the moments when she could see her reflection in them.

"Huh?" It was all she could come up with.

How did Cameron Blake, the constant rock in her shoe, make her lose her train of thought so easily these days? Easy. He did it in the same way he brought her frequent smiles, moments of sweetness and pure insanity. He made her forget what it was like being a Hayes in Acacia Falls.

He'd become her escape. The drug that transported her away from the small town without taking a step. He was her sanity, shutting the door on the monster's shadow. He was hers and hers alone. She didn't have to share him with half their high school.

His lips curved into a half smile as if he knew just what she was thinking about. "When I got here, you wanted to talk but...sorry about that." The smile deepened just like it had before he pressed her against a tree and pulled her shirt over her head.

He wasn't sorry.

Neither was she.

He shrugged his black Henley on and shot her a smile as bright as the sun. He was satisfied and happy, and she was about to ruin all that.

She pressed a hand to her stomach. "Tommy called. He's coming back tomorrow."

He paused long enough to drop the pressure in their atmosphere. The barely-there reaction roared louder than cracking thunder. "Did you tell him you moved on?"

She shook her head. He nodded and bent down. He didn't look at her as he put his shoes on.

Her pulse hiked, at a different kind of speed this time. Unlike minutes before, her heart wasn't racing toward the orgasm that rocked her body. This time it was a reverse spiral toward one of their ugly fights. Adrianna was desperate to steer away from any explosive argument.

"I'm going to tell him. I just didn't want to do that over the phone," she tried to reassure him. "I owe him at least a face to face. We were together since sophomore year."

"You don't owe him anything. Not when the guy was fucking all of Acacia High," he shot at her, derision etched in the curl of his lip.

"I know that, but I'm not him!" she retorted. She'd played the fool for two years. She knew it, the whole school knew it, but never again.

"You know what? Maybe you don't mind that. Maybe you still love

him, and you think he won't do it again."

He, more than anyone else, knew how to make her madder than hell. Adrianna swallowed her anger to reassure him.

"I don't love Tommy anymore. I am with you, Cam. I love you. I just want to tell him face to face."

He looked at her hand on his shoulder and then back at her face, "You've been with him for three years. He's been cheating on you, even with some of your friends. And you want me to believe you need to be face to face to tell him the truth?" he scoffed. "Everyone knows you and Tommy break up three times and make up four. I'm not going to be your in-between guy."

She didn't say anything. Because, you know, fuck him. How could he even say that to her? She turned away from him as the last three months flashed in her head like someone's life in their last moments.

"Wait. You think I broke up with Tommy to get with you, to then go right back to him again? You pursued me all summer. You told me you always had feelings for me. You made me fall for you and now you're throwing it in my face? You are basically calling me a cheating whore."

"I never said that, Adrianna. I would never think that. And don't turn this on me." He gave her a half smile. "You're the one that had a chance to tell Tommy to go to hell but didn't. Because you never intended to. I'm just your summer fun and summer's over, so it's back to the real world."

What a dick.

"Oh, that's the way you feel? Then maybe it's for the best this is over now. I don't fit in with the sophisticated Blakes anyway. So, do me a favor and stay away from me. You and your freaking necklace . . ." She pulled the necklace he'd given her over her head and threw it at him. "...can go straight to hell. I don't ever want to see you again."

She turned on her heel and walked away.

"You got yourself a deal, Babe. Better yet, a promise." He called after her.

With bitterness exploding all over her tongue, she turned around and looked at him one last time. "That's a promise I intend for you to keep."

1

New York City
Present Day

"Your father and I would like you to come to dinner."

Fuck.

A kink broke out in the back of Cameron's neck. He didn't attempt to stifle the curling of his lip. Instead he colored it with every single ounce of disgust the invitation evoked. He would rather spend a week being serenaded by the Fenway Park fanatics than two minutes at his parents' table.

"I'm a little busy right now, Mother. We can talk after my trip."

The humph from the other end came soft but loaded. Marilyn Blake never had to raise her voice to show her displeasure with her children. She always saved the screaming, yelling, and outward nastiness for her rounds with her husband Walter.

With her kids, she could convey her disapproval in small, covert-to-anyone-else noises that could still make them cringe but wouldn't qualify as abuse to anyone watching. Sometimes it was her loud charged silences that could make a priest squirm.

Cameron was almost thirty, freed from her clutches, and almost immune to her. *Almost.* Marilyn could still get under his skin in ways only her husband came close to.

"I have a lot on my plate with the show and I'm getting on a plane in a couple of hours. This can wait till I get back."

"There are art galleries all over New York City, Cameron. You are beloved here, the ace in the New York Emperors rotation, for God's sake. All the fine art galleries would have given you weeks just dedicated to your pieces. Your name would bring them a lot of customers. I don't know why you had to choose some unknown hole in the wall in D.C. for half a day."

He chuckled. "Goupil is one of the most prestigious galleries in North America. It's small but exclusive. They don't choose just anyone for a show. So, even though it's only a day exhibit, I'm going with prestige."

"I've never heard of it, but you should know what is good for you. You don't even bother to ask for my opinion or listen to reason. Like I've ever steered you wrong. You left a successful career to pursue a hobby full-time. I guess your parents don't deserve a heads up on their son's plans."

Heat stoked up on his lower spine, but Cam stomped on it. He was too old to let his mother drag him into an argument. No, he wasn't going to feed her need for drama.

"I left the game because I am done with it. I gave you ten years. I think that's enough. Anyway, I really have to go——"

"Cameron. We want to see you when you get back. It's not so hard. We live in the same city and we don't ask you for much."

The fuck you don't. You ask for everything and always give nothing but grief.

The beep of an incoming call opened the escape door. He'd be a fool not to go through it. "My agent's calling. We'll talk about dinner when I get back." *No, we won't. I'll book a trip to Siberia to avoid you.*

"Fine." She cut off the phone call without a goodbye.

Cam placed his phone in his back pocket, grabbed his iPad, and headed out the door. He'd call his agent from the car.

Any other time, his mother would have put a damper on his day, but you can't dampen what's already soaked in shit.

The prospect of traveling to Washington, D.C. had already done that.

He never set foot anywhere near Maryland unless the Emperors were playing the Orioles. And even then, he stayed in his room most of the time and hightailed it out of there like the Inner Harbor was on fire.

He couldn't pass up the offer from Goupil. Not if he wanted to continue with his life's passion.

His mouth grew sour. Acacia Falls was seventy-fucking-six miles away from D.C. *Still too close*. Maryland reeked of anger, sadness, and heartbreak. His ears still echoed with his parents shouting at each other. They had been more focused on their own vices, and hurting one another, than on their children. Marilyn and Walter Blake are the kind of people who should never procreate but did. Three fucking times.

Cam swore to himself years ago that he wouldn't make that mistake. He was going to keep his misery to himself and never pass the fucked-up Blake genes to anyone. That's why he already scheduled the vasectomy for the day after his return. The only children he would ever have were the ones he forged on canvas.

Washington, D.C.
The next day

It's almost over.

Cameron strained his face muscles to stay pleasant. Since he'd left Major League Baseball to follow his passion for painting, he'd encountered two types of people: those who were shocked that he could do something else than put up strikes on a scoreboard, and the sycophants waiting for the right moment to convince him to return to baseball. The general managers of the two local teams had come today, and something told him neither was interested in his brush stroke technique.

Cam wasn't interested in them.

He sipped the glass of wine and plotted a disappearing act. His publicist could take care of everything else. He would catch the next flight back to New York. *Screw marketing and publicity. You're not doing this shit for the money.*

The excitement of his artwork being on the walls at Goupil extinguished after the first hour. He couldn't even enjoy his dream of an exposition. He needed the distance, the skyscrapers, not the pleasant smiles or the *'welcome back, hon'* he got from everyone. He was on the front page of the Baltimore paper. The article dripped with sentimentality and purple prose describing how good it was to have the prodigal son back. And, of course, speculation that maybe he could paint and play another ten years while bleeding Orioles' orange and not the odious white and blue.

It was like his parents commissioned the hack-job article. He needed the fuck out so fast he was even willing to drive.

"Well, it's not very good if you ask me. He's done better."

The gasp bounced against the walls, dragging him away from the clutches of boredom. Cam, and everyone else, turned to follow the small feminine voice. His interest piqued for the first time since he walked in the room. No one had criticized his vision so harshly until now. The Arts Time editorial section had once tried. That article ended up making a name for him instead of breaking his art career. Goupil had called the morning after.

Well, this should be interesting.

Cam searched the faces around him. Then he looked down and there she was. Four-and-a-half feet of girl crowned by a mane of loose honey brown curls.

With sharp green eyes, her face was angelic, like one of Raphael's own cherubs. She wore glasses and an air of ten, going on twenty-five, years old. A whiplash contrast with her skinny jeans and blue Converse sneakers. Her long sleeve t-shirt had an image of Frida Kahlo's painting, 'The Two Fridas.' It wasn't exactly what you would see a child wear, and yet it was as natural on her as the golden raw sienna tinge of her skin.

Cam was a good reader of people, and he'd bet his last MVP bonus that the kid asked for the design on the shirt. He also knew he would put her face on canvas. He was already memorizing the diamond angle, her deep-set eyes, and heart-shaped mouth.

"And you are?" he asked.

"Bronwyn Alyxandra," the child said with so much pride he couldn't help but smile. "Mama was in her Jude Deveraux reading phase when she was pregnant with me. Don't ask." She finished with a wave of her hand.

Cam's mouth opened, but he found himself at a loss for words. Who was Jude Deveraux? Maybe a relative of hers? "Nice to meet you, Bronwyn Alyxandra. I'm…"

"Call me Bron. I know who you are. Artistic genius, nasty curve thrower, moody after every game, womanizing jock." She continued, "I read all about you on *Daily Mail*. Mama says I can't believe everything the gossip blogs say, but Uncle Nathan says it's *all* true."

Cam blinked. How old was this kid? "What do you say we get something to drink and continue chatting? You can tell me why you think my painting is not good."

Bronwyn's eyes narrowed and she shook her head. "You're famous and all but you're still a stranger. I can't go places with you."

She was smart. Cam smiled. "I didn't mean out. I meant get something from the refreshment table over there." He tilted his head toward the hors d'oeuvres.

She peeked at the table and then looked back at him. A smiled flowered on her lips and the air stuck in Cam's throat. He knew those eyes, that face, and mostly, her attitude. She also mentioned an Uncle Nathan, who'd talked about Cam. He didn't believe in coincidences. It wasn't hard to deduce who her mother was.

"Bronwyn, what's your last name?"

He didn't need her to say it. It was written all over her, in her every move.

"Arenas. Come on." She took his hand and began to pull him towards the table of goodies.

His heart slammed against his ribcage, his feet rooted to the ground. Arenas was Adrianna Hayes' mother's last name.

"What's your mom's name?"

The little girl's shoulders drooped. She looked away and mumbled softly, "Adrianna."

He almost staggered back. Adrianna must have taken her mother's name. Bron was her daughter. He tugged at her arm until she turned around.

"Who are you here with?"

"Um…" Bronwyn stared at her feet. He knelt on the floor before her and tilted her chin up with his index finger.

"What's wrong? You can tell me."

Worry clouded over her eyes and his cold, unfeeling heart bent a little. She had her mother's expressive, haunting eyes. He needed to get away from her. The last thing he needed was to see Adri again. *Fuck*, this is exactly what he had wanted to avoid.

She grabbed his hand tight into her smaller ones.

"They wouldn't bring me if I told them I wanted to meet you. Not Mama or Aunt Lauren. You were my favorite player and I just love your paintings so much, even if Mama says you're not even trying. Is it true? She said you're probably not even showing your best stuff." She paused briefly as if to give him a chance to answer but continued talking. "Anyway, I snuck out of school and took the train here. I only told my best friend Ayla because I planned to be back after recess."

It was amazing. In less than twenty minutes, this kid had rendered him speechless countless times. "Your mother must be worried sick." If she were the Adrianna he remembered, she was on the phone with the local police, the FBI, and the National Guard by now. "Do you know where you live?"

Her eyebrows snapped together. "I'm not a baby."

Her voice was so indignant, Cam mustered all the strength in the world not to smile.

"No, you are not. I can see that." Amazed he could keep a straight face at all, he cleared his throat. "Come on, let's get you home."

He took her hand and started walking, but she stayed rooted.

"Mama's going to be mad. Nuclear. She's going to ground me forever. She'll take away everything, like my salsa lessons and school dances. I love to dance. But, I'm okay with that because I would have to dance with boys. Boys are gross anyway. But I dance with Ayla and all my other friends. What if she takes away my pretty dresses or my painting supplies? What if she forbids me from painting again?"

He tugged at her hand to get her to stop babbling, "I don't think your mom would take away your art supplies, Bron. Even if she is um…nuclear, she wouldn't do that."

She nodded but didn't seem convinced.

He needed to give Adrianna her child back. The kid was making Cam's heart ache in the worst of ways. And he planned to do just that. Then he would get on the next flight the fuck out of the area and never come back. He would also get a lobotomy or hypnosis or Voodoo if necessary to forget this little episode. He would banish Adrianna to oblivion again.

Now, all he needed to do was face the past he'd put in the rearview mirror so many years ago.

2

Adrianna added another pink tulip to the bouquet for better balance, placed the candle holders on each side of it, and stepped back. She smiled. Every table was set with just a small variation on the center-pieces, to make them look unique but cohesive. Everything was as it should be, the walls and tablecloths pristine white, and the accent brick wall gave it a pop of color that made it chic, lived-in, and very Baltimore.

After five years, she still set the tables every day for opening. It was a pleasure, an indulgence, and it saved her money. She didn't need the staff as early. The only time she loved doing this more was during the weekends, when Bron was around to help her. Her daughter's artistic eye showed in her suggestions, and the customers got a kick out of their arrangements. She made a mental note of picking orange and purple flowers for the weekend. In the summer, there would be ranunculus and hydrangeas. *Let's see what Bron does with those.*

Adrianna went around the room, checking for garbage or dust hiding in the corners. *Mi Tesoro*, named after her greatest treasure—her daughter —was ready for the lunch crowd.

She peeked out through the glass panel. Canton Square was still pretty much empty, except for the late morning dwellers and the familiar figure sashaying down the block. She unlocked the door and her best friend, Lauren, walked right in. Ripped skinny jeans, sky-high stilettos and a white tank top with the words *Adios to the B. S.* clung to her skin. The shades, the shirt, the hand she held up, Lauren was in a mood.

"Don't say anything, I'm not human yet." Her friend strolled past her and made her way to the kitchen.

"Fine by me. I'll be in the office," she called out.

She'd barely made it through the office door when her phone rang. She placed it in her ear and began to riffle through her to-do tray.

"Miss Arenas?"

"Yes?"

"This is Loraine Walker, from La Salle Academy."

Her hands stilled. Why was her daughter's school director calling? "Did something happen to Bron?"

"Ma'am, please stay calm. I want you to know that we have dispatched a car there and called the police—"

"The police. What the hell are you talking about? Where is my daughter?"

"She left the premises. One of her friends says she went to a gallery in D.C. for some exhibit. This has never happened before. We don't know how she was able to sneak out."

"Are you telling me that my daughter bailed on school to go to some art exhibit? And you didn't know she left? Where were her teachers? Where was your security? And who did she supposedly go see..." It was on her desk, front page of the *Baltimore Galaxy*. *Maryland Son Returns Triumphantly*.

The blood drained from her head and the phone slipped from her hand, landing on the glass-topped desk. She had to find Bron. "Oh God."

She grabbed her purse and ran out of the office, heading toward the door, but it swung open and her daughter walked in.

Adrianna dropped her purse and ran to hug her. "You are so grounded, for like ever. I can't believe you left school like that. What were you thinking, Bronwyn Alyxandra? You're not ever going anywhere, not school dances, not even to the bathroom by yourself. You'll stay in your room forever with your books, where I know where you are at all times."

"Mom, you're suffocating me." Bronwyn tried to pull away from her.

"I'm so angry with you right now. Your friend told the teacher you left to go to an art exhibit. Where was Miss Winter? How did you get here?"

She couldn't make her hands stop roaming over Bron's face and body.

"Miss Winter got sick earlier and she had to go home. I would have asked her to take me, but this was my only chance to meet him." Her eyes drifted up and her head tilted back toward someone behind her.

It was then that Adrianna became aware that there was someone standing by the door. The looming shadow, the prickling on the back of her neck, the way her breath lodged in her throat. *Oh God*. Her head came up and face to face with the past. Summer days at the state park, kisses under the falls, posing for him by the lake, his body over hers, screaming fights…and heartbreak. Month after month of teary heartbreak.

Her lips parted but not even air came out. His green gaze cut through her and it was like time never moved. Except, his shoulders had almost doubled in size, filling his six-foot-three frame. His face no longer softened by boyish features. He was older, manlier.

"Cam." His name whooshed out of her lips.

"He gave me a ride here, Mom. He has a limo with a driver! It's nicer than Uncle Nathan's panty dropper."

Heat exploded all over her face. She looked down at the floor, urging the earth to swallow her. He was going to think she was a bad mother. "Language! What have I told you?"

Bron lowered her head. "I'm not supposed to repeat the things I hear Aunt Lo say because she's an adult and I'm not."

Adrianna ran her hand through her hair and looked at him again. Thanks to the scare, she probably looked a hot mess. "Thank you for bringing her. Would you like to sit down?"

He nodded, his gaze shifting between her and Bron. Adrianna's mouth grew more and more dry by the second.

She knew one day he'd find out and he'd come. She'd waited for this moment and tried to prepare for it. No, she wasn't ready.

"I'll get you some cake!" Bronwyn offered cheerfully. "Would you like coffee? I'll bring it!"

If she weren't dying inside, Adrianna would have smiled. Bronwyn didn't even give Cam a chance to answer and left him staring after her. Her daughter was like a tornado at times. "Sit down, please."

He turned to her and she almost staggered back at the intensity of his gaze. Adrianna's knees turned into jelly. She hurried to take the chair across from the one she was offering him.

His head tilted toward Bron. "She's amazing, smart, and so much like you. I can't believe how much she knows about art, brush strokes, and baseball. She told me she plays with her school."

Those were his first words and spoken with so much emotion the pressure in her chest built. She swallowed. "I wrote you. I wanted to tell…"

"My father told me." Cameron's voice turned into ice. "I guess Tommy is a great husband and father. You look more beautiful than ever and she's…everything."

"Tommy?" she asked. What about her old high school boyfriend?

"Yes, Walter said you called to tell him that you and Tommy were getting married and having a baby and that you expected me to keep my promise to stay away from you…"

Her stomach rolled, much like the last time they'd been together. She smoothed a hand over it and shook her head. "Oh God, no. I've only seen Tommy once since the day after I last saw you." She stood up. "Cam, listen, there's something you need to know."

"I have cake for you," Bronwyn announced, placing a thick, glazed slice in front of each of them and then addressing Cam. "What kind of coffee would you like? We have a lot of different kinds. Colombian, French Roast, Hazelnut, Ugandan—which everyone swears by and we highly recommend."

"Ugandan. Do you have milk and sugar?" Cam asked her.

She formed her lips into a pout and pressed her index finger to her mouth as if thinking hard and then pointed at him. "Yes!" She walked away giggling.

His mouth drifted open a little and he grabbed the corner of the table with one hand. He turned widened eyes on Adrianna. It was all written there.

Cam knew.

3

It was Luciana's expression. Cameron saw his sister on Adrianna's little girl's face. The devilish curve, the dimple, and the giggle his sister had yet to lose, even though she was in her twenties.

His heart set off into a gallop and his thoughts exploded into his skull. All the pieces swam around one possibility.

"How old is Bronwyn?"

"She's nine. She was born April 7, 2008."

His mind raced back to the summer they spent every second they could together. When he'd shrugged off baseball practice and scout appointments to sneak into her bedroom after her mother went to work. They'd kissed like they were starving for each other, fought like bitter rivals, and fucked like they'd invented it.

It had been the happiest time in his life. The aftermath of it was what Luciana referred to as the dark ages. He stole a glance as the child poured the coffee into a mug like she'd done a thousand times. She turned to look at him and gave him a smile he'd known all his life.

"She's mine, isn't she?"

Even as the question left his mouth, he couldn't fathom it. How was this possible?

The moments before her response were pure agony. No matter the answer, it would hurt like a baseball to the shin.

Tears shimmered in Adrianna's eyes and she nodded.

The blood furiously rushed to his head. His hand shook. He wanted to stand up and pace but was rooted to the chair. His world flipped upside down and Cameron drifted. When Adrianna's hand touched the back of his, he secured it in place with his free hand. He used her to steady himself.

Her teary eyes bore into his. "I wanted you to know, but your dad…it's a long story." She swallowed. "Can you stay? Let me ask Lauren to manage the bistro so we can talk."

He nodded, not trusting himself to speak. She brought up his father again and along with it, a rage inside him. Because Walter had known about this all along. He'd always encouraged Cam to stay away. His blood boiled and his hold on her hand tightened. *Walter. Always fucking Walter.*

"Here's your coffee," Bronwyn said to Cam. "Grape juice for you, Mom."

Both Cam and Adrianna removed their hands. Adrianna put her arms around her daughter, who looked at her tears and immediately frowned.

"What's wrong?"

There was such vulnerability in her voice and her eyes darted between them like she wondered if Cam had done something to her mom. Adrianna smoothed her hair and softly ran her hands over her face, smiling through her tears and for a second, Cam had to look away from the scene. He never forgot Adri's touch.

"Nothing's wrong. I'm just emotional. You know I get like that sometimes." Adrianna hugged her.

"Yeah. Like when I lost my first tooth and my kindergarten graduation?" Bronwyn turned to look at Cam. "She cried for a long, long time."

It hit him. He'd missed her whole life. For some reason a lump formed in his throat and he swallowed it back. "I bet it was a nice day."

"She also cried when I won the school art competition and when I made my painting of her for Mother's Day." Bronwyn said, coming closer to him.

His hands itched to bring her closer, to touch her face and make sure she was real. She couldn't be his. She was too perfect, too sweet. Instead, he balled his hands into a fist and placed them in his lap.

"Bron, would you like to keep Cam company while I talk to your aunt Lo? Then we'll go home."

Bron's eyes lit up. "Okay! Does this mean you're not mad and I'm not grounded anymore?"

"Oh, I'm mad and you're still getting grounded until the Orioles win the World Series." Adrianna leaned to pinch her cheeks before walking away.

Bronwyn turned to him with a smile. "I'll make her forget that she's mad."

Cam could see the hint of mischief in her eyes so much like his brother Chase's. "How?"

Bronwyn shrugged. "She can't resist this face." She leaned towards him and rested her elbows on the table with her face in her hands. The smile spread and her cheeks strained towards her eyes.

Even though it was a game, and he was not supposed to give in, Cam's lips curved on their own. *Definitely Chase.*

"Oh cool! It works on you too."

She leaned back and dug into the cake and juice she'd brought for her mom.

4

"What's your favorite thing to eat? What's your favorite thing to drink? What's your favorite painting? Where do you go for fun? Isn't Ed Sheeran the best? Do you know him?"

The questions kept coming at a fast pace and Adrianna was amazed that Cam didn't lose his patience. He answered all of them, rarely taking his eyes off Bronwyn. He was under their child's spell. Adrianna understood. Bron had bewitched her from the moment she'd laid eyes on her after twenty-three hours of active labor.

She kept her gaze on them as she worked on dinner. Her own inner turmoil was hidden behind the hectic stirring of her spaghetti sauce.

She'd pictured this reunion at least once every day. In none of those scenarios, or her wildest dreams, did she see Bronwyn proudly showing her father her artwork displayed in their family room.

Cam praised it, told her it was impressive, and Adrianna smiled. He too recognized it for the masterpiece it was. She had it mounted on floating frames and hung in the most visible place in the room, over the fireplace.

"I don't know. My wings don't look as good as yours did in your *Faceless Angel* piece."

Cam's gaze snapped to Adrianna. She smiled and nodded. "She actually does know all your published pieces."

"Yours are very good, Bron. You just need to work on making your strokes longer and dragging them out."

The little girl began to practice the movement with her right hand and he took it in his and guided it.

"Will you show me how to do it on canvas?" Bronwyn asked him.

"Of course. I will give you anything you ask me for," he answered and when his eyes drifted to Adrianna, her heart slammed against her ribs. For a second, she thought the offer wasn't solely for their daughter.

Don't be ridiculous.

She went back to her panicky stirring, hoping to hide the way her hands shook.

They didn't get the chance to really talk until long after dinner. Bronwyn asked Cam a million more questions. She got him to talk about winning the World Series, how to hook your wrist to throw a curveball, even more painting, and the technique he used to sketch wings.

She also filled him in on the people in her life, her cool aunt Lauren, and how much fun she had with her uncle Nathan, whom she missed like crazy since he'd joined the Peace Corps. Her aunt and uncle always bought her things, took her to great places, and watched shows with her. She also told him about her best friend, Ayla, and her school nemesis, Suzanne, who probably—she whispered—snitched on her to the substitute teacher today.

Adrianna got her ready for bed way past her bedtime.

When she was dressed in her pajamas, she came out of the bedroom and sat by Cam on the couch. She put her arms around him and kissed his cheek.

"You'll be here tomorrow, right?" she asked, uncertainty betraying her tone.

He brushed his hand over her hair and tucked it behind her ears, "I'll be here."

Adrianna's stomach sank lower through the whole scene. Her

daughter was sweet and affectionate, but she was that way with the people she knew. Why the sudden affection for Cam?

She lay on the bed next to her daughter, and Bronwyn cuddled her head on her chest, with her arms around her. It was their nightly ritual, one Adrianna refused to part with, though her heart was thundering and her insides shaking.

"You like Cam a lot, huh?"

Her little girl nodded emphatically and yawned. "He's nice and not that *A* bad word the girl on TMZ said he is. He stares at me a lot."

"That's because you're so beautiful," Adrianna said, pinching her daughter's nose.

Bronwyn looked up and put her little hands on Adri's face. "He stares at you a lot, too."

Adrianna sidestepped the statement. "Why do you like him so much?"

Bronwyn gave her a sleepy smile. "That's personal, Mom."

Cameron listened from the door and rushed back to the couch when the bed shifted and soft footsteps tapped on the hardwood. By the time Adrianna came out of the room and closed the door, he was rifling through the magazine on the coffee table, Bron's school catalog. She looked around the room, her hands clasped together like she couldn't figure out where to sit. He could look at nothing else but her.

He'd found out he had a child today, his world flipped on its axis, and it all came back to Adrianna. Everything about her was the same and radically different at the same time. She still had the same bright, wide-as-a-mile, smile. The endless shade of rich, creamy skin he'd sketched over with his tongue and once immortalized in brown ochre. The color came close but would wither next to the real thing, the *Faceless Angel Queen* forged from a burning red hibiscus.

Their eyes met, and it was charged, like lightning through metal wires. His pulse revved up enough to force a hitch in his breath. His gaze slid down her no-longer rail-thin, but fuller, curvier body. Her breasts were now larger than a handful and her thicker ass made his mouth dry and his slacks tighten. She was a woman, no longer the eighteen-year-old girl who dumped, broke, and cursed him.

Would her skin still be as soft against my lips? The blood rushed straight down, tightening his groin. He squeezed the catalog too hard, crumbling the paper. He smoothed it out and set it aside.

She took the other end of the couch. A full cushion was between them as she sat and turned to face him, with her legs tucked under her. It took all his willpower not to move closer to her. Too many things stood between them, but his fingers itched to lose themselves in her hair and to kiss her mouth. He needed to know if her lips still tasted like summer peaches and glory, or if his imagination had embellished her with every passing second. *No, I definitely should not touch her.*

Her voice jarred him away from his thoughts.

"I found out I was pregnant when I was about six weeks along. I wasn't feeling well for a while, but I thought it was something else, so I didn't go to the doctor until I was forced to." She pressed her thumb to her hand as she spoke.

"What did you think it was?" he asked, leaning closer, like a dog chasing the soft floral scent of her body.

"I was sad and crying a lot."

He frowned. "Why?"

She peered at him under her lashes with eyes full of yesterday's regrets. "You left."

"You told me to leave and never come back, Adri."

She nodded. "I know. I just never thought you would actually do it."

It had been the most ridiculous fight two people had ever had. His stupidity and quick temper that day still plagued Cameron.

Her gaze dropped to her feet. "I was seventeen and immature. When I got mad, I would tell everyone I didn't want to see them again. I said it to Tommy with every breakup. I said it to my boyfriend in first grade. I even said it to Nathan, that time we kissed when we were ten. You were the only one that listened. You, who followed me around all the time, chose the one time I didn't mean it to listen to me."

She shook her head and shot him a sad smile. "The next day, I went to Tommy's house early in the morning and told him we were never getting back together and I was in love with someone else. Your parents were there having breakfast with his. I figured they would tell you they saw me crying when I left and then I planned to make you suffer before I forgave you. I was so ready for you to come crawling and asking for forgiveness."

He looked down. "When they got back from Tommy's parent's house, they were talking to Luciana at the table and telling her you and Tommy reunited and seemed really happy. I told my father I would take the baseball contract and left that day for New York."

She waited until he looked up. "When I found out I was pregnant, I came by Mr. Blake's office. I told him I needed to talk to you, that it was urgent. He told me you had taken the contract with the Emperors. That you needed to focus on what was important. I broke down and told him about the baby. He said he would call and tell you. He called the next morning and said you didn't think the child was yours and offered me money for an abor—"

Cam didn't let her finish. He shot up from the couch. "I'm going to kill him."

Adrianna got up and went to him. "He's your father. You can't kill him…"

"No, he's not! He's never been. A father is someone who loves and supports you. I was just a pawn to him and my mom. I spent my whole life trying to please them and he convinced me to take the fucking contract. I never wanted to play. You know that."

Adrianna nodded.

"I'll kill him with my hands. He took everything from me." He clamped a hand over the back of his neck. "You don't know the things I did."

She crossed her arms in front of her. "Killing Walter won't give you any of it back. You can't get the time you lost with Bron, but if you kill him, you'll have no future with her either." She placed a hand on his shoulder and the other to his cheek. "Now you have a chance to be in her life and help me raise her. Don't let Walter take more from you than what he already has."

Her eyes sparked with warmth and somehow, they were closer than before. He rubbed his cheek against her palm. She'd been one of the things taken away from him. *No, he had been stupid enough to let her go.*

He reached for her, but she took a step back and cleared her throat. "We can work out ways for you to start getting to know her and spend time with her."

He stamped a foot on the desire surging through him. There were more pressing things they needed to decide. "Okay, let's talk."

5

Cameron's brain was clogged with so many thoughts and emotions, he found himself reeling. The door to the limo had barely closed, but it was like he'd been caged for years. He was practically jumping out of his skin.

Something he couldn't name came over him when he thought of Bronwyn. So small, so smart, so beautiful. If he had ever thought of having a kid, she's the kind of kid he would have wanted. But he'd never wanted a kid and now he had one.

With Adrianna.

He laughed out loud. Life sure played an ugly joke on him. All these years, he and Adri had had the strongest of ties and he hadn't known it. He hadn't known it because one person had kept it from him. *Walter.* His father had always been Cam's biggest nemesis. Cam didn't prepare to face the Red Sox with the intensity he had to talk himself into, just to go to his parents' house.

He'd taken the baseball contract to please them. How encouraging and proud Walter had been the day he'd left Acacia for New York. It was the only time in Cam's life when he had behaved like an actual father, instead of a tyrant who ruled over his children with an iron fist.

Cam had been fooled for a long time and even told himself how whatever he was suffering over his breakup with Adri was worth it because he'd made his dad proud.

It'd taken him six months to figure out the truth. That was when the money Walter had gotten illegally from Cam's agent ran out. Walter had been up to his neck in debt, with bookies calling around. Cam's ears still rang with the desperate calls from Walter and Marilyn, saying if he didn't pay the people he owed, they'd harm them or his siblings.

Cam couldn't let that happen. Chase and Lux were younger and he'd do anything to protect them. He'd completely thrown himself into preparing. He had no life except training and breezing through the Emperors' single, double, and triple A farm systems. Thanks to his talent he was one of the youngest players to make it to the majors. That's when the endorsements started to trickle in.

Walter had used Cam as his cash cow. He'd done it for years, getting into impossible situations with his gambling and forcing Cam to bail him out. It'd lasted until Cam had enough and set him up with a monthly stipend. He didn't want to deal with the phone calls, or the visits, or the worry it put on Luciana. He needed to center his efforts on keeping Chase from getting killed.

He'd parented everyone except for his child. *Bronwyn.*

All because he hadn't known. Because Walter kept her from him, so he'd still have access to Cam's money.

Do not call him. But his thumb scrolled through his contacts until Walter's name appeared on the screen.

"Cameron, this is a surprise." Walter always sounded like a debt collector. He was pleasant to start every call until you told him what he didn't want to hear, then came the threats.

"The surprise was all mine. She's a bouncing nine-year-old and laughs like your daughter." The acid churning in his stomach mixed with the wonder that still swirled in Cam's heart when he thought of Bron.

"Excuse me?" Walter asked, confusion stumbling on his words.

"I found the secret you kept from me, Walter." Cam wouldn't ever call him father again.

Walter's hmmph echoed through the line. "Now, Cameron, don't jump into conclusions. Let me explain first."

"Explain what? You kept a child, my child, from me." Heat clouded Cam's vision. He had to take a breather. "It's an asshole move."

"Watch your mouth, boy. You weren't ready to be a parent. Neither was that girl. You threw tantrums at the smallest provocation. What you were was a legend in the making and nothing was going to ruin that." Walter said.

The worst part was that his father wasn't wrong. Cameron had been an over-sized child at the time and, had he not been so impulsive in his fight with Adri, things could have gone differently.

But that didn't erase the wrong Walter had done him and Cam wasn't going to let him weasel or insult his way out of it. "That wasn't your call to make. It was mine. I deserved to know."

"I'm your father and I made the best decision for you. That's what a father does. He chooses the well-being of his children above everyone, including young girls whose mothers don't teach them the basics like making sure the boy wears a condom. You had a brilliant future and I wasn't going to let Fausto Hayes' brat get in the way of it. Plus, for all I knew that kid was Tommy's."

"You're lying, Walter. Adrianna went to you. She told you it was my baby. Tommy hadn't been around all summer."

"Women lie, Cameron. Even pretty ones with doe eyes and long legs. Who the hell knows who else she was opening them for? You couldn't have thought you were the only one."

The condescending tone made him want to punch a hole through the car window. "Adrianna didn't go around spreading her legs. I know she's not lying about this. You do too. You haven't even bothered to deny you knew."

That's what was pissing him off the most. Walter was cynical enough he didn't care that Cam knew.

"You think Adrianna doesn't lie? Then why didn't you believe her when she told you she had broken up with Tommy all those years ago? Because I remember you being really upset about it. You were so worked up, you signed a contract without reading it and left town right after."

It was a sock to the gut. Walter wasn't wrong about that. He hadn't believed her then. He'd thrown a tantrum and walked away. "I didn't believe her. You're right. I was stupid then but that doesn't change the fact that you exploited it. You encouraged me to leave and later, without me asking, you told me she married Tommy and she never did. She had a baby, *my baby,* and you hid it. Just so you could have access to my money. So you could milk me at your will whenever your fucking addiction got the best of you."

"I'm your father, Cameron. You need to respect me."

"No, you're not my father. You're not anything to me. You lied and used me. And since you deprived me of what could be the most important thing in a man's life, I'm going to take what's most important in yours. The only thing you've ever loved."

"What the hell are you talking about?"

Cam chuckled, the sound so ugly it turned his own stomach. "Find a way to fund your gambling elsewhere, Walter. As of today, the stipend stops. I'm taking your name off the credit cards. You won't get another dime from me. I hope you don't fucking owe anyone shit."

"You can't do—"

Cam didn't let him finish. He cut off the call and threw his phone on the other side of the seat. It began to vibrate again almost immediately. Walter's name appeared on the screen time after time. Cam ignored it the rest of the way to D.C.

***

Adrianna sighed and shot to her feet. She strolled to the window and looked out into the square. She twirled the stem of her wine glass around her fingers. Canton was practically dead on weekdays unless the Orioles or Ravens were playing. It was a shame. She could have used a little distraction tonight, and people watching probably would have done the trick. She wasn't holding her breath.

Neither music, TV, nor yoga had done the job of calming her

nerves. Usually, she could lose herself in the lotus, downward dog, and tree pose positions and let them empty her mind. But there was too much there. Too much emotion, too much fear, too much Cam.

He'd strolled back into her life with the finesse of a category-five hurricane, blowing everything all over the place. The life she kept as meticulously organized as her dresser was now turned on its side with all her feelings hanging out from the drawers.

This wasn't about her. It was about Bron finally getting to know her father and Cam finally knowing the truth. Adrianna just happened to be stuck in the middle, trying to shield her daughter from getting hurt and preparing for Cam's anger. It would come. She knew it would. He would want all the answers but she wasn't ready for that. Not yet.

The buzzing of her phone had her whipping her head around. Her pulse rushing, she stared at it for a couple of seconds. It couldn't be Cam. She wasn't expecting to hear from him until tomorrow. Plus, they'd exchanged numbers and she didn't recognize this one.

She crossed the room and grabbed it. She didn't even get to greet the caller.

"You just had to look for him, didn't you?" The thick voice was familiar. Not because she heard it every day but because Adrianna had only heard it a handful of times in the past ten years. It was flat and dry like surgical soap. Walter Blake was always frigid with her. He'd been that when he'd recommended she get an abortion, and with the same tone when he threatened to destroy her and her mother's lives if she went near Cam.

She should be used to his tone. She wasn't. She still got light-headed. Her knees gave out and her butt plopped on the ottoman. The wine swirled and spilled over the rim of the glass. Red droplets landed all over Bron's school newsletter. It was the same one Cam had been rifling through on the coffee table.

She took a deep breath and recited the same mantra she had for years. *You are not a pregnant eighteen-year-old girl. He can't hurt you or Bronwyn.* Except he could.

"I didn't go looking for him. I told you that if Cam ever came, I wouldn't lie to him." *Nice and steady, you have to stay that way.*

"Liar," Walter spat on the other end of the line. "But you're not going to get his money."

"I. Don't. Want. His. Money." She made sure to enunciate every word. "I don't need Cam's money or your family's. My daughter and I live very well. We're not rich like you but we don't need to be."

"Go feed that hogwash to someone who doesn't know a Hayes like I do. Your kind sells their own flesh for a few bucks."

Ice coated her stomach hard and fast. Yes, that had been her father's legacy but she had her mother's. Those roots were stronger. She'd always put Adrianna first and that's what Adrianna would do too. She'd always put Bron's interests first.

"You should know a Hayes better than anyone, Mr. Blake. But I'm no longer that. I also don't have time to talk to you right now. Don't call me again." She was so proud of how firm her voice came out.

"Walk away now. Send Cam away and tell him it's not his kid. You don't think I'll make good on my promises but I can go to the police any day. I will destroy you. You know I can. And what's going to happen to the kid then?"

The air wooshed out of her lungs. Anxiety scaled the walls of her chest but she banished it with a forced breath. Bron would never be alone. She had made provisions for that and she needed to stop reacting to Walter's threats. He was nothing but a sixty-something-year-old bully.

"Leave us alone. I didn't go looking for Cam. He came here. I kept quiet and never did anything, but I can't control what your son does."

"I don't care. You need—"

She cut off the call. She couldn't stand to listen one more second.

Her hand still shook and she punched the wrong numbers and had to erase and type again. She started talking as soon as Lauren picked up. "Are you still downstairs? I need to talk."

Thirty minutes later, after closing, Lauren sat on the other end of the couch, the spot Cam occupied a couple of hours ago.

"Adri, you have to stop getting all worked up when that old bastard calls."

"I know but I can't help it. He said he would make good on his promise. I can't let that happen. I just…" Adrianna buried her head in her hands and breathed.

"He's not. He's had years to do this and you've kept your end of the bargain. Shit, you made *me* keep that promise when all I've wanted for years is to go slap him. Plus, Cam knows about Bron. There's nothing Walter can do. Even if he could, Cam won't let him."

"Cam wouldn't be able to do anything, Lo. Walter can still hurt us."

"He won't. What you need to do is tell Cam everything. Why didn't you tell him today?"

Adrianna shoved a hand through her hair. "I don't know. There were too many revelations and he kept saying he was going to kill Walter."

"Listen, for the past ten years, that man has made you afraid. He's threatened you and made you keep Bron away from her dad. What he feared so much has already happened. Now all he's doing is talking shit. Don't let him scare you anymore. When will you see Cam again?"

"Tomorrow. He's going to come to talk about what will happen when he gets back from New York. I imagine he'll want a paternity test."

"Wait, what? Why? Does he have doubts?" Lauren started getting up.

Adri's hand clamped over her wrist. "I don't think he does but this is only normal. Athletes always have kids coming out of the wood-work. I'm sure his lawyers will advise him to get the test. We can't blame him if he wants that."

"I don't like him or anyone having doubts about our girl."

Adrianna smiled. *Our girl.* Yeah, Bron was Lauren's girl too. "I know but I don't want anyone to ever point fingers at her. I want it to be left all in the clear in case his parents decide to start something."

"His fucking parents. Tomorrow you need to cut all that shit at the root. Walter has to stop being a pain in our ass." Lauren leaned in. "How was everything? The bistro was so busy all day I didn't get to call. What else happened with Cam?"

Adrianna remembered their afternoon and evening, his interactions with his daughter. She smiled. "He's in awe of Bron."

"Well, duh. She's the most amazing girl in the world."

"That's what he said. You should have seen them. He couldn't take his eyes off her. They talked paintings and baseball all afternoon. He taught her stuff and talked about his playing years. It was a bit off because it was like he didn't really want to talk about that."

"Why would he want to talk about baseball? He found Bron..." Lauren shot her a saucy smile. "...and her hot mama. I'm sure the only thing he wanted to reminisce about was that summer and afternoons by the falls—"

"Stop. Don't put things in my head." The last thing she wanted to think about was anything like that. Because she and Cam would never be like they were that summer. "Cam wasn't thinking about that and neither was I. We just happen to have a kid together. He's just..."

"Your baby daddy? He was totally checking you out when you headed up here. And I dare you to tell me you didn't notice the way he fills out that shirt or, dearly lord, those arms."

Adrianna's mouth drifted open but her denial never came. Yes, she noticed how much bigger his shoulders were and how his pants clung low to his waist and those thighs against his trousers, or the pangs of raw need in her belly when he got closer...

Lauren threw her head back and laughed.

Adri shook the thoughts along with her head. "All he is to me is Bron's dad. There's too much bad blood between us. If he wants to be there for her, and he says he does, I'll let him but there is no way in hell I'm jumping into anything with him. Things with Cam always get crazy and we're stupid around each other. I'm a mom. Moms don't get to be crazy or stupid."

Cameron returned to his hotel room too tired, too wired, and with the day's events swirling around him. The call to Walter had taken the fight out of him.

He arrived in the city for one exhibition and in less than twelve hours, everything in his life had changed. He was a father to the most beautiful little girl he had ever seen. Her mother was the woman that'd broken his heart, sent him spiraling, and tainted him forever.

The last time he'd seen her, she'd been an angry girl damning him to hell. Now she was a mom and in true Adrianna form, she excelled at it. Just like she'd managed to always have good grades in high school, despite what was happening with her parents, she managed to have her own business while raise an amazing kid.

Bronwyn was beautiful, polite but outspoken, smart, dedicated, sweet and loving. Cam couldn't take his eyes off her. She was also a bubble in his chest that grew larger and larger. He looked out into Sixteenth Street. The quiet street should have helped him think but nothing could help him now. A child, Adrianna and everything he'd missed in the last ten years plagued him.

He needed to make sure he was there for Bron. He and Adrianna talked about the next steps. He would secure a house in the area and get to know Bronwyn and then they would tell her he is her father. He needed to travel to New York in two days, tie up some business ends and attend his next big exhibit. It was the last one on his schedule.

His cell phone flashed. Probably Walter begging again. *Fuck Walter.*

There were two people occupying every part of his mind right now, leaving no room for anything or anyone else.

The knock on the door yanked his mind off the little girl and her mother. He wasn't expecting anyone, but his hotel was exclusive and discreet. It wouldn't be some dumb reporter looking for an exclusive or anything like that. More than likely, it was someone knocking on the wrong door.

"Open the door. No one else wants to visit you but me."

Cam stopped midway to the peephole, smiled, and flung the door open to the man in the three-piece suit and brown bag in hand. "You dressed up for me. You shouldn't have."

"Shut up and move aside." Elias moved past him and waved the brown bag in his direction.

"How did you find me?"

"It's not hard when you know where to look. How many times did I have to come have dinner with you in seclusion? I can't believe you're still hiding out when you come to the area."

It jabbed at Cam's side. For the last ten years he'd come to the Maryland/D.C. area multiple times, only to confine himself to this hotel room and Camden Yards. Had he gone out or stayed with the team, he may have found out about Adri and Bron. It all seemed so stupid now.

"Hey, snap out of it." Elias pulled a six pack of beer from the bag and placed it on the table. The familiar white label with black letters brought back memories he didn't care to indulge.

Cameron ignored his question in favor of another. "Washington's top shark attorney, Elias Sanders, slumming like a high school senior? Did you really bring a six pack of Shiner?"

Elias laughed and cross the distance between them. He slapped a hand on Cam's shoulder. "It's really good to see you. I'm sorry I couldn't make it to the exhibit. Grayson had me chained to his side. I've never seen anyone more married to his work than my boss."

Spencer Grayson had a hand in everything, and his ventures were topped only by the Amazon empire. Elias often bragged about the important work he did for Grayson.

He gave Cam plenty to tease his friend about. "Hmmm. Sounds like you found your soulmate."

Elias popped the top of one of the beers and handed it to Cam. "Shut up. Why didn't you bring Sophia?"

Cam scoffed. "I haven't been dating Sophia in years."

"Who said anything about dating? Didn't I see somewhere she got caught by the paparazzi leaving your house recently?"

No, she'd tried to come see him, but Cam hadn't been home so Luciana had put her out on the street. "We're into gossip now?"

Elias tipped the beer into his mouth and then shrugged. "I just happened to open the *New York Daily* website and there was my college buddy's ex-girlfriend."

Sophia was the last thing he wanted to talk about. This day was too big, everything weighing too heavy, and the only female on his mind was a nine-year-old with a huge smile. Well, that wasn't true, there was also her mother looming in the background like Jupiter.

"What the hell is wrong with you tonight?" Elias waved a hand in front of his face.

"Sorry. Um…I got a lot on my mind right now."

"Like what?"

The painful bubble in his chest wouldn't let up and he would have to share it with someone. He and Elias went way back. Cam let the words fly out of his mouth. "I have a daughter."

Elias' gaze dropped to the floor for a brief second and when he looked back at Cam, he burst into laughter. "A kid? You?"

"I just found out today."

"You hate children, Cam. Even the ones that revere you and always ask for autographs. You never hit anything bareback and swore you would never have one. Remember that time I had to talk you out of a vasectomy? You were twenty-two."

Cam winced. It was true. Up until a few hours ago, he'd still been planning the vasectomy. It wasn't that he hated kids. He just never wanted to get trapped by some opportunistic woman trying to get an eighteen-year stipend.

You didn't hate Bron, though. Total opposite, since the moment he'd laid eyes on her, his reaction had been adverse to the usual. He'd engaged her even before he'd known who her mother was.

"I know I said all of that, but it's different. She's…different. She's smart, knows about art and baseball and…she's Adrianna's too."

"What? And she just showed up out of nowhere, saying she's your baby mama? Cam? Are you crazy? Don't tell me you're falling for this. This is the most common trap ever. Athlete makes it big and every gold-digging mama in the world sets on pursuit."

Cam pressed a hand to his chest. "No, the skeptic in me would have kicked in but she didn't know anything. Bron, that's her name, came looking for me. Adrianna was shocked to see me. She also told me of the times she tried to contact Walter."

"Anyway, women like that teach the kids all kinds of trick too."

Cam's jaw went so tight it hurt. Adrianna was not like that. Even if he hadn't seen her in ten years, he knew that about her. "Watch your mouth."

Elias lifted both hands. "Hey, don't shoot the messenger. People change, Cam. If your father didn't say anything, it's because it's not true."

Cam scoffed. "Come on, Elias. All Walter cared about was me signing with the Emperors and making money out of his investment, as he called Luciana, Chase, and me. He wouldn't have let anything get in the way of that."

"He was only being a dad. They meddle because they care. You need to be smart about this. No one accepts a child after all these years without a DNA test, and some explanations of why Adrianna didn't come to you. She could have contacted you without Walter knowing. Why didn't she?"

"You're right. She still has a lot to explain, but that kid is mine. I know it. Everything about her says something about me and my life. She laughs like Lux and she's curious like Chase and I see so many things in her. You know?"

"Cam… You were always kind of crazy when it came to that girl. You lost your head. You need a DNA test. And you need to get Adrianna talking. You were too hung up on her and that breakup. Make sure she answers all your questions."

Elias was right. Things changed. People changed. But could Adri have changed that much? Could she be a gold-digging liar like Elias said? Cam couldn't wrap his mind around that. There was also Bron. Everything told him she was his. That's what made this all so fucked up.

"I'm going back to New York tomorrow night and I'll reach out to my lawyers."

"Good. Thank God you're not that far gone. But make sure that kid is yours. I can recommend a place here. I know someone that works there really well. They'll be discreet," Elias said.

"I'll just let my lawyers handle it because they'll also handle the rest of the situation." Cam said.

"I can do this for you. It's not a big deal and you don't even have to pay me," Elias insisted.

Cam laughed. "That's generous. Don't worry. I pay the firm a lot of money. It's time they earned it."

Elias' lips went flat, a glare replacing the friendly look in his eyes.

Shit, he'd hit the sore spot. He hadn't hired Elias to handle his affairs, though he'd always intimated he'd gladly do it. He just didn't want to mix friendship and business.

"Suit yourself."

"Come on, let's get tipsy on that cheap beer."

Elias laughed.

After he left, Cam dropped himself into the bed. Yes, he would go home and settle things there and then he'd come back. He would have to arrange his life to include Bron.

His eyes drifted close and the question he'd been dying to ask all evening, but had not dared, popped into his head. Adrianna had not married Tommy, but was she seeing anyone?

6

Cam walked into *Mi Tesoro* the next morning, determined to get some of the answers he and Elias talked about. He'd barely slept and woken up earlier than he would during his spring training days. One of the waitresses pointed toward Adrianna's office and told him she was waiting for him. All the questions that had kept him up at night and tortured him into the early morning hours crashed together and went up in a smoke cloud when he saw her again.

Adri was standing behind a glass-topped desk, hair up in a no-nonsense tight bun, whispering to herself and placing papers into a tote bag. She didn't notice his presence and he took a second to watch her in her environment. He didn't get to see how she ran her business the day before, but the bistro was beautiful and tastefully decorated with some quirks punched in.

The office followed the same pattern. The pristine white walls with raw wood shelves housed cookbooks lined by subject. The ladder bookshelf filled with photos of Bronwyn, her mom, and friends, balanced and organized in a way only Adrianna could.

When she was his Adrianna, and he used to sneak into her bedroom, everything was organized and not even a hair clip was out of place. She was still a compulsive cleaner, but she wasn't his Adri. He didn't know much about this woman. Her summer dresses had been replaced by blazers and her wild curls subdued, away from her face. Only her slightly faded jeans broke the business monotony into chic. She'd always been like Sargent's *Madame X* painting. A straight line combined with a sex bomb. The most exciting of conundrums for him.

On the brick wall behind her desk, a large framed photograph of a laughing one-toothed baby Bronwyn stared at him until Cam smiled.

Adri looked up with slightly startled eyes like a deer in the woods. "Cam."

And there went his thoughts again. "You're going somewhere?" he asked. *Well, duh.*

"Um no. Yeah. The school called. Bron's not feeling well and she's coming home early."

The words were barely out of her mouth and he went still. What was wrong with Bronwyn?

She waved a dismissive hand. "It's probably some kind of bug. Kids get them all the time. I hope you don't catch it before your flight."

He didn't care about his flight. He could grab one at any time. "I'll come with you to pick her up."

"No need. Lauren is on her way back with her. She's on the list of people who can sign Bron out."

Of course, Lauren was on the pickup list. Everyone was on a list for Bron. *Except him.* He was her dad but got left out of everything.

"We'll go upstairs after they get here." She walked around the desk with her cell phone in one hand. "I have to do inventory and you get to entertain her and play butler to her," she laughed. "Be warned. She's as lovely a sick person as I am."

He remembered the one time he had to take care of her. The whining, snapping, and screaming. "Oh God. That has to be impossible."

She swatted him with the back of her hand. "I wasn't that bad."

His hand quickly shot out and trapped hers in place on his chest. Ironically in front of the heart she'd once broken with eight words.

I don't ever want to see you again.

In that moment, they were back in time, when she was the queen bee star of his wet dreams. All alone and eye to eye, it seemed natural and almost involuntary when his other hand reached for her waist and pulled her to him. Her gaze drifted to his chest and she grabbed the front of his Henley.

"I love that you still wear these," Adrianna said, bunching it in her hands and inching her mouth toward his. Her warmth breezed over his lips and he could almost taste her. His entire body buzzed in anticipation and he leaned into her and just as they were but a hair's breadth away, she released his Henley and turned away. His lips brushed against her cheek instead.

Why?

"Adri, we're here." Lauren called from the bistro and both jumped back.

Shocked, wide eyes stared back at him. Her hand pressed to her cheek, she turned and left the room. He followed.

In the main area, Bronwyn was pressed to Lauren's side. The little girl looked sad and sickly.

"What's wrong, *princesa*?" Adrianna asked, bending over and pressing the back of her hand on her daughter's forehead.

"I'm not feeling so good," Bronwyn whispered, her gaze on her feet.

Adrianna placed a loud kiss on her forehead. "We're going to go upstairs and Cam is going to hang out with you all afternoon. You can talk about painting and drawing. I'll make you *sopa de pollo*, like *abuela*."

"Her grandma's chicken noodle soup is Bron's favorite. It's going to make her feel a lot better," Lauren explained to Cam.

Bronwyn shook her head. "No, thank you. I'm not hungry." She shot Cameron a brief look that didn't go past his chin and then looked back to the floor. "I just want to be alone."

She walked toward the stairs that led to their apartment upstairs.

Adrianna turned to look at Lauren, a deep frown etched in her face. "What just happened?"

"She didn't say two words on the trip and Winter said she's been withdrawn the whole day. Winter also told me she didn't participate in art class," Lauren paused, "Sorry, hi, Cam."

He gave her a nod and a brief smile.

"She was really quiet this morning, but I thought she was just tired," Adrianna told them. "I'm going to talk to her."

Adrianna knocked on Bron's bedroom door and opened it. Her daughter sat in the middle of her bed hugging her knees with her head resting on top of them.

"Bron?"

No answer.

The uneasy pinch in her stomach grew. This was very unlike her kid. Bron was almost never sad and never stopped talking. "Is there something you want to talk about, *princesa*?"

"No, I'm fine," Bronwyn said not looking at her.

Adrianna placed her phone on the night stand and sat on the bed, facing her. "You know, I think we are more than mother and daughter. You and I are best friends too. Best friends confide in each other when something is wrong. That way they can help one another. I want to help you and you can always come to me when you need me."

Bronwyn turned to look at her with glistening eyes. "You can't help me. He's leaving you too, again." She swiped the back of her hand across her eyes. "I know Cam's my dad—" her voice broke off.

The floor dropped out from under Adrianna's feet and she was lightheaded. She wasn't ready for this moment. How could she explain everything that happened, and the secrets she carried, to a nine-year-old?

"Is it because of me that he doesn't want to stay? I thought he liked me, but he doesn't." Bronwyn's lip trembled, crushing Adrianna's heart against her ribs.

She scooped her baby up onto her lap and rained kisses over her face. "No, *princesa*, he adores you, like I do. He thinks you are the most amazing and beautiful girl ever. He's going to come back. He just has business to take care of and he wants to tell his family about you."

Her little girl shook her head against her chest. "He won't. He said he's going to take care of business. Ayla's mom never came back after she left on her business trip."

"He never left us. He didn't know about you. I promise you, my love, he will come back." Even as she said it, Adrianna prayed Cam didn't let them down.

She held Bronwyn until she fell asleep and would have been happy to hold her all day, but Cam waited outside. Her chest hurt, thinking of Bron torturing herself with this.

She got up to leave but her phone was flashing. She grabbed it and noticed she had an email alert from The Law Offices of Sanders & Associates. She frowned. The name rang a bell but she couldn't place it. Cam was outside waiting but curiosity got the best of her. She opened the email and scanned through it. Her body grew cold with each letter she read.

A formal request that a paternity test is carried out in order to establish whether Bronwyn Arenas is the biological child of Cameron Blake...

She stopped reading after that. A fissure formed along her chest sending waves of anger and shame through her. He didn't fully believe her. No matter what he said, Cam had doubts and for some reason that hurt like hell. She pressed her hand to her chest, trying to quell the pain and reminding herself that this was only normal.

You've been out of his life for ten years. This is a natural step like you told Lauren. Still, she wished she could feel nothing. Bron sighed and her attention was back on her child. This was all for her because she was all that mattered.

Adri used that to steel herself. She tiptoed out of the room and closed the door. Cam and Lauren waited for her in the living room. She exhaled deeply. "She knows you're her father."

"What? How?" Lauren asked but Adrianna's gaze focused on Cam's bulging eyes and pale face.

"I didn't ask her. She's too upset." Adrianna took a deep breath. "She thinks you're leaving again because of her."

"She thinks I left her?" He dropped to the couch and put his head in his hands. "I'm really going to kill Walter for this."

Adrianna stood in front of him. "We are not going through that again! Your daughter thinks you are abandoning her. Instead of concentrating on what you'll do to your father, why don't you start thinking of ways you can reassure her?"

He gaped at her for a few moments. "I'm not leaving."

"You have to go. If you arrange everything like you said, you'll have a lot of time to spend with her and you have to tell your brother and sister."

"Then maybe she can come with me?" he suggested.

Blood rushed to her head. *No way in hell.* Adrianna shook her head. "You're not taking my child anywhere without me. I don't want her anywhere near your parents. I won't have them shaming her," she almost shouted.

He stood up and they were toe-to-toe, face-to-face when he shouted back, "One, Bronwyn will never have to interact with Walter. I cut him off last night, so you don't ever have to worry about him being anywhere near her."

Adrianna's mouth drifted open, but he held up a hand to stop her from saying anything and continued, "Two, I wasn't suggesting we would go without you."

"That's what you said, and I can't go anywhere with you. I have a business to run."

The air was thick and both of them were more than ready to have it out.

"Let me play the devil's advocate here, no offense Cam," Lauren said. "Adri, you can go. I may not be as thorough as you, but I can manage the staff. You can do the books and the ordering from anywhere. You have yet to take a vacation this year and Bron will be out for spring break the week after next."

Adrianna shot Lauren what could only be defined as a death look and then began shaking her head. "That's out of the question. His exhibition is not until two weeks from now and Bron would miss an additional week of school. We can't be gone that long. I can't do this to you, Lo. You have exams for your certification coming up."

"I'm more than okay to handle it. I think Bron should go spend time with Cam and you." Lauren smiled and there was something Cam couldn't catch happening.

He didn't care though. Lauren was helping him for some reason. He would take that. If anyone knew how to make Adri agree to stuff, it was Lauren. They'd been best friends all their lives and you rarely saw one without the other.

He could practically see the thoughts scrolling through Adri's brain. She didn't want to go, that was sure, but he couldn't leave Bron to think he was abandoning her. He needed to be around his daughter. Adrianna would have to swallow her discomfort.

"I think that settles it. Don't you?" he asked, earning his own murderous look.

Adrianna pressed a hand to her belly and breathed. "Okay, fine. If you say that we don't have to deal with your father, we can go with you. Lauren is right. I can do the scheduling and booking remotely." She spoke through clenched teeth and her breath was choppy.

Cam was careful not to smile. "Thank you. I know it's not easy for you to just leave and I appreciate you doing it for—"

"Bron. I would do anything for Bron. She needs to feel secure and if what it takes is to be away for a few days, then that's fine. Tomorrow, I need to go meet with the principal about the incident yesterday. She wants to discuss it and make sure it doesn't happen again. I can talk to her about our impromptu vacation and coordinate with the teachers for her work and homework." The color in her face was darker and her eyes glowed like flames.

God, she was hot when she got mad. Cam dismissed the thought as soon as it came. Nothing good could come of that. *It would be a lot harder to dismiss the tightening in certain areas.* "I'll come with you and Bron to the school tomorrow."

Adrianna gave him a brusque nod. "Good. She will love showing you around."

Cam smiled this time. It was hard not to. He'd get to spend the day with them.

"I did some research. The Maryland Diagnostics Lab is twenty minutes away from her school. They can take us in after," Adrianna said.

"For what?" he asked.

She squared him with a look. "The paternity test. As your lawyer stated in his email, we might as well get the wheels in motion. You can run it by him but it's a legit place."

Lauren humphed low, turning cold, accusing eyes on him.

His good mood evaporated. She'd blasted it away with two sentences and fucked up his day with the rest. "Adrianna, I don't know what you're talking about. My lawyer wouldn't have contacted you without my permission and I don't need that right now. We can wait 'til New York."

She shook her head. "Elias Sanders is right. There's no point in waiting, as it's the norm in these cases. You can get the results while we're there. Let's just get it over and out of the way quickly."

7

"How did she manage to leave this place without anyone noticing? Everyone here knows her," Cam asked.

"That's what I'm dying to know," Adrianna replied, her gaze fully on their daughter.

Bron's cheeks bloomed into a pretty pink that almost made Cam smile. *Almost.* After the twenty-minute lecture from Ms. Walker, the school director, the danger of what she had done had punched through his senses. He'd been so caught up on meeting her and then finding out that she was his daughter that he hadn't stopped to think about everything that could have gone wrong.

Someone could have grabbed her or hurt her. Adrianna had been pale through the whole conversation. She'd been ruminating about all those things and worried about them. Guilt took over. He shouldn't have to be told about those dangers. He should be thinking about them. *You can't afford to go through life like you don't understand that there are people who can hurt her.* You're a father now. *Her father.*

"Well, we should be glad she won't be suspending Bron. I'm guessing it's because of your casual mention of a donation to the teams," Adri whispered the last part of the sentence just for Cam's ears as soon as they were out of the school director's office.

"She said it was because Bron is one of their most talented and usually well-behaved students. I'm sure that played a bigger part."

Adrianna scoffed. "Right. She's already envisioning you at the school fair and planning how much more to charge the people to attend because you promised that clinic for students on the baseball team."

"I was trying to be helpful."

She sighed. "I know. Hey, Bron, why don't you show Cam the art studio? I'm going to set up the petition for remote homework and virtual interaction."

The little girl's face brightened. Her eyes danced with excitement. "Okay, Mom."

She took his hand in her little one and pulled, but Cam's gaze was on Adrianna. Her hips swayed along with her purposeful stride. She'd worn a fitted dress that stopped at her knee. It was tailored to her form, with buttons starting at the collar and going down the length of it. It was sexy as fuck, leaving no doubt about the curves hiding under it. Her ass called to him and for a second, he indulged in the view and put everything else out of his mind.

"Come on," Bron pulled him the other way in the direction of a glass exhibit. "There," she pointed.

His head refused to move and he had to remind himself about the innocent girl tugging at his hand. *His daughter.* That's the word that managed to shake him from his lustful haze and in the direction Bron was pointing to. In the middle of all the sports and science trophies was the wood framed painting. It was Canton Square. All the businesses in the area were there and the yellow light straight from the sky shone above *Mi Tesoro*, like the treasure it touted to be. The painting was done by a young artist but the talent was there, raw, undeniable, authentic. Resting under the painting, was a hexagon-shaped award with an easel and a brushed etched in it and his daughter's name engraved in it.

He turned to look at her and her smile was wide. The lump formed in his throat and grew large. He knew she was talented. That was obvious from the work she'd already shown him. But seeing it here, recognized and guarded, it filled him with all kinds of different emotions.

It was just an art trophy. *What the hell was happening to him?* Cam had to clear his throat a few times. "That's amazing, Bron." He could barely recognize his own voice.

"Thank you. Mama cried. She always cries when I win something."

He nodded. "You told me." *But now I understand.*

"Bron, are you not coming to class today?" A raspy feminine voice called out from the other side of the hallway.

Bron's gaze moved beyond him and she smiled. "Miss Alexander."

She rushed toward the woman with Cam's hand still ensconced in hers. Even if Bron and Adrianna had not mentioned the woman several times, Cam would have known she was an artist. Her curly hair was held back by a scarf but it did nothing to hide the bright green highlights. Her jeans had paint splotches, but it was the printed top and minimal but big tribal earrings that called her out. She was a bohemian, a true one. Her clothes were authentically worn and not matched.

It was the kind of look women paid top dollar to recreate. That his sister, Luciana, often featured in her fashion blog.

Her eyes narrowed and she pointed at him. "You're Cameron Blake. I love your Cloisters Series. It inspired many day trips to New York. I'm Winter Alexander, Bron's art teacher."

Cam didn't get to introduce himself.

"He's my dad, Miss Alexander."

The woman's eyes widened, her mouth opened and closed.

"Bron, we talked about this. We have to keep it to ourselves for now." Adrianna rushed in and shot Cam an apologetic look.

He wanted to take her hand and tell her he didn't care that the whole world knew. But it just wasn't practical. It was sudden and the last thing he needed was the sharks from the press getting all over this while he tried to sort out how everything was supposed to work. "I'm sure Miss Winter can keep our secret. It's just until we work some things out."

"Oh, I won't say anything. Don't worry." Winter smiled.

"How are you feeling? Adrianna asked, adding, "Bron told us you went home sick."

The smile faded. "I'm doing better. I'm sorry about that. If I had been here, I would have noticed Bron was gone right away."

"You would have taken me to the art exhibit. Right, Miss Alexander?" Bron asked but she didn't give her a chance to answer. "We both love painting and she just paints without sketching sometimes. We talk about your paintings a lot."

Winter shook her head and the smile was back in place again. "Now I get Bron's interest and why you're her favorite artist. Not that you're not amazingly talented but there's always been extra pride in there."

Cam patted Bron's head. "I'm proud to be her favorite."

"You have to be really proud of Bron too. She's so talented. Her work in class leaves me in awe. She's a fast learner and dedicated to her craft. Sometimes, she and Ayla come to paint with me during lunch," Winter said.

"What do you paint, Miss Winter?"

"Just Winter please. I like to work on portraits mostly."

"She's also a sculptor. Her work has been displayed at *Artscape* the past three years. Last year she got her own booth. I bought one of her pieces for *Mi Tesoro*," Adrianna added. Cam intuited that the women were friendly and not just in a parent-teacher way.

Winter stared at her feet and fidgeted with the hem of her shirt. "Would you like to see our art lab and student stations?"

"Yes, I want to see where Bron does her magic."

His daughter giggled. The sound, so new yet familiar, did funny things to his chest.

"It will have to be a quick tour. We are running late for our next appointment."

Adrianna's reminder sent a cold wave through Cam. Their next stop was the laboratory for the paternity test. He didn't have doubts, and even though it was Adrianna's idea, it still felt disingenuous to go through with it. As if he was trying to deny the smiling little girl next to him. He'd been telling himself to get over it since last night. This was a logical and practical step. Anyway, Adrianna seemed determined this would happen now.

His lawyer said the place was reputable and affiliated with the ones they'd worked with in the past. They could work out an expedited result. Cam just wanted to get it over with. He was the biggest of assholes, looking at Bron in the eye when they were at the lab, trying to rule out she wasn't his.

Thanks a-fucking-lot, Elias.

A day later, they flew to New York first class. Cam still refused to go anywhere near Acacia Falls, even if it was passing through on the highway at seventy miles an hour. Even though the person he'd tried to avoid the most sat at arm's reach in the seat across from his, ramrod straight and staring out the window most of the time.

He couldn't blame her. Though the ordeal at the Maryland Diagnostics Laboratory was behind them, it was far from forgotten. He didn't know how they'd gotten through it. Her face had been taut throughout the visit to the facility. Her teeth clenched, despite how friendly the staff had been and the smiles she put on for her daughter.

His lawyers had arranged for a visit with the utmost privacy. One of them had taken the train down to accompany them. They'd explained the procedure and the steps they'd have to take later.

Do we need a test because you don't think I'm really your daughter?

Cam would have preferred a baseball to the head without a helmet than to look in Bron's eyes when she'd asked that. He wanted to say he didn't need it, but Adrianna had stepped in and explained that this was all routine like getting fingerprinted for a passport. The little girl had smiled and said she understood.

She'd moved on to ask the lawyer if judges were as mean as they seemed on TV. Anger bubbled inside him at Adrianna for keeping her a secret and putting them all in this position. He'd turned to Adrianna, intending to blast her with the venom inside him, but the tears she blinked away so fast stopped him. The slight tremble in her lip and death grip she kept on the armrest made him feel like an asshole for even wanting to unleash his anger on her.

She'd pulled out her cell phone and texted Lauren. Cam didn't make out the whole text but the words *mortified,* and *earth to swallow me*, were clear as day, even with a seat between them. Seconds later a barrage of messages kept her phone vibrating for a while until Adri chuckled and the tears disappeared.

They'd gone inside the lab room five minutes later. The rest of the visit was a blur, relatively painless. Now all they had to do was wait for the results.

But…

Adri had been colder with him since then. They returned to her place, she'd left him with Bron and gone to work. In the evening, they'd come down and had dinner at the bistro. She was pleasant but her only real smiles were saved for Bron.

Elias deserved every swear word Cam had vented during their conversation last night. He stopped short of telling him to shove his apology straight up his ass.

"Wow, is this how you always travel?" Bron's words yanked him back from yesterday's drama. "This is so different from when we went to Los Angeles or when we went to Atlantis, right, Mama?" Bronwyn gushed. Adrianna smiled back though it wasn't in her eyes. That damned remote look in her face had become a new annoying norm.

Cam just didn't get it. He had not pushed for the paternity test. But he had pushed her to come to New York, though she'd made it clear she wasn't one hundred percent comfortable with the trip. He spent the evening yesterday and all night worrying she would back out. He hated to put her in this position, but he couldn't leave Bronwyn to think he abandoned her.

He only needed a couple of weeks and he wasn't going to take any risks. He wasn't going to knowingly put his child in the position to wonder why her father wasn't around. Bronwyn never again would.

His thoughts were interrupted when a set of hands grabbed his face on either side of his cheeks.

"Are you listening to me? Am I talking too much?"

Eyes identical to his own blinked at him, a smile played on her lips. He doubted that there was another child in the whole world as beautiful as her. He shook his head.

"Atlantis is that awful place with the rides, right?" he asked.

Her eyes widened. "It's not awful. It's fun. Mama didn't like the rides and she stayed with Aunt Lauren by the poolside, but Uncle Nathan went on all the big rides with me." She lowered her voice and moved closer to him. "He even paid the guy to let me get on some of the ones I was too short for. Don't tell Mama."

"I already know," Adrianna said, looking away from the window and back at them. "I gave your uncle Nathan a piece of my mind after that." She leaned forward to be eye-to-eye with her daughter and asked, "How did you know Cam is your dad?"

Bronwyn looked down at the floor. "I heard you talking about it the night I found the magazine article about his paintings."

"When you were supposed to be asleep? I tucked you in! Oh my God, that's how you knew Cam was going back to New York. You eavesdropped on your Aunt Lo and me." Adrianna was so shocked that Cam wanted to laugh, but he strained to keep a serious face. He didn't want to ruin the moment of levity or the fact that she was no longer looking like she wanted to puke on him.

"I also read your diary from that year," Bronwyn admitted. "You said you were shocked by the growing attraction between you and Cameron. He was a nuisance, a pest, and worst of all the town bad boy. You were kinda mad at yourself for liking him." His daughter turned to Cam, "What kind of bad things did you used to do?"

He looked from Adrianna's flushed face and then at his daughter's inquisitive one. "How about a nap?"

Bronwyn crossed her arms in front of her and gave him a look worthy of her mother when she was in a mood. "I'm nine not two."

"I...I'm sorry. I didn't mean to imply that. I just thought you might be tired from the day." Cam worried he might have hurt her feelings.

"It's okay." She leaned and kissed his cheek. "I'm going to ask the flight attendant for a drink."

She got up from the seat and walked away. When he looked back, he found Adrianna staring at him.

"You're not going to make it. She is already playing you like a cheap guitar."

8

He'd fucked up again.

Cam pushed the door to his East Side townhouse open only to be assaulted by the blaring music and the familiar female voice singing at the top of her lungs that she's in love with the shape of someone.

"You do like Ed Sheeran!" Bron gasped behind him and it was all Cam could do not to swear out loud.

He took a step inside the foyer and turned to Adrianna. Recognition was written in her flat lips and the upward roll of her eyes. Cam sighed. This wasn't going to be good. And why should it be? Things never went the way he needed them to. It would be nice, though. *For once.*

He wanted to take Bron's hand to walk her in, and not just because he was afraid her mother would bolt, taking their child with her. He forced himself to step inside the living room where his sister lay on the couch, her iPad in hand, her foot draped over the back of the couch, still singing.

Luciana's gaze landed on him and the smile bloomed on her face. She jumped off the couch and headed his way until her gaze drifted beyond him. She halted, spotting Adrianna, and her mouth twisted into a lemon pucker.

"Oh God, not you again! Why would you bring her here?"

"Trust me, the feeling is mutual," Adri snapped back.

Here we go again. The high school rivalry between both women materialized all over again.

"Lux, calm down. I need to tell you something—"

His sister cut him off. "What is there to say? You went to D.C. for an exhibition and stopped in Maryland to pick this one up. Like she didn't mess you up enough the first time around."

"It wasn't…"

"He didn't pick me up from anywhere. And I messed him up? You don't know anything…" Adrianna muttered, her tone dry as a cup of sand.

Before Cam got the chance say anything, Bron stepped forward and extended her hand. "You must be Luciana. I'm Bronwyn."

Luciana took one look at Bronwyn, blanched, and backed away, plopping back down on the couch. "Oh, God. Oh. God."

Luciana's eyes ping ponged from Bron to Cameron and back to the little girl.

"Is she okay?" Bronwyn asked him.

He nodded. "She's fine. Just a little dramatic."

Adrianna scoffed, "You must mean a drama queen."

"Like Aunt Lo," Bronwyn said walking closer to her aunt. "But they were wrong. You don't have any warts and your skin is not green."

"Who told you I had warts?" Luciana snapped out of her shock and was on her feet all over again.

"Lux, we should get going before…"

His brother, Chase, stood at the top of the stairs looking down. His hair was over-grown, and a thick stubble covered his chin. It was his brother's vacation look and Cam would bet his life he'd been staying over while he was gone. Chase walked down the steps, his gaze landing on Bron and then her mother. The smile was instant and irreverent. "Adrianna. Even more gorgeous today. How is that possible?"

He passed Cam like he wasn't even there and headed for Adri, hugging her. Adrianna smiled genuinely for the first time that day. It made Cam's mouth go sour. All he'd gotten from her were surgical or tiresome looks.

I guess all the fond smiles are for Chase today.

Chase turned and saw their little girl. "Well, you're beautiful and I never forget a beautiful face. You are—"

"Obviously Cameron's child," Luciana spat.

Cameron sucked in a breath, his gaze snapping to his sister. "How did you know?"

Luciana waved an upward palm in Bron's direction. "Look at her. She's you." She then turned feral eyes on Adrianna. She took a step forward, shoving a finger in Adri's direction. "You had a baby by him and never told him? You're…"

"Lux—"

Adrianna jumped in. "I went looking for him. He was gone. All of you were. I told your father. Instead of helping me get to Cam, he got in the way."

Lux halted midway and shot her an incredulous look. "Father? Why would you tell our father? You could have contacted Cam directly or me or Chase. God, this is so like you…"

Cam wanted answers too, but that wasn't the moment. Not with the set of young eyes watching them all with curiosity.

"Stop. We can talk about this after we've settled down." His gaze drifted to the child, hoping all the adults would get the hint.

Luciana sighed.

"He means when I'm not around," Bronwyn whispered out loud.

Chase laughed and mumbled for Cam's ears, "Yeah, this little smart-ass is definitely ours."

He glared at his brother. "Can we all sit down and talk about this?"

Neither of the women made a move and Chase's eyes danced with mischief.

Adri cleared her throat. "Bron should eat something. If we get her something to eat, she can watch some TV and we can talk."

Cam nodded. "Lux, why don't you order us all something to eat? I'll show Adrianna the guest room."

"I bet you will," Chase said. Cam was dying to punch the smirk off his brother's face.

Except it made Adrianna laugh. "Are you ever going to grow up?"

Chase shrugged. "Growing up is overrated. My brother grew up and look at how boring he's become. Now you—" he pointed at Bron "—look like you're a lot of fun. How about you and I go watch some TV in the family room while these adults find us something to eat?"

Bron smiled and nodded.

Adrianna stared after Bron.

"Don't worry. They're the same mental age anyway. I'll go order us some dinner." Lux walked away to the kitchen.

"Come upstairs. I'll show you the room you and Bron will be staying in. The driver will bring your things upstairs." Cam started walking but Adrianna waited a few seconds before following him. He breathed a sigh of relief once she started moving again. She wasn't going to bolt. There was no way she'd leave Bron behind.

Still, the tight air between them was something he couldn't take for much longer.

Adrianna was both delighted and freaked the hell out.

Once everything was explained, everything took a whiplash kind of turn. It all had to do with Bronwyn. She won over both Chase and Luciana.

Maybe it was what Adrianna's grandmother used to say about the call of your blood. She would always say there was an affinity to people who shared your genes. That something in you recognized them, even if you didn't know their name. That had to be the case here.

They had been in New York for a week and already her daughter lived a completely different life. Cam and his siblings bought her all sorts of expensive gifts that would take Adrianna years to give her. Just earlier today, Luciana brought a catalog of children's furniture so Bronwyn could choose before she called the interior decorator.

It sent Adrianna straight into their home gym where she ran for forty minutes straight. It wasn't the Canton harbor side trail or the cobblestone streets of Fells Point, but it gave her peace, which lasted until her daughter intercepted her to show her the huge iPad Pro her father had gotten her. Adrianna loved the smile on Bronwyn's face as she told her of the new software to help with her stroke precision and the sketching apps Cam downloaded for her. Yet, she couldn't help the apprehension growing every minute they spent in New York.

It was too much, too fast, too intense. She needed air, lots of it.

"Adri?" Cam called out from behind her. Just the sound of his voice rasped over the walls of her belly. She turned around fast, only to find herself a few steps from him.

"What's up?"

His eyes lingered a little too long over her running capris and she fought not to fidget. She also wasn't going to linger on his bed head or the way his jeans hung loose. And she was *definitely not* going to notice the way that white T-shirt clung to his arms and torso. Nope, she was going to keep her eyes above his shoulder. Just nowhere near his kissable mouth.

You need air and distance, like blocks and miles away from him.

"You have a sec? I wanted to talk about plans moving forward."

She shook her head. "Huh? What plans?"

He shrugged. "Well, I was talking to my lawyer about something and when I brought up Bronwyn, he asked if I wanted him to start getting together the paperwork to change her last name and add mine to her birth certificate."

She tensed, the heat rising all over her face. He said it so calmly that she wanted to punch him. She took a deep breath and pushed the words through her teeth. "You talked to a lawyer about changing her name? Without telling me?"

"It just came up when I brought up her name, Adrianna. It's not like I'm going behind your back."

"That kind of stuff doesn't just come up. The test results have not come back yet. Why did you even bring her name up?"

He sighed, "I was dealing with some acquisition deals and eventually, I want to put some things in Bron's name."

"Without consulting me?"

"I don't have to ask your permission for every gift I give my daughter! You already have an opinion on all the small things we give her." His voice rose, his face taking a familiar dark turn.

She was more than ready for him. "Are you fuc—"

"Why are you guys fighting?" Bronwyn asked from behind her.

Adrianna shoved her fury into her back pocket. The last thing she wanted was to scare Bron. Arguments with Cam had always ended in one of two ways, all-out combat with words sharp enough to cut flesh…or clothes ripping and bodies sweating. There would be no chance of the second, so she needed to diffuse the first.

She rubbed a hand over her daughter's head. "We're just having a disagreement. No need for you to worry. You know I yell a lot."

Bronwyn nodded and peeked at Cam. He was shell shocked.

"Cam sometimes gets like your Aunt Lo in the morning when she gets no sleep."

"Ohhhh," Bron nodded. "Let's get you some coffee. That would fix you right up." She reached for his hand and began to drag him.

"Go ahead. We'll talk later," she said to Cam.

"You're in a lot of trouble," Bron whispered loudly when they were a few feet away.

Adrianna laughed as soon as she closed the door to her room. She filled the soaking tub and sank into it. She wished she had a tub this big at home.

She was happy that Cam and his siblings accepted Bronwyn, but things were moving way too quickly for her. It was downright scary to think about. She wasn't trying to control Bron's relationship with her father, but she didn't want her daughter to become spoiled.

Adrianna needed to get in the right mindset. A little alone time might just do the trick. She rose from the tub, got dressed, and made a list of places she wanted to go.

She was reaching for her purse when her phone rang.

"Start spreading the newssssss, Adri Bear," the teasing voice on the other side of the phone made her smile.

"Thank God, Lo. I'm losing my damned mind."

"Oh? I'm guessing you and Cam didn't shed your clothes yet."

"Shut up, *loca*." As if Adrianna needed to picture him naked, anymore than she did. "He just ticked me off so bad."

"And who is this?" Cam asked, trying to keep his voice light despite the urge to fling his daughter's new tablet into a wall.

She was showing him her photos and they came to one of Adrianna and Bronwyn with a tall, muscular man. All three smiled and the man's arm was around Adrianna, his other hand on Bronwyn's shoulder. They looked like a happy family, which made the bile in Cam's stomach churn.

"That's Evan, Mama's ex-boyfriend. He is so cool. He used to take us to the museums and games and to the state fair. He was a really good shot. He won me like five stuffed animals. I miss him a lot. He always calls on my birthday and Christmas and sends me presents. He still loves Mama. That's what Aunt Lauren told *Abuela*. She also said it's too bad the relationship didn't work for Mama, 'cause Aunt Lauren says Evan is all kinds of right."

"She said that to you?"

"No, I heard them talking once. Don't tell Mama."

Cam opened his mouth to say something about her eavesdropping, but her mother walked in the room.

"Bron, it's for you," Adrianna said, waving the phone at her daughter.

The little girl leapt and took the phone. Her face lit up and she squealed, "Aunt Lo, wait, hold on. I'll call you on FaceTime."

She hung up and began to walk to the other side of the room.

"Where are you going?" Cam called out.

"To the dining room. Mom, can I talk to you?"

They moved away where Cam couldn't hear what they said. His daughter was talking a lot and Adrianna nodded. Then, Adrianna gave her a hug, then a kiss and whispered something in her ear. Bron sat in a chair by the window with her iPad.

"What was that about?" Cam asked as Adrianna walked back toward him with a smile. Luciana joined them.

"She wanted to talk to Lauren in private because she doesn't want you all to get jealous. She says that when she mentions Lauren or her uncle Nathan, you guys get like Suzie, her school frenemy, whenever Bron gets anything new."

"She's so considerate and kind. It kills me that you're responsible for that," Luciana said.

Adrianna's face shifted from amusement to pure joy. "Thanks." Then she turned to Cam and the warmth faded out of her gaze. "I'm going to visit a couple of bistros for new ideas and do a little shopping. We can talk later or tomorrow. Today, you can bond with her."

His stomach knotted. He had never spent time all alone with Bronwyn except for the car ride from the exhibit to her mother's. What if he said or did the wrong thing? And damn it, he didn't want to see Adrianna go. He could kick himself for losing his temper earlier on. He'd made her cold and distant, again.

She ran down a list of instructions and stuff he shouldn't let Bron do and answered some of his and Lux's questions. *Don't let her eat too much or whatever she wants* and *please do not buy her everything she asks for* were among the most stressed sentences. She repeated them a couple of times.

"Are you guys going to be okay?" she asked with wary eyes.

Fuck no. He didn't know anything about entertaining kids. Still, he had too much pride to prevent her from walking out, which she did without so much as a glance back.

"What's going on with you and Adrianna?" Luciana asked as soon as the front door closed.

"Nothing," he said quickly. The last thing he needed was his sister's meddling.

"He made her mad earlier," Bronwyn said, walking back to the family room. "It doesn't look good for him."

"How was your talk with your Aunt Lo?" Cam asked. He wasn't having this conversation. Especially not in front of the kid.

"It was okay." Bronwyn answered.

He ran his fingers through her hair. "You can tell us. We won't be upset."

"She got me an Eli Manning Jersey and tickets to go see the Giants play the Ravens in the fall." she gushed. "If Mama lets me, we're getting our faces painted blue."

"Why?" Luciana asked.

"'Cause that's how you show love for the team." Bronwyn looked at him. "Can we go do something outside?"

"How about a little sightseeing?" He was rewarded with a big smile and a nod.

"Can we go see the Statue of Liberty?"

9

Adri wished she could cartwheel as easily as she had in high school pep rallies. Fancy s'mores made with chocolate mousse and shortbread cookies and chocolate hazelnut lattes. Those would be new items at the bistro. The pear, walnut-gorgonzola salad would be a hit. It had been a wonderful day for her business mind. She couldn't wait to see Lauren's and Mom's faces over the gifts she bought for them.

She splurged like she rarely did but it would make them all happy, and that was all she cared about. Her mom and her best friend had always been there for her. These gifts were not enough to show how much she appreciated them. And Bronwyn would squeal over hers.

Adri headed back to Cam's more in control of her emotions. The call with Lauren and the day in the city had centered her. She couldn't wait to see her baby. She could now trust herself to talk to Bron's father without screaming. She and Cam were in a tricky situation but it was not unheard of. Millions of parents who are not together raised children every day. They just needed to get on the same page. The most important thing was that Bron was dealing well with all the changes. She planned to call the school and ask them to recommend a professional to advise her on how to deal with it.

She and Cam needed to learn to work together and share the

responsibilities. It was no longer solely up to her. She was scared and relieved at the same time.

Luciana intercepted her at the door. Her normally sleek and styled former nemesis seemed frazzled and her hands clasped tightly together. "Thank God you're here."

Adrianna froze. "Did something happen to Bron?" she asked but moved past Luciana.

In the living room, Cam was holding a sobbing Bronwyn.

"You see?" he said. "She's here."

Adrianna walked over, sat down and wrapped her arms around Bron, kissing her teary cheeks. "What's wrong, *Princesa*?"

"I thought you left me." She burrowed in Adrianna's chest.

"Left you? Where would I go?" Adrianna asked her.

"Back home," Bronwyn said, sounding even younger than her nine years.

"Without you? I can't go without my heart." She waited until her daughter looked at her. "I will never leave you. Nothing's changed. It's just like when you go to school. You understand?"

Bronwyn nodded.

"I brought you something. I think you're going to like it." Adrianna signaled to Luciana to pass her the bag. She looked through it and pulled out a T-shirt. She handed it to her daughter.

Bronwyn unfolded the garment. Her eyes widened and she let out a high-pitched squeal.

"Las Meninas. I love it, Mom."

Then she stood up, her face still wet with tears, but it was like nothing happened just seconds before. She went around the room, showing the shirt to Lux and Cam, who seemed dumbfounded. Then she turned back to Adrianna.

"Can I wear it now? Please, Mom!"

"Yes, after you've had a bath," Adrianna said, secretly patting herself on the back for buying a backup and two other art T-shirts.

"But I bathed this morning…" Bronwyn complained.

"Yes, and it's seven o'clock and you've been out and about, right? How about you head upstairs and take your clothes off? I'll come to the bathroom and fix you a bath with bubbles in the big tub. You can tell me all about your day and I'll tell you about mine."

"Okay," she said and ran up the stairs.

Cam and Luciana, whom Adrianna had completely forgotten, stood around in shock. She tried to lighten the mood. "*Las Meninas* is one of Bronwyn's favorite paintings because my mom calls her *Mi Niña,* which, to Bron, sounds like *Menina.* She also bought Bron a replica of the painting. When Mom visits, they come up with stories together about how *Las Meninas* was a group of girl spies working for the crown."

Stop rambling, Adri. They don't care.

"I don't understand. She was having fun and laughing and then she was crying hysterically asking for you." Cam seemed so confused.

"She's nine. Kids are super dramatic at that age. She still doesn't know you all very well. But she needs you, too."

"It's like she thought we would hurt her." Luciana smoothed her hair.

"She's had huge changes in her life the last few days. I was thinking about that earlier," Adrianna said to Cam. "We should probably have her see someone. Just to make sure she is taking everything well."

"That's a good idea," he said.

"I also think we need to get her back into her routine. We can take turns helping her with her homework and making sure she is doing more reading than the basic." She turned to Luciana. "You and Chase are an important part. She's always had an aunt and uncle around and she needs you. No more faces when she mentions the people she loves, no matter how much you hated them in high school."

Luciana nodded, but Adrianna wasn't done, "And no more gifts. You're going to spoil her. No matter how hard you try, you can't make up for your absence all these years with presents. Lauren doesn't always give her presents. She gives her love, attention, and affection. She doesn't need another iPad, but she would love it if you played with her outside, watched a movie, or taught her painting stuff."

"I noticed. She screamed louder for your T-shirt than she did for the iPad," Luciana murmured.

"It's better if you get to know her and you let her get to know you. And don't do everything she says either. You're the adults," Adrianna pointed to them. "I'm going to go give her a bath."

Cam nodded and she headed upstairs, almost feeling sorry for them. They weren't used to being around kids.

She got Bronwyn to lay down after her bath. Adrianna pumped her fist in the air and walked out of the bedroom. Bron almost never napped anymore but the meltdown probably got the best of her. In the alcove outside her bedroom, she found Cam sitting in one of the chairs. His back was so straight it looked like it could shatter.

She smiled and sat in the chair across from his.

"I should've noticed something was wrong," he said looking down. "She mentioned you so many times. At one point she said she wished you were there during the helicopter ride. Then we went somewhere else and as we headed home, she asked for the time and began to cry when I told her."

"She realized a lot of time had passed."

He nodded. "I'm a stranger to my own daughter. She can't stand to be with me for a few hours."

So that's where Bron got her dramatic nature. All this time she'd blamed Lauren but nature and nurture worked together in her little girl. *My poor baby.*

"She just found you and too many things are happening. She got scared for a minute. Did you not see how quickly she bounced back?"

He said nothing. Adri got up and stood before him and soothingly touched his hair like she did with their daughter when she was upset.

But this wasn't their daughter and when he looked up to her, it wasn't a child's eyes she saw. Something had replaced the sadness, an emotion she associated with Cam's name. It provoked a gnawing deep in her belly, releasing a desire pent up for almost a decade.

This. Was. Bad.

He kissed her stomach and circled her lower back with his hands as he rose. His mouth bee-lined for hers and she waited for him with hers a little open and when their lips met, it was like the room caught on fire.

His tongue slipped into her mouth and he pressed his body to hers, searing her skin. She moaned and tried to press herself closer. His hands closed around her ass. Hers roamed his back. He rubbed himself against her, sending her blood straight to her head.

He walked her back until she was up against a wall next to the door. She instinctively got on the tips of her toes to align herself with him. It was her favorite thing, to feel him, all of him, this way. He groaned. Their bodies brushed against each other in a dance as familiar today as it was their last time. His mouth attacked her neck as he rocked his hips against her, kissing his way up to her ear.

"Let's go to my room."

She began to nod and then remembered where they were. "We can't, Cam."

"Okay, here, then," he said, strangling another moan out of her as he captured her lips again, making her dizzy and drunk on the taste of his mouth.

Make it stop, Adri.

He was wearing out her resolve and she had to use the one thing she knew without a doubt would work on both of them.

"Your daughter's in the next room."

Cam lifted his head, confusion and frustration waging a silent battle in his eyes. He pulled away slowly and it took every ounce of self-control in her not to pull him back. He turned around, putting distance between them. His hands buried in his hair, he turned around again.

"Are you seeing anyone?"

His question caught her by surprise. "What? No, I'm not dating anyone. That's not why…"

"What about this Evan guy?" he countered. "The one you're all smiling and happy in pictures with," he spat at her with enough spite to make her wince.

Screw that. She knew where this was going. He was jealous. Yet, he had no right.

"Um, Evan and I ended our relationship long ago. Not that it's any of your business."

"Did you love him?" he whispered

"Does it matter?"

His eyes darkened to an impossible green. It had been the wrong thing to say. He stalked forward until he was right in front of her.

"Yes, it matters. You seemed happy with him. Meanwhile, I was in hell," he bit out with force.

Heat flushed over her body hard and fast. She had to laugh. That's how ridiculous it was. "Yes, Cam. You were really miserable, escorting around every supermodel and actress on her fifteen minutes of fame. It was especially beautiful and awesome to read, or watch on TV, while I changed dirty diapers or spent sleepless nights soothing our crying baby. How did you ever make it through that?"

She wasn't making things better, but *he had some fucking nerve.*

He closed his eyes briefly and took a breath. "I would have been there all along. You have to know that…" His voice trailed off in the end.

He was being honest. It didn't change what she went through. "I know, but unfortunately it doesn't change those times, and you have no right to question who I saw then, because you were doing your own thing. We were not together. It's unfair of you to do that."

He came closer. "I may not have a right, but I'll ask anyway. Because, yeah, I dated those other women, but none of them meant a thing. Every one of them was a stand-in for you. When I held them, when I kissed them, when I fucked them…it was you I saw, your face, your lips, your body—" Cam's eyes widened and he clamped his lips together like he could take the words back. "Fuck it all."

He kissed her again and this time it was deeper, more charged. His lips were slow this time and she melted into him. No one ever kissed her the way Cam did. From their first kiss, he'd made her insides twist, filling her with the need to wrap herself around him. She'd looked and tried to erase those memories of him. She never could.

Her arms went around him despite the screaming in her conscience. She kneaded the muscles in his back and gave in to the kiss, caressing his tongue with flashes of hers.

When they broke for air, the words flew from her lips, "God, I missed your mouth." She pulled him back to her again, but he suddenly jumped out of her reach.

Her thoughts were fuzzy. She frowned. Had she come on too strong? He wasn't even looking her in the eye, but to the side. She followed the direction of his gaze. Bron stood there, watching them with widened eyes.

Adri's heart threatened to sledgehammer out of her chest. Their shit had hit the fan and spread all over the place.

She looked at Cam, not knowing what to say, and the look of absolute panic in his eyes indicated he'd be no help. She needed to say something, fast.

"*Princesa*, I didn't know you were up," she managed to croak out.

"I heard loud talking and I thought you guys were fighting again but when I opened the door you were not fighting…"

A new kind of heat crept up Adrianna's neck and flooded her face. Time for the earth to swallow her whole. There was some relief: Bronwyn didn't hear the conversation between her and Cam, but how was she going to explain what she saw?

"No, we were not fighting." She smiled and then looked back at Cam, who stood there like a frozen statue with cartoon wide eyes.

Thankfully, he caught her meaning and jumped in the conversation.

"No, no fighting here. We were just…"

"Making out." Bron finished for him and turned around to go back to the bedroom.

Adrianna followed open mouthed with Cam trailing behind her. Bronwyn went into the bathroom and closed the door.

Adrianna turned to Cam and whispered, "Oh my God. What are we going to say to her?"

He raised his hands as if not knowing what to say. "Let's tell her we're dating."

"What? Are you crazy? We can't tell her a lie to cover ourselves. How would we get out of it later?"

"What do you suggest then, Adrianna? Your parents can't keep their hands off each other and were halfway to hooking up. Does that sound better to you?"

If she weren't so worried about Bron, she would swear at him until the green fell off his eyes. "Just shut up." She dug her fingers into her hair. "What are we going to do?"

"I thought you wanted me to shut up?"

She crossed her arms and blasted him with a look, "Seriously?"

Anything else she thought of saying was interrupted by the sound of the sink water running. The door opened and Bron walked out. "Mom, I'm hungry."

"What would you like to eat? We can order whatever you want, or do you want to go out to eat? Your choice, anything you want." Though he sounded desperate and pathetic, Adrianna couldn't even fault Cam for trying so hard.

But their daughter shook her head. "I want chicken and rice and beans."

Adrianna exhaled the breath she didn't know she was holding and laughed at the look on Cam's face. "It's her Dominican side. What can I say? I think we could manage that. You both can help me. We'll talk while we make the food."

10

An engrossed Bronwyn watched TV in the family room. Adrianna made dinner in Cam's kitchen like she'd always been there.

Cam stood close by to watch. "I must say, seeing you move around the kitchen these days is a delight. I still remember that time you tried to make that chicken recipe from the magazine." He patted his stomach and fought back the queasy memories.

She laughed. It was loud and musical. Cam had always loved her laughter and the way it reached her eyes first and spread through her body. He didn't realize how much he missed that sound until now.

"Chicken Merlot. I thought it was okay to use my mom's Moscato. I still can't believe you ate all of it. It was the grossest dinner ever." She turned to him, touched his cheek. "That's how I knew you really loved me."

He laughed, tilted his head and moved a bit closer to her. "What did you think before that?"

"I thought you wanted me for my long legs."

How did they do that? They were in trouble after getting caught making out in front of their impressionable child and not even thirty minutes later, they were flirting again. With her, rules, rationality, and everything else went out of the window. It's what she always did to him.

"It was both." He leaned closer to her, "It still is, Adrianna. I..." He was less than a breath away from her lips and she leaned towards him.

"Are you going to kiss again?" Bronwyn chimed in and Cam jumped back.

"She gets her laughter and timing from Luciana," he said, and Adrianna laughed a little.

She didn't look as panicked at getting caught as last time. She tilted her head towards the child and he understood.

"Come here, Bron. We want to talk to you."

She walked over and he scooped her up and sat her up on the kitchen island.

"We want to talk to you about what you saw upstairs," Cam said as Adrianna came away from the stove and closer to them.

"When you guys were making out?" Bron said, staring at him until Cam's face burned. "It's cool. It happens."

"Um. What do you mean?" Adrianna asked after giving him a look.

"You're boyfriend and girlfriend, right? Boyfriends and girlfriends kiss all the time."

It was the most logical thing in the world, which is why he had suggested they went with that, but now he could see the danger in this. If something happened, how would they explain it to Bron? He glanced at Adrianna and the frown in her face said it all. They were both backed into a corner. He chose to speak with as much honesty as he could.

"Your mother and I are getting to know each other all over again. We care for each other but there's still a lot to learn after so long. You understand?"

Bronwyn nodded, "I think so. Can I go back to watching TV?"

Cam helped her down and she scampered off. As soon as she was out of earshot, Adrianna turned to him.

"What the hell are we going to do now?"

"Mama's not back yet."

Cam walked out of his master bathroom to find Bronwyn standing in front of his bed.

"She's with your aunt Lux downstairs," he said, coming closer and touching her hair. "Do you want me to go get her for you? Or I can stay with you until you fall asleep?"

She chewed on her bottom lip, as if considering the offer. She smiled. "I can stay here with you until she comes to bed."

Cam smiled back, relieved that she wanted to spend time with him alone after what happened yesterday during their tour of the city.

"Do you have a TV?"

"Yes, I do." he grabbed the remote and clicked a button. A panel rolled out, revealing a 60-inch flat screen. Her mouth opened into a perfect circle. "I take it you like it."

She nodded emphatically, her eyes still engrossed on the screen. "Can I have one?"

"Of cour...um...what do you want to watch?" he changed the subject.

"Let's watch *Vampire Chronicles* on Netflix." She clapped her hands happily.

Thirty minutes later Cam was more confused than ever.

"Wait a minute. Why do these people go through so much trouble to help Elsa? She's whiny and annoying and why are the two brothers always fighting over her? What about Carla? She's beautiful and sexy but she's with that cowardly werewolf. Why can't we have more of her? She's so bubbly." How could anyone like this ridiculous show?

"I know! I love Carla too. She's kickass." She covered her mouth. "Sorry."

He nodded. "And this guy, what's his deal? He's a vampire and a werewolf too? How does that even work out?"

She giggled out loud. "It's called a hybrid, Daddy."

Cam's heart banged against his ribs and he froze. Her eyes were wide and his own welled up.

"It's okay, right?" she asked, uncertain.

A lump lodged high in his throat. He tried to swallow but couldn't.

Daddy. One simple word took the ground from under his body. He released a shaky breath and nodded. "It's perfect."

She smiled into his eyes. "You're sentimental like Mama."

The adrenaline pumped faster along with his heartbeat. Adri was right. He wasn't going to make it. He'd never wanted this. But being called Daddy was euphoric, like getting a strike out with the bases loaded. He'd done that plenty of times and never experienced this kind of tremor. A little girl not even half his size was doing to him what playing in the world's biggest stage never did. She was bending him.

Bron leaned against his chest and settled back to watch the show. She was perfectly content while he struggled to breathe normally.

Play it cool. Don't be weird.

"You said you and your mom watch this show together?"

She nodded against him. "Yeah, the hybrid's her favorite. I think she has a crush on him."

He grunted, "Now I really don't like this guy."

"You're funny, Daddy." She snuggled closer to him and yawned.

His heart jumped in his chest. Jesus, would he ever get used to hearing her call him that? Probably not, but he smiled. The word he had never wanted to hear, Daddy, wasn't all that unpleasant at all.

11

"I haven't heard from Jacob in ages. Last I heard, he's in the Marines. Connie still keeps in touch with him."

"Of course she does," Luciana replied. Two seconds passed before they burst out laughing.

Adrianna tipped the bottle of wine into the glass and it was less than a mouthful. Had they really polished off the whole bottle? "We need more wine."

"I'll get another bottle." Lux stood up, leaving Adri to wonder how the hell they'd gotten here.

It was almost shocking they drank a bottle that quick, but it explained the last two hours. She laughed, gossiped, and even shared photos of baby Bron. She was having a great time with Luciana Blake, the person she could barely be in the same room with ten years ago.

When had Lux become so nice and fun to talk to? Their fights now seemed all sorts of ridiculous. Then again, they'd been teenagers, vying for the same cheerleading roles. Not to mention how cliquish they all were back then.

Luciana walked back in, flashing her best wine-induced smile. "Thank God for Cam's collection. I'll have to blog about this. I would

76

make it a list about choosing the right wine for your date. 1985 was a great year, don't you think?"

"First, neither of us were born back then. Second, won't he miss that?"

Lux shrugged and poured. "Who cares. Besides, I think my brother can more than afford another and my audience loves any fancy thing I post."

"It's must be a fun way to make a living," Adrianna shook her head.

"Being *Bougie Girl* has its moments. I'll have to show you my swag collection. You'll drool and I'll let you pick some things for yourself." Lux slow-nodded.

Adri couldn't wait. Maybe she could snag some things for Lauren. "Thanks. This is nice. Who would've said we would be laughing at the fights Lauren and I had with you and Connie."

"Ugh. I bet Connie's still a raging bitch."

"She's worse now." Adrianna said, flexing her tingling fingers. Connie was more than that. She was an adult bully who constantly manipulated and guilted Lauren into giving her money. Lux didn't need to know that, though. "You and she got close for a while."

"That's only because she was trying to stick it to her sister. She wanted to get back at you for being so close to Lauren," Luciana said with a smile. "That's when Cameron was going around moony-eyed over you. Connie liked him. She hated that."

Adrianna's mouth dropped. "What? Your brother didn't like me. He used to make my life miserable. He used to make Tommy look like an idiot."

"Duh, because of you. He was crazy over you. He tried to hide it but I know him too well. Whenever you were around, he watched you, and you didn't give him the time of day. You would antagonize him and he would take it. Cameron doesn't take shit from anyone." Luciana poured herself a drink. "He forbade me to come see you. Threatened to never speak to me again if I went to talk to you."

Adrianna frowned. "When?"

"That day dad said he saw you at Tommy's house. He said the two of you got back together. Cameron went upstairs and began to throw all his stuff in bags. I begged him not to go. He was so pissed." She stopped to have a drink from her glass, "He told me everything. I didn't like you but I knew he was crazy about you. I wanted to go talk to you and explain that he's a hothead and says and does crazy shit when he's mad. He wouldn't let me. He said he was getting the hell out of town. Chase and I left with him that day. There was nothing for me there."

Adrianna let out a deep breath. Things could have been so different between her and Cam, if only… "I can't believe how everything changed after a stupid argument. We went through so much unnecessary shit."

"But you're back together now…" Luciana began tentatively.

"I don't know. We have this connection. We always did. He's always been in the back of my mind," Adrianna said looking at the other woman.

"But?" Luciana asked.

"Bronwyn. I'm afraid we'll hurt our daughter. We're volatile and crazy together. We're either all over each other or fighting like crazy. What if we try and fail? She'll end up paying the price."

"It's normal for you to be worried, Adri. You wouldn't be a good mom if you weren't."

Adrianna contemplated her wine glass. "Less than ten days ago I was an only parent that made all the decisions and counted only on me. Now everything's changed and it scares me. Cam wants to change her last name. She's been mine all her life, but now we won't even be sharing that."

Adrianna didn't know why she was confiding all that in Luciana. "Don't get me wrong, I'm happy Cam and Bron are getting to know each other and that he's in her life. It's just…"

"You're scared and you have a very precious reason." Luciana said. "I would be petrified too, but let's take things in parts. You and Cameron have feelings for each other and you owe it to yourselves to find out where that goes. Let's be honest, neither of you is going to be able to date other people unless you give each other the chance first.

The two of you continuously get all gaga around each other and trust me, it's not cute to watch."

Adrianna sighed. "But what if we try and it's a disaster? What if we go ape shit on each other again? I would die if I hurt my baby."

"Adrianna, of course you are going to fight with Cameron. The man is impossible and he's my brother. But I think you both know what's at stake now. I don't think either of you would let it go too far. Especially because you both remember what happened the last time you did."

That made a lot of sense.

"And then there's your parents." Adrianna's chest tightened. Walter and Marilyn Blake would not be happy about this. She was afraid of Walter, of the secret he held over her head.

"Cam doesn't give a fuck what Walter and Marilyn think. Neither do Chase and I. We are all tired of their bullshit. We won't let them mess with you and Bron."

Adri smiled. "You're offering me your protection? God, pigs must be flying all over Central Park."

Luciana laughed. "You're my adorable niece's mom. And you're totally not the bitch you were in high school."

"Thanks."

They continued talking but Adrianna stopped drinking. Bronwyn woke up early and she would rather not have a headache in the morning, since they planned on doing things outside. Two hours later she was grateful for that decision.

She helped Luciana to bed and it brought back horrible flashbacks of getting Bronwyn to sleep when she was three. Cam's sister was completely plastered. She finally fell asleep and Adrianna headed to her room. She went to the bathroom first, on her tiptoes and not turning on the lights, as not to wake up her daughter.

She brushed her teeth and grabbed some pajama shorts and a tank top from the drawer. She put them on and went to the bed but when she got close, Bron wasn't there. *She must be with Cam.*

She made her way to his bedroom, intending to usher Bron to bed quickly. It was way past her bedtime and she'd be cranky in the morning. She almost stumbled at the door.

Cam lay on the bed, one arm on the pillow, his head nestled on his bicep. Bronwyn's face was tucked on the side of his ribs and one hand on his chest and a foot on top of his legs. It was her favorite sleeping position when she slept with Adrianna. Cam's left arm curved protectively around her. An enormous TV was still on, illuminating the room.

Adrianna told herself she should go back to her room, but her feet were already walking towards the bed. She stood on the side on the bed for a bit, trying to convince herself to leave. Instead she climbed on the other side of Cam.

A warm body slipped next to Cam, enveloping him in the sugar and berry notes of

a familiar perfume. "Adri?"

"Do a lot of women crawl in bed with you while you cuddle with your daughter?" she giggled.

"You're drunk?"

"Nah. Luciana's drunk. I'm just happy." She lay on her stomach and scooched up closer to his face. Her face was on her hands as she leaned on her elbows. The minty notes of mouthwash washed over his face.

"Is Lux in bed?" he asked, trying to distract himself from how close her face was to his.

"Your sister is plastered. I put her to bed before she could drunk-dial and tell her ex to fuck off." The light from the TV illuminated her face. Adrianna smiled a little too hard, making Cam's insides shift a little. She was drunk adorable.

"How much did you two have to drink?"

"We had a bottle of wine together, and I had a glass of another and she had the rest."

"She'll be a pain in the morning," Cam sighed. Lux never did well with hangovers.

"I feel bad. She's still so into him," she sighed, her face morphing into a wistful, dreamy expression. "I know the feeling."

It was late and they both needed to go to sleep but he couldn't help but ask, "You're into Mateo?"

She laughed, "No, you, dummy. I mean you." She jammed her finger into his chest and moved her head closer. "I'm still so into you."

He gaped at her and his mouth dropped open just in time for hers to descend upon it. It took him a bit to recover from the shock but his hand automatically wrapped around the back of her head and he pressed her close. His tongue followed her lead. He began to turn towards her when the weight on his side reminded him that their daughter was in the bed. He pulled away and she frowned at him.

"Bron," he said and she turned her head towards the sleeping child. She then looked back at him and smiled.

She brought her face closer. "We'll finish this another time," she promised. "What did you and Bron do?"

"We watched that awful show with the vampires. Just terrible," he yawned.

"*Vampire Chronicles*?" she whined. "You guys watched it without me? Was the hybrid on?"

"Yes, Bron told me how you love him," he said disgusted. "He's a mass murdering sociopath. What are you even thinking?"

"He's a tortured soul. He kinda reminds me of you." Her wistful voice made him roll his eyes.

"How?"

"He's hot, with a bad temper, and very kissable lips." She gave him a quick peck, buried her face on his neck and went to sleep.

It was a while before Cam could sleep. He gazed at both sides. On his left side, his daughter slept pressed to him. On the other side Adrianna lay her head on his arm. He never could have predicted this. He wasn't going to dwell because tomorrow he intended to cash in on Adri's promise.

Adrianna groaned. A warm hand shook her from the most amazing dream. She lifted her head and all she saw was Cam's sleepy face. His mouth was slightly open.

"He snores a lot."

Adrianna turned her head towards the voice and saw her daughter hovering over Cam's body. "You do too."

"How long have you been up?" Adrianna smiled and reached over the sleeping body to kiss Bronwyn. "Good morning, my baby."

"I'm hungry. Can I have pancakes?"

"Yes, you may." She stretched and poked Cam. "Are you having breakfast with us?"

He barely moved. "I'm dying. She kicked me all night and you snore."

Adrianna swatted him on the side. "You have some nerve, complaining about someone else snoring."

"Go away, both of you. I need an extra hour." He struggled to get the words out.

"Daddy's grouchy in the morning," Bronwyn said, giggling.

Adrianna's eyes widened and she looked at her. "Daddy?"

"She calls me that now." Cam smiled in his sleep. "Now, leave."

Adrianna laughed. "Let's go Bron. The baby needs his sleep."

As she was opening the door, she heard him say, "You made me a promise."

What promise? Oh God.

She needed to have a stern talk with herself. She couldn't allow last night to repeat. She'd jumped into bed with him. Granted, nothing happened. Still, it couldn't happen again.

Once they bathed and got dressed, Bronwyn ran downstairs ahead of her mother. She got a call on the house phone and rushed out.

Adrianna was coming down the steps when she heard her daughter squeal. She stifled a groan. It was probably another gift from either Luciana or Chase. She should be mad, but Bronwyn's happy laugh never got old.

She reached the bottom step, took one look at what caused her baby's happiness, and was immediately ready to kill whoever got her the gift. Bronwyn held in her arms a tiny, white British Bulldog. It had a brindle patch that covered his right eye from the top of his nose over to his ear.

By the look of absolute guilt when he saw her, Adrianna's best bet was on Chase.

"Look at what Uncle Chase got me, mama! We can take him home, right?"

"He's beautiful." Adrianna breathed out and it was true. It was the cutest puppy Adrianna had ever seen. As she bent to touch its head, she looked above her daughter's head to Chase and mouthed, "I'm going to kill you."

For the past few months, Bron had been campaigning for a puppy. Adrianna stalled on getting one. They lived in an apartment above the bistro and not a house, which meant there was no yard for the dog. Now, she was going to have to figure it out because, as angry as she was at Chase, she couldn't take the joy out of her daughter's face.

"We can take him home, but he is your responsibility from now on. You will look after him and make sure he doesn't do anything bad around the house. He better not chew on my shoes or leave any sort of puddle. You will feed him and bathe him. Do you understand?"

"Yes, I promise!" Bronwyn said, smiling as she hurled herself at Adrianna.

"I mean it, Bron." She tried to be stern but the way her daughter smiled made it impossible. Instead, she directed her annoyance at the offender. "Does he have all his shots?"

"Um, yes, but he does need a few things I didn't get a chance to get. I was thinking I could take Bronwyn shopping for them."

Adrianna didn't say anything.

He continued, "I meant both of you, of course. Maybe I can get you…a Ferrari? Would that erase that Hannibal Lecter look from your eyes?"

"You and Bronwyn go. I have to talk to Cam about our arrangements for next week, and we have some decisions to make. You take care of her and *do not* buy her another thing."

Luciana finally took mercy on Adrianna and spoke. "I'll go with them."

Adrianna smiled at her, "Thank you, Luciana. Now, Chase, come give me a hug."

Chase walked over and when he hugged her, she whispered in his ear, "I'm going to murder you and eat your liver for dinner."

12

Cam reached downstairs to find Adrianna talking on the phone and leaning on the kitchen counter. She had pulled her hair into a ponytail that swung away while she talked. She had a notepad in front of her with a list of entries almost the length of the page. He noted she'd crossed out several completed items.

The fourth one, "speak to Dr. Perkins," caught his attention.

"Lo, I know you got everything covered but you know how I am. I'll worry anyway. I can't thank you enough. You *are* doing a great job and it's not easy." She paused and laughed. "Cam's exhibit is Saturday night and we'll be there Monday. I'll see you then."

When she turned around, he was waiting for her and pulled her to him by the waist of her jeans. He pressed his lips to hers for a moment.

"Good morning," he whispered, breaking away from her mouth for a second, only to go back.

When he finally let go she was smiling, "It's afternoon."

"Where is everybody?

"They all went out."

He raised an eyebrow and came closer to her. "Perfect time to fulfill promises made last night."

She smiled coy, unlike herself, and put her hands on his chest. "About that... we need to talk first."

He sobered up, biting back an oath at the words no man wants to hear.

"Your brother gave Bron another gift." The tightness in her voice told him to tread carefully.

"So, that's what has you all freaked out." He rubbed her arm and pointed at her list.

She shook her head emphatically. "Not freaked out. Well, maybe a little. Normally, I de-stress by cleaning, but your maids take care of it. Speaking of, how come we rarely see your housekeeper or anyone that works on the house or the yard? It's like elves do the job and no one ever sees them?"

Cam cleared his throat. "They like to do things out of our way... they don't want to bother us." He walked to the refrigerator hoping she wouldn't ask any more questions.

Adrianna moved to the other side of the counter. "Why do I get the feeling there is more to this story?"

He pulled out the sparkling water and sighed, "There was...a small incident..."

She served some of the salad she made for lunch on a plate and added the grilled chicken. She grabbed his hand and took him to the dining area, passing through the archway dividing both rooms. Cam and his siblings rarely ate in the dining room. It was too big, done by a decorator and all of them preferred the large kitchen island or the family room.

But Adri was apparently a stickler for eating in the dining room and they ate there now.

Cam didn't mind anymore. She and Bron made the room less big. He sat at the head of the dark wood dining table and she took the chair to his left, facing the wall full of photos of different places he had visited.

The center image was of the lake behind his family's property in Acacia Falls. It was the last place they'd been together. Every time he looked at it, he remembered pressing her against the rock and the way she'd arched for him when his fingers slipped through her folds.

"Tell me everything," she said.

He didn't want to, but she was leaning on the table with her elbows, her chin on her closed fists. She looked so much like their daughter, he couldn't resist.

"There was this one time I was painting in the yard and I walked away to go to the bathroom. The gardener hit my easel with the mower. It fell on the grass. The maid was trying to help him clean stuff and ruined the painting. I found her using a rag on it…"

He finished the story five minutes later.

Adrianna slowly leaned back on the chair with her lips pressed. First a whimper came out of her mouth, followed by a snort, and then she dissolved into laughter.

She was holding her stomach. "You threatened to disembowel them? And they believed you?"

"I was quite mad, Adrianna." He struggled to stay serious, but her laughter was contagious. "What gift would make you angry enough to make lists?"

She took a little time to compose herself. "Chase made us grand-parents."

"Come again?"

"Remember what I said about no gifts?" He nodded. "Your brother bought Bron a puppy. She's been wanting one for the longest time."

"He bought her a puppy?" He stopped eating his salad and stared down at his plate. *Shit*. This wasn't good.

"The thing is, I was planning on getting her one. I just wanted to wait another year. I live in an apartment and there's no yard to walk him." She sighed.

"I'm buying us a house with a yard," he announced tentatively.

Adrianna went still, her face unreadable. "Well… that still leaves the time she is at home with me."

He put his fork down. "You know that's not what I meant." He reached for her hand. "Adrianna, I think we need to…"

She leaned back and crossed her arms. "We should date first."

If she told him she came from another planet, he wouldn't have been this shocked. "Pardon?"

"You told Bron we were getting to know each other again and it's true. I don't want us to move too quickly." She placed her hand over his. "We can't jump face first into this. We can't afford to hurt each other like we've done in the past. Not with Bron between us. You understand?"

He nodded. "I do, but I don't want to take it slow with you. I've missed you too much, for too long." He pulled her out of the chair and into his lap. "I want you full blown in my life. In my arms and in my bed, under me." He paused each time to kiss her softly and fully. On the last kiss, his tongue slid inside her mouth, making her moan before she caressed it with her own tongue.

His hand slid under her shirt to draw circles on her lower back. "Do you really think we're going to be able to hold out?

She ground her bottom against his lap and gripped his shoulders while her tongue continued to tease his. "We're going to have to."

The front door slammed shut and Adrianna practically jumped off his lap. Cam didn't want to move, especially because she had made his pants so tight. He had no choice but to follow her to the living room. They made it in time to see Bronwyn walk in first, hugging the puppy tight to her. Behind her, Luciana and Chase walked in, their faces somber.

"I'm going to take a shower," Luciana announced right away. "See you later." She smiled faintly at her Bron.

"Lux?" Cam called out.

"Not now…" She took a breath and looked at her brother. "I have a bit of a headache. I'll be down soon."

"I need a drink," Chase said and left the room as well.

Adrianna and Cam exchanged confused glances, then turned to look at their daughter.

Bronwyn sighed, "Let them go. It's been a difficult day for all of us."

Cam wanted to laugh at the dramatic words but there was something more in the way his little girl tightly clutched the dog in her arms, with the puppy's face cradled on her neck.

"Bron, did something happen while you were out?" Adrianna asked, moving closer her to her daughter. "Your aunt and uncle seem a little upset."

Cam loved the natural way Adrianna had with Bron. She sat down on the chair closest to them and when Bron came closer, Adrianna touched the puppy's ears. She was making her daughter at ease. In turn, the little girl went to sit down by her.

"Their mom was really mean to them," Bronwyn said.

Cam stiffened and Adrianna's gaze flew to his. *Shit shit shit.* "Their mom?"

Bronwyn looked at him briefly, then down at her lap and nodded.

The pressure in his stomach built at the sad look on her face. Where had she seen Marilyn? Worse yet, had his mother said something mean to his child? He knelt on the floor in front of her.

"Why don't you tell us what happened, Princess?"

She shook her head without looking at him. "You're going to be mad at me and Diego."

He took her face in his hand. "I'm not going to be angry with you." He smiled and gave her a kiss on the cheek, then frowned. "Who's Diego?"

She pointed to the dog and looked away from him again.

"Why did you name him Diego?" Adrianna asked.

"'Cause he's Frida's husband, of course," Bronwyn said looking at Cam with a smile for the first time since she came in.

"Bron…" Cam tried to get back to the subject quickly. Adrianna's eyes burned holes through the side of his head. He turned to find her glaring at him.

"She's not getting another dog," she turned to Bronwyn. "You're not getting another dog."

Cam put his hands in front of him. "I didn't know Chase was getting her one. We picked Frida out the other day, before you put a halt on presents, and she should be here tomorrow morning."

Adrianna came off the couch. "This is not happening!"

"But Mom, please, we can't just throw her away," Bron pleaded. "She's already part of our family."

"We don't have space for two dogs. We barely have room for one!" Adrianna was getting more and more worked up by the second.

Cam began to shake his head, trying to stop what he knew would come out of his daughter's mouth next.

"But Daddy's getting us a big house with a humongous kitchen, and there's a huge yard and Frida and Diego can run happily. I helped him pick it out already and there is plenty of room for all of us and two painting areas, one for me and one for Daddy. And it's supposed to be a secret, but I promised Uncle Chase that he would get his own room. You see? It all works out, Mama," Bron exhaled after saying all of that in one breath.

Adrianna seemed stunned. She wasn't moving or saying anything. Her widened eyes stared straight at her daughter. She turned her gaze towards Cam. Her eyes now had a feral quality to them.

He opened his mouth, but she lifted a hand to stop him. "We're not going to talk about this now." Then she turned back to her daughter. "Tell us what happened today."

Nonplussed, Bronwyn went on to tell them how, as they were leaving the pet store, someone called out Luciana's name. They turned to see Marilyn Blake sauntering their way. "She was talking to Aunt Lux, but she kept looking at me. I introduced myself, but I don't think she liked that because she began yelling at Aunt Lux and Uncle Chase. She screamed about someone not getting the Blake money and she called my aunt and uncle traitors and said she would cut them off. Aunt Lux told her she doesn't have any money and Uncle Chase told her to go home and have a drink."

Cam moved close to her again and put his arms around his daughter to prevent himself from exploding. "I'm sorry you had to meet her. She's not important."

Bronwyn shook her head. "But, she's your mom, and I'm sorry if this makes you mad, but I don't like her. She's mean and she shoved Diego with her foot when he peed on her shoes. She kept screaming at me, asking if I knew those were Valentinos." She paused to look at Cam with big rounded eyes. "I didn't know."

"Bron, it's okay. I'm sure Mrs. Blake was probably having a terrible day," Adrianna said. She sat on the armrest of the chair next to her daughter. Bronwyn laid her head on Adrianna's lap. "You don't have to like Cam's mom, but you have to respect her. Do you understand?"

The little girl raised her head to look at her mom. "Yes, I have to be courteous and polite even if I don't feel like it because I'm a lady and I've been raised to know better."

"That's my girl," Adrianna said, then bent to kiss Bron's forehead before hugging her to her chest.

Cam watched the scene with a heavy heart. A week and a half ago, he'd thought there was nothing his parents could say or do that could hurt him anymore. Knowing Bronwyn had to face Marilyn's disdain and her insinuations about Adrianna made his blood boil. It was worse than any of the things Walter had said or done to him. Cam was slowly learning that now there could be worse things than the ones already done to him.

He looked up and found Adrianna watching him. There was something in her eyes, an emotion, he couldn't describe. She hugged Bronwyn tighter to her. "I want you to call and see if the paternity test is ready."

She always knew what to say to make him go from boiling into an eruption.

13

"…and her amazing ability to catch all the elements. I don't think I was that advanced at her age."

Adrianna sat back and took another sip of her wine to hide the smile that had been threatening for a while now. The courting had begun and they had gone out to dinner at a restaurant in the city that touted the best wine collection on the Upper West Side. When they'd stepped through the doors, it'd taken Adrianna's breath away.

The dining room was not very large, about the size of Cam's family room, which was still pretty impressive. In the middle of the ceiling there was a rectangular skylight roof. Under it a vine of leaves and blooming flowers served as a canopy above the dining tables and down the walls. String lights intertwined with the vine, which, along with the skylight, provided sunlight and warmth, allowing the flowers to grow all year long, as the waiter explained to Adrianna. In the far end, there was a roaring fireplace, completing the exquisite and beautiful effect.

Adrianna fell in love with it instantly. She began to think of ways she could recreate a similar effect in her bistro. She did have a fireplace and she could emulate the skylight with a faux tray ceiling and 3D ceiling wallpaper. She could section that part off as an exclusive area for romantic dinners.

Cam's voice brought her out of her reverie.

On the way there and for the first thirty minutes, he had not stopped gushing about Bronwyn's talent, her maturity, and how kind she was.

"You're in love," she said.

His face reddened and he looked down into his wine glass.

Adrianna put her glass down and reached for his hand. " If anyone understands, it's me. I've been in love with her since my second trimester."

He wrapped his fingers around hers. "You've done an amazing job with her. You make it look easy but today was proof that it is not."

Adrianna laughed. For the first time, Cam had told Bronwyn no and she hadn't taken it well. Still, she'd bet the bistro that Cam took it harder than Bron. "Did you honestly think she would be mad at you forever?"

He looked away, making her laugh even harder.

"She makes your angry face. It's very convincing." He looked back at her. "I just don't want to hurt her. After ten years of not being together, I don't want her to hate me."

Adrianna squeezed his hand tighter and reached to touch his face with her other hand.

"That girl could never hate you. She already loves you. When she came back in the room and didn't see you today, she was worried. I think she thought you left. It broke my heart a little—I already scheduled an appointment with Doctor Perkins when we get back—but we cannot be 'yes parents' because we're afraid of hurting her feelings. The harshest no in her life won't be the one she hears from you. When you say no, at least it will be for her own good."

He nodded, and they stayed silent for a while, still holding hands.

Then Cam smiled devilishly. "You just like saying no, Adrianna."

She arched an eyebrow. "I didn't say no to you, Cam. I just wanted to date before we jumped into bed." She paused and tasted her wine before continuing. "Of course, that was before you and our daughter decided to gang up on me and buy two dogs and a house."

"So, are we sleeping in separate rooms like we do now?"

"When was the last time we actually slept in separate rooms? Whenever we don't go to your room, you end up coming to ours. We are co-sleeping with a nine-year-old. Bad parenting on our part." She chastised both him and herself for it but there was no real regret in her words.

"I love sleeping with you both. I love her cuddling up to me but I would love to sleep with only you." His smile was so mischievous, his gaze— the penetrating eyes of the boy who marked her body and heart with his kisses and bites. Thousands of butterflies circled and dived in her tummy.

The candelabra's accent over them was now dimmed. If you looked up the words "mood for a perfect date" on Google, you would get the image of this place. It was perfect all the way to them holding hands over the table.

They never got to do this the first time around. They'd loved each other in secret. He came over to her house when her mother left for work in the afternoons, or they would meet at the edge of the Blake property, and other times by the falls. Whenever they went to the fair or local hangouts, they hid who they were to each other, acting like they barely tolerated one another.

A tug at her hand had her blinking back to the present.

"Where did you go?" His voice was uncertain, and a frown adorned his forehead.

"I was just remembering us ten years ago." She pulled at his hand to bring him close to her and leaned in. She pressed her lips to his and let her hand slide up his arm and behind his neck.

Slow kisses followed one another and Adrianna took her time. She led, dragging them both until both were lost in the soft feel of their mouths, the strong taste of the wine, and the velvety caresses of tongues that flicked, teased, savored, and retreated. And came back again.

"Adrianna." He moaned against her mouth while his hand snuck to the back of her head to press her closer. "We need to get out of here."

She laughed softly. "You're still courting. I don't put out on the first date."

"If we stay here, we're going to give a steamy show."

She gasped and pulled back. Her face was on fire and she looked around to see if anyone noticed. "We need to do better. We're not kids anymore."

Cam smirked at her, making Adrianna even more unsettled. "Stop."

"You know what's funny about you?" he asked.

"What's that?" She reached for her water goblet and took a sip.

"You get so embarrassed about kissing in public and yet you are the same person who initiated the most erotic experience of my life that day at the state fair when you took your clothes off under the Fire Ball."

The memory hit her with full force. The water she drank went down the wrong pipe; soon Adrianna was choking and coughing loudly.

Acacia Falls
Ten years ago

"I think I see a better prospect than you to go on the ride," Chase said, eyeing Lauren as she made her way toward them.

Normally, Cam would have rolled his eyes at his younger brother, but Lauren wasn't alone. She walked with the girl that never left Cam's thoughts, who had been torturing him for the last two hours, sending him looks under her lashes and slight smiles when no one was looking. But as they got closer, Adrianna eyed him like he was something on the bottom of her shoe.

Though maddening, Cam couldn't deny how exciting this was. For the past two months, they had been seeing each other in secret. Everyone thought they hated each other but every minute they were away from the prying eyes of others, they spent talking, arguing or making out passionately.

Adrianna had been in his every fantasy for the past year. He pursued her hard, knowing she was with Tommy. Cam couldn't understand how that guy could spend his time screwing with every other girl in town when the prize was already his. When they'd broken up and Tommy's parents had sent him away, Cam doubled his attempts. Adrianna still rebuffed him. Then came the day when she found him reeling from a fight with his father by the side of the falls. She berated him for stalking her. They'd had an all-out screaming fight that ended with them kissing.

They had yet to have sex and it drove Cam crazy. His body was constantly feverish, his erections made training uncomfortable. She wore shorts all the time or dresses that caressed her mid-thighs. All he wanted was to lose himself in her, running his hands up and down her beautiful limbs.

"What do you say, Cameron?"

Chase's voice pulled him out of his thoughts and he found both Lauren and Adrianna directly in front of him.

"What?" He asked, staring at Adrianna, who wore an enigmatic smile on her face.

She knew the effect she had on him. And loved it.

"Lauren agreed to go on the Fire Ball with me. Are you coming? You can sit across from us. Maybe Adrianna can sit next to you?" Chase offered, looking from Cam to Adrianna.

Before Cam could respond, Adrianna jumped in, shaking her head. "Nope, that's not for me. You guys go. I'll catch up with you later, Lo."

She walked away towards the opposite side of the ride. When she got to the end, she turned and threw him a suggestive look over her shoulder. In awe, Cam watched her dip underneath the ride, behind the operating cabin.

"You coming?" Lo asked him, but laughter danced in her eyes and her lips pressed to barely contain the knowing smile. She was Adri's best friend. Of course, she knew what was happening between them.

Cam shook his head and waited for them to board the ride, almost laughing at the giddy look on Chase's face, then went to meet Adrianna.

He found her sitting on the floor, her legs crossed in front of her under the big metal beams. He kneeled in front of her, making a bee-line straight for her lips.

"Why didn't you want to go on the ride? I would've held your hand so you wouldn't be scared," he taunted.

She shoved him. "I'm not afraid of rides. I just think they're juvenile."

He smirked at her. "Aha. You just like to be safe."

She raised an eyebrow. "Are you saying I'm not adventurous? I'll have you know, I'm plenty adventurous. Just because I don't want to sit on a fair ride operated by people not much older than us and who don't look like they can read all that well, doesn't mean I'm scared. I like my life. I have tons of plans…stop laughing at me!"

Cam lay on his back, holding his stomach, trying to calm the waves of mirth her speech caused to roll through him.

"Come on, Adri. I'm sorry. Don't be mad," he said trying to do some damage control. Her back was to him now and her arms were crossed. "Come on, babe. I'm sorry. I take it all back."

"You know, there are better ways to be adventurous than to get on that death trap," she said, turning around to face him.

He leaned on his elbows. "Like what?"

The smile she gave him froze the laughter in his throat. Then she reached behind her dress and pulled down the zipper. She pulled her arms from the straps and let the short dress fall slowly. He stopped breathing at the same time his heart began to race. Her tits bared for his eyes to feast on, followed by the planes of her belly, then the curves of her hips and finally her long legs. He tried to swallow but found that he couldn't.

She was naked before him, except for pink, lacy boy shorts. She stepped out of the dress and walked over to him, not stopping until she was towering over him one leg on each side of his face. His hands shook.

"Tell me, Cam, where would you rather be, on top of the ride or under it?"

"I don't think I stopped smiling for a week," Cam confessed.

"I know," Adrianna laughed, stopping the spoon on the way to her mouth. "It was weird and so cute."

"Cute?" His lip curled.

"Mmmhmmm," She answered him with her lips around her spoon but her shoulders shook, trying to suppress more laughter at the pained face he made.

"Cam?"

She'd been so caught up in Cam and their memories, Adrianna didn't see the tall brunette with eyes as green as Cam's approach their table. She wore a form-fitting dress Adrianna saw in Marie Claire last month. It was a designer number that seemed like it was molded from the woman's body.

Cam mirrored her warm smile as he stood up and embraced her, Adrianna couldn't remember where she knew the woman's face from. He turned to introduce the woman and the memory struck Adrianna like brick on a glass, shattering the warmth in her chest and breaking the mood.

"Adrianna, this is Sophia."

"Hello." Adrianna ignored the heat flushing up her neck and managed to smile, extending her hand towards the woman. "It's nice to meet you."

"Likewise." Sophia smiled and gave her a limp noodle handshake. The woman's eyes were sharp, searching, measuring, assessing. Apparently not finding, she turned back to Cam. "I'm so happy to see you. It's been a while since you called." Sophia pouted a bit. It was pretty and perfect, the kind of pout that sells lip-kits.

Her fingers drifted over his forearm comfortably, making Adri stiffen. Cam put his hand over them, removed them and pressed them on to the table.

"It's been a busy time and you could have called as well," Cam said, his tone soft and friendly.

"Cam and I used to date but we've stayed really good *friends*." Sophia explained to Adrianna. The slight waggle of her eyebrows and emphasis on the word "friends" was lost on no one.

Bile crept up Adri's stomach, taking hold of her belly. Adrianna wanted to hurl her wine glass at them.

She chuckled instead. "Yes, I remember seeing you on the red carpet one time. You wore that beautiful, long, green dress with the deep V. I watched from the TV in the hospital the night I had to take my two-year-old to the emergency room. She was running a fever of one hundred and four."

"Adrianna…" Cam started but Sophia cut him off.

"That was so long ago when we attended the Met Gala. If your baby was two then, what is she, ten now? Are you into the whole family thing now? You hate children." Sophia said, her eyes widening before she let out a laugh. "Cam, the family man."

The maliciousness in the woman's voice was obvious, but even more glaring was that Cam didn't set her straight. That's what set Adrianna off.

"My daughter's nine, actually. You know, I remember hearing about your breakup and wondering why such a perfect couple would break up. You are obviously made for each other." She stood up from her table, ready to leave.

Cam reached out and stopped her. He moved closer to her and whispered in her ear. "That was long ago. There's no reason for you to make a scene."

"Oh, that was not my intention at all. Should I apologize to your girlfriend?" she asked for his ears only. She turned to face Sophia. "Excuse me, I need to retouch my lip gloss. I'll let you both catch up. It was nice meeting you."

She pried her arm from Cam's grasp and made her way to the bathroom.

Once there, she resisted the urge to pull at her hair. She wasn't a teenager anymore. She was a woman and a mom. Jealousy fits should not be part of her life. Still, no matter how much she lectured herself, she couldn't get her blood to cool or her breathing to slow down. She retouched her lip gloss while giving herself a you're-better-than-this talk. She took a deep breath, squared her shoulders and walked back to the table. Cam waited alone.

He stood up. "I settled the bill. I figured you wouldn't want to stay."

His tone was sedated, the kind you use when you're afraid someone will go mental. A fresh wave of anger set off through her but this time it was directed at herself. She'd been immature and she couldn't forgive herself for that. Why couldn't she fall into a black hole before she'd made a fool of herself?

"That's for the best. I'm tired and would like to go home," Adrianna said, proud of how steady and casual she sounded. Home didn't mean his house but her apartment over her little bistro. It meant her bed, watching TV with her baby, where she never had jealousy fits. He wasn't back in her life even a month and she was already reverting to her teenage self. It was a sign. One she'd be a fool to ignore.

They walked out of the restaurant in stark difference to how they came in. There were no provocative looks or small touches. When he opened the door for her, she thanked him but didn't look at him.

The ride home was mostly silent, except for the time he tried to talk.

"I don't want to be rude, Cam, but I don't want to talk about this right now. I have a headache and just want to go to bed."

14

Crab was going to leave her broke. Adrianna groaned and hit the enter key harder than she had to on the spreadsheet cell. They'd spent more than usual on crab meat for the bistro in the past two weeks. *Damned that market price bullshit and the shortage of crab pickers.*

"It's pitiful."

She looked up from the laptop to find Luciana at the foot of the bed.

"Ever heard of knocking?" she snapped.

Unfazed, Luciana climbed into the bed and scooted closer to her. "You look awful."

"Thanks," Adrianna muttered and bared her teeth. "Now, get the hell out."

"You and my brother left this house disgustingly in love last evening. You were like lovesick teenagers with all the lingering looks and small touches. I considered taking Bron and going to a hotel somewhere because I thought we were going to hear some ungodly noises." Luciana paused. "Instead, I wake up next to my snoring niece. Both my brothers are passed out drunk in the living room and you're here looking like a city bus full of hobos ran over you."

"I hate you so much," Adrianna practically growled.

"No, you don't." Luciana reached for the laptop, closed it, and placed it at the end of the bed. Then, she sat back against the headboard and patted the spot next to her. "Now, tell Doctor Lux all about what happened."

Luciana lost her mind. There couldn't be any other reason and the last thing Adri was going to do was indulge her crazy. She wanted nothing more than to flick the other woman on the forehead with her finger and kick her the hell out of the room. Instead she sighed and moved to sit where Luciana indicated. The miserable four hours of sleep caught up with her and left her without fight. She gave up trying to sleep at four in the morning. She spent the time since then doing the books for the bistro, organizing inventory, double checking Bronwyn's events for the next two months. She was exhausted but not sleepy. Mostly, she was hurt and embarrassed.

"We were having a great evening," she began. "The restaurant was beautiful and everything was sexy and we were in this haze, you know? Then, this woman came to our table and began talking to Cam…" Adrianna went through the whole eventful evening, all the way to the point when they got home.

Luciana was silent for what seemed like hours to Adrianna before she began to laugh. "Thank God!" She threw her arms around Adrianna and kissed her cheek loudly.

What the fuck. She tried to pry herself away from Luciana, to no avail.

The other woman continued talking, "This is such a relief! I thought you turned into some kind of patron saint of maturity and poise. I am so glad to see the old Adrianna is in there. I mean, don't get me wrong. New Adrianna is a great mother to my niece. But it's nice to see traces of the girl who dragged Stacy Morris by the hair when she found her with Tommy near the bleachers."

Adrianna covered her face. "God, I was awful back then."

Luciana shook her head. "You were fun."

"You hated me," Adrianna reminded her.

Luciana smiled. "We hated each other. We also made that fucking hick town tolerable. What are you going to do about Cameron?"

Adrianna sighed. "I don't know. It wasn't exactly my best moment, and God knows I don't want to face him right now." She was mortified at the way she acted the night before. She should have known better. There were better ways to handle something like that. She was always preaching to Bron about being a lady and look what she did.

"You don't have to face him now."

Adrianna frowned. "What do you mean?"

"We can go have a girls' day. Do some shopping, grab some food and maybe a movie, or hit the spa so they can make you look human again," Luciana said, lifting one of Adrianna's limp curls between two fingers. "I can make a call and get us into the Green Goddess Spa. They're dying for a review from me."

She ignored the dig Lux buried between sentences. "What about my daughter?"

"She has a father now, Adrianna." Lux winced right after she said the words but plowed on. "And don't you want to face him when you're looking your best?"

"I couldn't do that to him. You said he's hung over. Bronwyn is a ball of energy and she has two puppies that require constant attention. It would be torture." Adrianna toyed with the hem of her tank top, a small smile tugging at the corners of her mouth. With Cameron not being a morning person, it would be pure hell.

She wasn't that evil, though.

"I guess it's good that you are so mature. I admire you, really." Lux studied her nails and sighed. "You're just so good. I bet you have never had a few drinks and then had to take care of Bron hung over or when you didn't feel well." Luciana got off the bed and began to walk to the door.

"It just wouldn't feel right," Adrianna called out after her.

Luciana stopped at the door and said one word, "Sophia."

Adrianna got off the bed. "Give me two minutes."

Five minutes later, they were tiptoeing down the stairs and to the family room. She checked on Bronwyn, kissed her and whispered in her ear that she would be back later. Her daughter barely stirred but nodded. Then, she and Luciana snuck out the door but not before stealing a glance at the two men asleep on the couches. Adrianna texted Cam as Luciana drove away.

"This is so bad," she said.

"No, it's not. It's co-parenting," Luciana countered.

The earth was shaking. Cam was sure of it. It was the big one that would sink the island of Manhattan forever. He was trying his hardest to remain still and ignore the buzzing sounds coming from his back pocket. Only, his phone wouldn't stop ringing. He reached back and pried it out, bringing it close to his face. He opened his eyes and immediate pain seared through his skull and his stomach revolted. He moaned. His mouth was dry, like he swallowed a cup of sand. He took a few shallow breaths and opened his eyes again. His phone screen flashed Adrianna's name.

He sat up too quickly, then heaved forward, praying for death's merciful touch. Hope filtered through the wave of nausea surging through him. It was a text message. He unlocked the phone and proceeded to blink a few times.

I went out with your sister. Bron's sleeping in the family room. Luciana threw away the empty liquor bottles but you and Chase may want to clean up before she wakes up. She is very inquisitive.

Cam wished he had the strength to fling the phone into a wall. Instead, he set it next to him on the couch. He planned to lie back down when a movement caught his eye.

Frida was licking at Chase's face while he slept on the floor and Diego was tugging at the hem of Cam's pants.

"I guess Manhattan's not moving. At least not today," he said, reaching for the puppy. Diego evaded his hand and began to bark.

"Make it stop," Chase groaned.

Cam tried again to reach for Diego but the puppy moved back, still barking. Cam got up and began to chase after him. Unfortunately, the puppy must have thought it was a game and began to run faster. Frida joined him and both puppies were barking soon.

"I'll kill you, Cameron, if you don't make them stop now." Chase now sat.

"Shut up, Chase. I think they may need to go outside. I'll go take them. You call the maid and tell her to clean up before Bron wakes up. And go shower," Cam barked.

"You're a mean drunk, Cameron," Chase said.

After praying for thirty minutes for death to come for him, Cam came downstairs to hear his daughter's voice coming from the family room. He made his way there.

"No, Mom's out with Aunt Lux. I'm home with Daddy and Uncle Chase. The maid said they were showering. She is always so nice and gives me cookies. She offered to make me breakfast but I said, no, thanks. She almost ran from the room when I said Daddy should be down soon."

Cam didn't have to be told his daughter was smiling. It was infused in her voice.

"What will you eat for breakfast, then?" a female voice asked on the other end.

"I'll let Daddy figure it out," Bron said.

"Does he normally sleep in this late?" the woman asked.

"No, Him and Mom…excuse me. He and Mom went out to dinner last night. They didn't take me. It was a romantic dinner. Mom looked amazing."

"Did she now? Who did you stay with last night while your parents were out?" The woman asked a lot of questions and Cam couldn't begin to guess who she was.

"Aunt Lux and Uncle Chase. We watched *Elf*! Can you believe they never saw it before? I don't know what people watch here, *abuela*." Bronwyn's voice was full of disappointment. She turned just then and saw Cam by the entrance to the room. "My dad's here now!"

Cam's stomach turned at the word *abuela*, grandma. *Shit*. He didn't have time to prepare or duck out of the way. Bron turned the iPad to face him. There, staring at him with schoolmarm eyes was Victoria Hayes. The last time he'd seen her was the week before he left Acacia. She caught him with his lips wrapped around her daughter's in a secluded area near a town function. The blood had drained from his head at how relieved he and Adrianna had been her mother hadn't shown up five minutes before.

To say this was an encounter he wasn't looking forward to, would be putting it mildly. The disapproving look in her eyes only made it worse. After all, to her knowledge, he'd impregnated her daughter and skipped town.

Cam cleared his throat and forced a smile. "Good morning, Mrs. Hayes."

"Arenas," she corrected. "Hello, Cameron. It's been a long time."

Fuck his life.

Cam struggled to keep his smile in place. Adrianna's mother was not smiling.

"Yes, it has. About that, um, I don't know if Adrianna told you. I was not aware—"

"I know," Victoria interrupted, "Nonetheless, we have a conversation pending. That is, when you are not taking care of my granddaughter while nursing a hangover."

Nausea rose in waves until Cam was ready to vomit right then and there. Her voice dripped with disapproval. Only he could have managed to piss off both the mother and daughter at the same time. The last thing he needed was for Victoria to call when Adri was pissed off at him.

He opened his mouth but before he could speak, his angel daughter saved the day.

"I'm hungry. Let's go eat something," Bronwyn said with a smile, flipping the screen back toward her, "Can we call you back, *abuela*?"

"Of course, you can, *Mi Niña*." Victoria's voice did a radical switch, becoming infused with warmth. Her love for Bronwyn was evident in every word. "I'm going to run back to work and we'll talk this afternoon during my coffee break. I love you."

"Love you too." Bronwyn leaned forward and kissed the screen.

Cam smiled and rubbed his temples.

"You don't feel so good, do you?" Bronwyn said coming closer. When he nodded, she smiled and put her arms around him.

Cam picked her up and she took his face in her hands. "Your head hurts?"

Cam nodded again. She kissed each of his temples and then both cheeks, making him smile. His heart ached, thinking of how he just met her and how lost he would be without her now. She was so sweet, so loving. Just like her mother when she wasn't angry, scowling, or giving him the cold shoulder. "That feels a lot better."

"When Mom comes home, I'll get her to do it too. She's the best at kissing boo boos."

Cam cleared his throat and put her down on the floor. "How about you go shower and change and I'll order us some breakfast?"

"Okay," she answered.

"Do you need my help with anything?" he offered.

"Nope. I can do it myself."

She began to walk away when Chase appeared at the door. "Hurry back, Bron. I have head boo boos that need kissing."

Bronwyn giggled. "You're so funny, Uncle."

"Even she knows you're beyond help," Cam said dryly.

"You're ugly," Chase retorted before adding, "And by the way, I think it would be a bad idea to ask Adrianna to kiss any part of you. She may take a chunk off."

"Shut up, Chase," Cam said reaching for his phone. He dialed and ordered the food.

"What are you going to do about Adrianna? Because your plan from last night is not good at all. She would probably break a heel in your face," Chase asked.

Cam frowned. "What was my plan? I can't remember. Damn you for bringing out that third bottle."

Cam went to sit on the couch. Chase sat down in the opposite chair.

"You asked for that third bottle, brother," Chase half-growled. "Last night, you planned to seduce Adrianna into forgiving you. Only a fool would bare his naughty bits around a woman that angry."

"Chase…For God's sake…" Cam ran his fingers through his hair. "I just had to talk to Adri's mother and she already knows I'm hung over."

"Fuuuuck! That woman scares the bejesus out of me to this day. I hear her name in my nightmares. She once caught me with my face near Lauren's secret garden." Chase shuddered.

"What?" Cam sputtered. "You got close to Lauren's…"

Chase shrugged. "You're welcome! We let ourselves get caught so you and Adrianna wouldn't."

"When?" Cam asked.

"The time you decided to get frisky outside of the Town Council celebration. I happened to look over to see Mrs. Hayes approaching and Lauren said it was better she caught her than Adri." Chase stopped to give Cam a mocking smile. "You thought you were so clever hiding stuff from me."

Cam didn't know what to say. "Thank you…How did you know?"

Chase laughed as he turned on the TV. "You were MIA for a whole summer and so was she. Then when I finally saw you both somewhere, you would sneak away." His smile turned malicious as he looked back at his brother. "I saw you walk out from under the Fire Ball and after… you had the most ridiculous smile for a really long time. Not even father could wipe it away."

Cam tried not to smile. "Nothing happened."

"I wouldn't call it nothing. My niece is darling," Chase teased. "Plus, thanks to you getting laid, guess who got to swim naked with Lauren the day after?"

Cam's mouth dropped opened.

Chase closed his eyes and smiled. "I told her the two of you were getting it on. She said she would do anything to keep my mouth shut. I'm so grateful to you guys."

Cam did laugh this time. "She didn't know you would never tell?

Chase shrugged. "She offered, and I really, really wanted to swim naked with her."

His brother stayed pensive, making Cam laugh again.

The sound brought along the puppies. Diego promptly attached himself to the hem of Cam's jeans.

"Good God, the mutts are back," Chase groaned. "By the way, thanks a lot for letting Frida get to second base with me earlier."

"I still have no clue what I'm going to do," Cam said picking up the two puppies and placing them on the couch. "I didn't do anything and somehow I messed everything up. She was jealous with no reason. I told her I want this to be between us. I'm wrapping up everything here so we can go back Baltimore. What else do I need to prove to her? Why doesn't she get that I'm all in?"

Chase grunted, "Women are complicated, Cameron. She probably knows all of that. I don't understand how she couldn't? Maybe last night, seeing you with Sophia, reminded her that she's been raising a kid alone for nine years. Think about it. She has had to see every relationship you've ever had on screen and in print."

Anger crept up Cam's neck. "Chase, you don't know…"

His brother interrupted him, "I don't what? Know you? Your reactions? How spiteful you can be when someone hurts you?" Chase was relentless. "You've purposefully dated only women that were very famous and whose lives were always caught on camera. For ten years, you've been trying to prove to Adrianna that you moved on from her, while assuming she was happily married to Tommy. She's probably tabloid witnessed your every relationship. I think she got the message you wanted, about how little she meant to you."

Cam's throat knotted, and he could only gape at his brother.

"I'm back and ready to eat," Bronwyn announced from the door.

She wore jeans and a yellow T-Shirt with a wolf on it. On her feet she wore knee-high Uggs over her pants. Her brown curls hung over her shoulders.

"Bron! It's about time. My boo boos are killing me. And only the kisses of the most beautiful girl in the world can fix it," Chase said, opening his arms to her.

Cam watched in amusement as his daughter stepped into her uncle's arms.

"I thought you said Aunt Lo was the most beautiful woman in the world and that's why I had to help you with her."

"Second only to you." Chase tickled her, making her laugh. "Now get to kissing."

The scene playing out before him made Cam chuckle but Chase's words continued to torture him.

15

Adrianna paused at the door. Truth be told, she was scared out of her mind of going inside. All day, she avoided thinking about coming home. She and Luciana treated themselves to the most delicious body treatments, massages, and scrubs. They got their hair and nails done, as well as makeup. They went out for lunch, then spent the last two hours shopping at some vintage boutiques in SoHo.

All in all, she had a relaxing day after putting her Cam woes in a box and throwing that box into the Hudson River as Lux suggested. The results of her spa day were impressive if she said so herself.

The perfect curls brushed her shoulders. The navy-blue shirtdress hugged her curves. She left the three top buttons undone. A thick leather belt cinched her waist, matching the four-inch, knee-high, oak leather boots with a buckle ankle strap. A "strickjacke" cardigan was in the crook of her elbow and her new handbag hung from her shoulder. Her lips were lined and painted raspberry pink. She thought it was ridiculous, but her spa mate insisted.

"You need to look seductive. If you take away his speech, you won't have much explaining to do. Trust me."

And that is how Adrianna found herself looking like a photo spread of *Vogue* while internally she shook like a leaf.

She heard a huge sigh behind her and before she could think, Luciana walked past her and threw the door open. Adrianna had no choice but to follow. They heard voices coming from the family room. They headed there, Adrianna's legs following the other woman's lead. They found Bronwyn and Chase playing Uno while the puppies lay at their feet.

"Mom!" Bronwyn ran to her. "Wow. You're like a movie star."

"That's so not right," Chase said, shaking his head. "You play real dirty, Adrianna."

"You hush, Chase. Do you ever go home?" Luciana asked.

Footsteps sounded behind her and Adrianna turned around. Cam stopped walking and just stood there watching her with his eyes widened and his mouth hanging open.

"Daddy, doesn't Mom look beautiful?" Bronwyn exclaimed.

"Yeah, doesn't she, Cameron?" Luciana went to stand by her brother, patting him on the back.

"Um," Cam blurted out.

Adrianna's gaze drifted to Luciana's, who winked at her.

"Like I said," Chase muttered under his breath. "Dirty."

Cam couldn't stop staring at her. Adrianna was like a vision that froze him in place. He knew both his daughter and Luciana spoke but he didn't hear what either said. Then Adrianna's lips began moving.

"Huh?" He shook his head.

"Can we talk?" Adrianna repeated.

"Uh. Yeah. Let's go to the living room." He waited 'til she walked by him before following. She wore an intoxicating fragrance that clung to him as he walked behind her.

When she stepped into the living room, she turned to face him, only to frown looking over his shoulder. He turned around to find the other three people in the house watching them.

Cam turned back to Adrianna. "I don't think we will get privacy if we talk here. We can go for a walk in the park and then go to dinner if you feel up to it."

She gave him a small smile and nodded.

"Wait," Bronwyn said. "You're going out without me again? That's two times."

She held up two fingers for emphasis.

"I know, Bron," Cam said, placing his hand on her shoulder. "I have to talk to your mom in private."

"Oh." The little girl's eyes rounded up. "She's mad at you again."

Cam opened his mouth, unsure of what he was going to say, when Adrianna intervened.

"I'm not mad at your dad." Adrianna sounded sincere and Cam looked at her.

"Come on, Bron. We'll watch your favorite show while they're out. I'm way behind," Luciana offered.

"Okay!" Bronwyn clapped but then she turned to look at her parents. "Next time, you're not leaving me behind."

Luciana waived at Cam and Adrianna. She turned her attention to her niece and said, "We can order cupcakes and ice cream from *Sweet Dreams*. They deliver."

Cam turned back to Adrianna, shaking his head. "Shall we?"

She nodded.

They walked in silence until they reached Central Park. Cam was nervous, not knowing what she would say or how he could start. They went in through the Strawberry Fields entrance side by side. He tugged at her hand and moved left. Then dropped it, not knowing if she would welcome his touch at the moment.

The silence unnerved him. His mind reeling from Chase's words clashed with the need to stop and pull her close.

"About last night, Cam..." She began, but he stopped walking and shook his head.

"I understand now..." He trailed off as they reached a park.

There were trees along the path, barely juxtaposed against each other. From their walking angle, the trees appeared to touch. It was like they held hands and made a pact to shield over and around them like accomplices. Or maybe that's what he wanted to think. That the world was on their side and wanted them to make up again.

"Solace," Adrianna said, her voice softer than the wind.

Cam blinked in surprise. It was the name of the painting in which he immortalized this place. "I come here to think and reflect."

They continued to stroll, past the Imagine Mosaic, where she stopped and paid her proper respect. His Adrianna was a dreamer. He had always been able to see that in her eyes.

His Adrianna. God. Cam shook his head and shook the thought. They made it all the way to the gazebo overlooking the lake before he spoke.

"I've spent the day going over last night. Most of the time, I kept thinking of what I could have done for you not to be jealous of Sophia." Her mouth opened, and he reached for her hand. "Let me finish, okay?"

She took a deep breath and nodded. They resumed walking.

"The rest of the day, I wondered how I would keep you from being upset when we ran into the other women I dated, and there's a lot of them, Adrianna."

Cam squeezed her hand to prevent her from bolting.

"I know that," Her voice was dry and coarse like a sand block.

"It wasn't until Chase put everything in perspective for me that I realized what this is really about," he sighed.

Her lips twitched. "Chase?"

Cam chuckled a bit. "He has this nasty thing he does. He's always horsing around and joking. It's like he takes nothing seriously, and then out of nowhere he drops logic and knowledge into a conversation. It's really annoying."

Adrianna giggled. "Lauren once said that about him too."

"He knew about us the whole time back then."

"She told me that too, and that she'd bribed him somehow. What did he say that clarified things for you?"

The gazebo was surprisingly empty that day. So they walked in. She went to the back of it and leaned on the hand rest to look into the lake.

"He pointed out that this was not so much about your reaction but my actions behind it."

Adrianna looked over her shoulder and quirked an eyebrow. "Chase actually said those words?"

"No, he just pointed out that I purposefully got involved in relationships that would get paparazzi coverage, in hopes you would see it and think you never meant anything to me. That I wanted you to think I was happy without you." He whispered the last words and leaned to look out.

Her body tensed as she held the wooden rails of the bridge, but she didn't move. "This reminds me of Acacia and the town square."

Cam stood. Sitting was too passive. He couldn't take it. "It's always reminded me of you, Adrianna. I used to come here and remember you, us, that summer, the square, the woods…"

She whirled around to face him. Her face was tight and red.

"Why are you telling me this? You're saying that for ten years, you set out to purposefully rub in my face your every relationship. That what I witnessed and convinced myself was not your fault, actually was because you orchestrated it that way?"

He stared right into her fiery gaze knowing he couldn't avoid this. "I'm telling you that everything in the last ten years of my life has been only about you. I ran from you but you were never far away. I sketched you without meaning to. You were in everything I did. You still are."

Emotions crashed all over her face and she pressed her lips together, then turned away from him to face the lake again.

You might as well let it all out.

"It didn't start that way from the beginning. The year after I left, my parents invited me to dinner at their house. Walter told me he ran into Tommy's parents. He carried on about how they gushed about their son and his beautiful bride and how happy they were."

A breathtaking woman and so in love. Their children will be beautiful and strong. Tommy has it all. Walter had said. Cam's anger rose at words that still echoed in his ears and his father's mocking eyes when he'd said the words.

"And to think it was all so stupid." His hands fisted at his side. "If I had looked it up or called you like I wanted to so many times. Instead, I just went and..."

"I did it too, Cam. You weren't the only one," she interrupted, her words surprising him. "I had a few relationships through the year. Some really good ones but...it never seemed enough. It wasn't until Evan said he wanted to marry me that I realized— "

"What," he jumped in. "He wanted to marry you? He asked?" Something about it, other than murderous jealousy, pricked at his skin.

She rolled her eyes. "Obviously, I turned him down. What's so wrong about him asking? Am I not marriage material?"

"Of course you are, but what if you had said yes? Would I ever have found out?" An enormous pressure built in Cam's chest because there it was. The thought that'd been torturing him. Had Adrianna gotten married, he never would have found out. He would've gone through life without Bron forever.

Her hand went to her heart, several emotions crossing her face. "Cam, I wanted to tell you. I was waiting until Bron was older. I tried but your father..."

"No! Don't tell me. I don't want to know right now. It will only piss me off more," he said, shaking his head.

"We have to talk about it, Cam. You do care. You need to know this," she insisted.

"No, it doesn't matter. I was just thinking that you could've married him and he would have been Bron's father." His stomach lurched and he could barely get the last word out.

"The point is, I didn't. Furthermore, I didn't because he wasn't what I was looking for, what I wanted. I went into every relationship looking for what we had that summer and without meaning to. It wasn't fair." She shook her head.

The floor dropped under Cam.

Adrianna continued, "It wasn't fair to them and it wasn't fair to me. I looked for you in every man while you..." She paused to exhale. "Sophia brought it all back. It really wasn't my best moment. The two of you just seemed way too friendly," she added with a laugh.

Cam winced. "Sophia was just a party friend. Nothing more. It's not like I had intentions of marrying her…unlike Evan and you."

"Seriously?" She advanced on him and Cam knew where they were heading again.

"I'm sorry," he said, moving closer to take her hand. "That was uncalled for." He tugged her closer to him, his arms wrapping around her. "Please, let's not fight anymore. We've spent a decade looking for each other in other people."

He kissed the corner of her lips in tender pecks, savoring her soft skin. Then, he did the same on the other side of her mouth. "Now we found each other again."

"Cam…" Her protest sounded half-hearted, weak to him.

"Adrianna…please." He touched his lips to hers briefly. "I need…"

"Me too," she moaned into his mouth.

Her hands went around his waist as his lips crashed against hers. Her fingers splayed against his back, and his went to each side of her face. She pulled him closer and he smiled against her mouth, desire melding with relief and happiness.

His memory had always been with her in the same way hers had always been for him.

Cam's tongue plundered her mouth, slowly undulating against hers. Her fingers dug into his skin; he groaned. He let go of her face, his hands needing to touch. They were on her shoulders, sliding down her back, and pressing her to him. He needed more of her. More feeling, more friction, more Adri. He cupped her ass, bringing her higher, against his erection.

A little gasp escaped her lips; he thrust forward holding her in place. Her head fell back and he nipped at her neck. He thrust again with his lips traveling up to her ear.

"I want to press you against a tree and fuck you until we both lose our minds. Let's go find a secluded corner." He started to pull her in the direction of the area he knew.

"Oh God. We're going to get arrested."

Or mugged or worse. Get it together, man.

Cam's heart was about to beat its way out of his chest. He looked back at Adrianna who kept blinking. Her lipstick smeared on her parted lips. He didn't want anything like he wanted her under him. Yeah, the woods it had to be.

"We're not going to get arrested because we're not going to be loud and I just can't make it—"

"No, Choco. You come back here. Bad dog. Sir, watch…"

Cam didn't get a chance to turn. A huge object pressed into the bottom of his ass like it was trying to make its way in. The distinctive wiggling of a dog's nose trying to get to know him better. And just like that, he knew he would get luckier in this park with Choco than he would with Adri.

Dogs were out to fuck…his day up.

16

After they got over the shock of the interruption, they went to get food and sat on one of the checker tables.

"I can't believe how people just bend over backwards to do things for you here," she said, taking a small sip of her wine, which was poured into a discreet to-go cup.

"Four championships," he held up four fingers. "New Yorkers like winning. Oh, I spoke to Mrs. Arenas today," he said, picking up a fry from her plate and dipping it into ketchup.

"Yes, she called me." *And gave me an earful.*

He leaned toward her, placing half a fry on her lips. "She hates me."

Adrianna closed her mouth around it, wrapping around his fingers as well. His lips parted and he shot her a warning look.

She chewed her food and lowered her lashes. Unable to stop herself, she leaned forward and crooked her finger for him to come closer. She reached behind his head and pulled him to her, brushing her mouth against his in a soft, slow kiss charged with all the warmth this evening brought into her heart. She nipped at his lower lip and ran her tongue over it, making him groan.

"She doesn't hate you. You didn't know."

Cam shook his head. "You didn't see her face. She's always looks at me like she knows everything before I say it. It's disturbing. She missed a successful career with the FBI. She noticed I was hung-over."

"Yes, she did…" Adrianna pressed her lips together to keep from laughing.

"She never thought I was good enough for you," he grumbled.

"If it makes you feel better, she didn't think anyone in Acacia was." This time, Adrianna did laugh at the way he glared at her. "She knew about us the whole time."

"Were we that obvious?" he asked.

"Well, she didn't know you spent the nights over or, and I quote, 'I would have taken him out on the field behind his family's property for a little Smith & Wesson lesson.'"

Cam swallowed hard. "I told you she hates me."

Adrianna drew circles with her finger on the table. "She's worried about Bron and me…and your parents."

Cam's eyes sharpened at the mention of Marilyn and Walter. "They won't be in our lives."

She looked away from him for a few seconds. They needed to talk about Walter and Marilyn. They had to stop putting it off. But, the hurt was hanging over his eyes and she just couldn't bring more pain to him. She moved to sit on the bench next to him and placed a kiss on his lips. It could wait.

"Let's not talk about them. We have so much more ground to cover."

"Oh, yeah." Gone was the pained look in his eyes and his voice dropped to a seductive whisper. "Like…"

"Tell me when you painted your *Faceless Angel Queen*."

He chuckled, "Oh, you want to hear about how much I missed you and how I painted you even when I didn't want to."

She smiled and nodded, tucking her face in the crook of his neck.

His arms around her, he kissed her forehead. "Did you know that was you from the beginning?"

"No, but Bron did. She was about four and we were having a movie night with Lauren. We saw the painting in an art magazine she had brought that day. Bron asked to look through it and when she came to the painting she turned to me and said, 'It's you, Mama.'"

"She recognized you right away?" he asked.

"That's your daughter, the art connoisseur! We checked who the artist was and there was your name."

"It is you." There was something sad in his voice. "I asked my agent to sell it quickly and cheaply because I couldn't look at it all the time. The new owner had it featured in that magazine. I'll have to find it now."

Adrianna pulled back and looked at him. "I have a pretty good idea where it is."

He frowned.

"It's in my storage safe. I wanted to buy her a copy, since she liked it so much. I saw the original was on sale, so I bought it through an art dealer."

"You…bought it…"

"I planned to tell her about you some day and when that day came, I wanted her to know that what her parents had was real. That painting proves it."

<hr>

They'd walked back into the house when Lux told them to go see Bron because she had a surprise for Adri. Cam let out a low groan as they made it up the stairs and she giggled. His mind had been on seduction and hers too. Their evening at the park had been beautiful and though she kept her expectations low, just having him near took her mind places and made her so wet.

The whole evening of closeness, eating from each other's hands, talking about how deep their feelings for each other still were. It all conspired to set her body on fire. She couldn't wait until they were alone. She was going to devour him tonight.

Adrianna barely walked through the bedroom door, took one look at her daughter, and her feet became rooted. The *Oh. My. God.* was at the tip of her lips and it was only sheer willpower that kept her tongue plastered to the roof of her mouth. There was just so much color, so much tulle, so much volume, so much contrast.

"Daddy took me shopping for tomorrow's show. What do you think, Mom? Isn't this the coolest dress you've ever seen?"

Except, they had not gotten a dress. It was…well…something you let a child choose all on her own.

Bron was a fantasy vision. From the sparkly combat boots to the tapered pants and printed T-shirt with the *Faceless Angel* print, to the detached, purple long-sleeved jacket with a sweep train that stretched a foot behind her. The inside lined in pink tulle made Bron look like a butterfly-ringmaster-steampunk-book cover.

She twirled around, showing Adri the detail work over the back of the jacket.

But her *princesa* was happy. Her beautiful little face glowed as it was meant to. A princess on her own terms. Adri wouldn't have chosen the outfit for her but all that mattered was that look, the confidence, her daughter reflected. She'd choose that look on her child's face. Always.

"You're beautiful, *Princesa*," Adrianna said. Tears clogged her throat, the knot expanding along with the blinding smile on her daughter's lips.

Where had time gone? It was just yesterday Bronwyn was looking up to her from the crook of her arm while Adri nursed her. Right now, she looked like a teenager, choosing her own party dresses.

"It's a vintage jacket. The lady put the poofy inside stuff while Daddy and me went for ice cream."

Adri turned to Cam. He stood there with a small smile on his face. He had taken Bron shopping after being hungover and the happiness was there, clinging to every part of him too. He'd been a jock. This is not the type of stuff most men enjoyed. But there was pride, shining in his eyes like he'd been to heaven and back.

"It was all Bron's idea. She knew exactly what she wanted," Cam said as if it was no big deal. As if he took little girls shopping all the time.

"Daddy also helped me pick a Day-After-Mother's-Day present for Aunt Lo. She's going to love it!"

Another wave washed over her chest and Adrianna smiled so hard it threatened to break her cheeks. "He did? Your dad was a hero today."

She had to stop staring at him. She was two seconds from jumping on him and there was a very eager, very smiley little girl in the room.

"Bron, why don't you let me help you out of the jacket and then we can hang your new dress. I want you to take a shower and go to bed. We have a long day ahead of us tomorrow.

"Okay."

When her daughter slipped out of the room, Adri closed the distance between her and Cam and took his face in her hands. She brushed small kisses on his lips, pausing in between, letting all the emotion swirling inside her drive her mouth and her fingers. Her heart threatened to burst inside her chest. She lay her head against his shoulder.

"Thank you. That was really sweet of you. She's so happy with the dress and it's so her."

"It was fun. She has so many ideas about what she wants. The seamstress was impressed," he said, pressing a kiss to her forehead.

"How did you know where to go?"

He cleared his throat. "Chase knows the woman."

"I bet." Adrianna laughed.

He shrugged. "Anyway, why did Bron buy Lauren an after-Mother's-Day gift? I asked her and she smiled and said she just does. That it's between her and Lauren."

"It's our tradition. We each get Lo something special on that day." She stepped out of his arms and grabbed Bron's jacket and put it back on the hanger.

"Why?" The baffled look in his face was adorable.

"Lauren is my and Bron's warrior. She was with me when I found out I was pregnant. We freaked out and cried for hours. She was there to hold my hand then. We made ourselves sick many nights, eating our hearts away. I think she gained sympathy weight during my pregnancy."

"I'm glad she was there for you." Cam said, and she didn't miss the hints of sadness in his voice.

Adrianna held on to his hand. "It was more than that. She left Acacia with me for Baltimore. We had a small apartment on the edge of Pigtown. The area was rough but it was all we could afford. Lauren was another parent. She watched Bron when I had to work. I didn't have money for babysitters and we were going to school. It wasn't easy…"

She looked away. She didn't want to make him feel bad.

His fingers wrapped around her chin and he pulled her face to look at him. "Don't stop. I need to know this."

"I remember this one night, Lauren went out on a date and I was alone trying to study. I had exams but Bron wouldn't stop crying. The walls were closing in on me with baby wails echoing and bouncing off them. She called me to ask me to turn off her curling iron, which she'd left on. I tried to pretend everything was okay but not even fifteen minutes later, she strolled through the door. She went to Bron's room, brought out warm clothes and dressed her. She told me to go take a twenty-minute hot shower, wash my hair and take a nap. She'd wake me so I could finish my homework."

"She cancelled her date for you and Bron." He shook his head like he couldn't believe it.

Adri smiled. "Nope. She made the guy take her and Bron to the Columbia Mall. They walked around with Bron in her stroller for hours."

"And her date went for that?"

She laughed. "You obviously need a refresher course on Lauren. Actually, it bought him some extra time. She didn't dump him as quick as she normally would have because he'd been so nice."

"No wonder she talks so much about Lauren."

"Oh, yeah. I was so jealous one day when she was five and she told me Lauren was her best friend."

"Oh," Cam said. "What did you tell her?"

Adri shrugged. "Lauren's my bestie and she needed to get her own best friend elsewhere, or there would be problems."

Cam gave her a deep, hearty laugh. "So, you would fight your five-year-old?

"Hey, we've shared the same body. We shared the same room. I love her more than anyone but as I once had to tell your sister: step off my best friend." She couldn't help laughing.

"Well, I'm throwing my hat in. I'm fighting the two of you to become Lauren's bestie. She took care of my girls when I wasn't around. It's meant to be."

Adri's heart skipped a beat. *His girls.* That's what she and Bron were.

She cleared her throat, pushing away the emotion. "You don't have a chance," she teased.

He shot her that playful smile that ten years ago always led to them both shedding their clothes. "Not only do I have a chance. I have an edge."

Her hands bunched around his shirt and she pulled him to her, crushing her mouth to his. There was something different about tonight. Lazy walks in the park, talks about their lives, his bonding with Bron, and now his appreciation for her best friend.

His arms went about her and she lost herself in his sandalwood and citrus scent, in him. His hard body pressed against hers, his hard-on against her lower belly. She needed him to take her clothes off and brush his talented fingers all over her skin. She needed his cock pressing inside her. Her core flexed and released, remembering what it was like to feel him. She never forgot. God knows she tried. She pulled him closer, needing the friction of his chest against her nipples.

The bathroom door flung open. Adrianna's heart gave a cold thump against her ribs. They sprang apart, panting, and she was sure the same look of half horror Cam was sporting was written all over her face.

"You guys are not going to do that in front of my friends, are you?" Bron asked, not looking shocked but more like the annoyed teenager she was bound to become.

How long had they been kissing? They needed to be more careful. "Your dad was waiting to say good night to you too."

Bron went to hug her dad. "See you tomorrow. You're staying with me. Right, Mom?"

Her stomach plummeted but there was no way she could say no. Not without explaining way too many things. "Yes, I am."

She didn't miss the light of disappointment dimming in his eyes but maybe it was better this way. They needed a little space and she needed to digest the day and everything she was feeling. She wasn't a teenager. She couldn't afford to act on hormones and feelings alone.

17

Cam was going out of his mind. He was in the middle of an interview with Barron Lyons, the head writer of *Giaconda*, a European art magazine. The man was doing a piece on tonight's exhibit. The review could open new doors for him outside the United States. But Cam's heart was about a hundred feet from it. Along with his gaze, it strayed beyond the man in front of him to Adrianna, who chatted with Chase.

Both were standing in front of a painting of the lake in Acacia Falls. It was one of the few older pieces on display and one of his first. Chase turned to look at Cam and then back to Adrianna and whispered something. Her eyes widened and she covered her mouth. His brother pointed back at a spot in the painting and said something else and she giggled.

The smile brought a new glow to her face. She was unaware of how beautiful she was and of his gaze that was glued to all of her.

The wine-colored dress fell above the knee. It was sleeveless, with a V neck mesh cut in the top front exposing the silhouette of her cleavage in a barely-there-teasing way that drew Cam's gaze. From her strappy heels to her long neck, she was a walking magnet. He would rather be alone with her, kissing that glossy pink lipstick from her mouth and weaving that teasing ponytail around his hand.

He couldn't chase the images of everything he wanted to do to her. They weren't teenagers anymore. His sexual repertoire had improved and the way she'd kissed him last night told him she was as ready as he was for the next step. He couldn't wait to bury his face between her legs. The scent of teenage Adrianna still made him wake up in long night sweats. He was dying to know if she still tasted the same.

He couldn't wait to head back to Maryland with her and Bron. She still had doubts but he'd erase those by showing her he was there for her. They could put the past behind them and start working on their new life. He was desperate to put that nagging thought in the back of his mind. Something that whispered that this happiness wouldn't last.

"I find my heart bursts with pride tonight."

As if he'd summoned his worst fear, his body went rigid at the sound of his mother's voice behind him. Tonight, Marilyn's voice rang with her polite-company cadence. That voice carried none of the acerbic or vindictive cuts she reserved for the moments she couldn't get her way.

Cameron didn't turn right away. He took a deep breath and assured himself he had nothing to fear. She'd be on her best behavior or he'd have security escort her out like he promised over the phone. He'd already banned Walter from the show. There was no way he'd allow him to be here on his big night. He would do the same to his mother, if necessary. But her stipend was on the line. No way she would risk it.

"Mrs. Blake." The reporter beamed, oblivious to Cam's reaction. "What a pleasure to see you. I was hoping I could talk to you and get a few quotes for my piece tomorrow."

"Of course, Barron. I'm sure we'll have time before the end of the evening. I want to catch up with my son first," Marilyn said.

She didn't know squat about art but Marilyn, like Walter, made it her priority to know what members of the media would be there. It was something they exploited at their whim. His mother especially loved seeing the family featured in the social pages.

The reporter smiled and excused himself. As soon as he was out of ear shot, Cam pounced.

"Mother, you came?" he asked.

"You're my son, Cameron. Where else would a mother be but supporting her child on his triumphant night?" she answered.

"It's funny you should say that because you deprived me of mine for all her life," Cam spat at her.

She waved a dismissive hand. "I came here in peace, Cameron. No need to bring up that child where people can hear."

"Bronwyn, my child," Cam corrected.

Marilyn chuckled, "You've always been obsessive and susceptible, Cameron. You were taken with the Hayes girl since the first time you saw her at the Smiths. All of Acacia knew. She was with Tommy one minute and then suddenly she went to Walter out of nowhere, saying she was having your child. Were we supposed to disrupt your blossoming career for a child that we were both completely sure wasn't yours?"

His pulse leaped, violent enough to almost make him stagger. Cam gritted his teeth and summoned patience. "You should have told me about her or let me find out on my own. Instead, you acted like Adrianna had gone back to Tommy."

"If we had told you, you would have run back and married the girl without even stopping to question the child's paternity. You left town because of her. This would have brought you back and tied you to someone below your status. No Cy Young awards, no MVPs, no world championships. You would have been a minimum wage husband and father, when you were almost still a child yourself. We watched out for you."

He scoffed. "That wasn't about me. That was about you and your gambling addict husband. You squandered your money and needed me as your cash cow."

"I've invested too much in your life. I bore your father's philandering and humiliations so the three of you could grow up in a stable home with both your parents. And look at you...You've made your own money, your own name. You are famous, admired. Because of us, you're practically King of New York."

Marilyn took a look around the room and released a breath.

"I wasn't going to allow you to throw all your potential away on a criminal's daughter. A girl who destroyed her future by getting pregnant when she wasn't even eighteen. She and her little fast-ass friend were probably looking for some fools to get them out of their situation. A child was a sure way to tie you down."

Cam grew hot with every word she uttered until he couldn't take it anymore. "First, Adrianna is not like that. She has her own business and doesn't need my money. She went to college and graduated. Second, you are my mother, Marilyn. Bronwyn is your grandchild. She carries your blood. You didn't even care if she struggled. What if Adrianna had not been able to give her what she needed? You shouldn't have been threatened by Bron. You're my mother. I would have always taken care of you."

"We don't know if that's truly your child, Cameron," Marilyn bit out.

Cam reached for his pocket. "Yes, you do. You saw her. She's mine. It's written all over her face. I'm there. Luciana's there and so is Chase. All your children, mother. You can see all of us at one time or another in the way she acts, smiles, walks. She's beautiful, brilliant and good."

He swallowed and kept his voice low. "She's never been touched by you and I am happy because all she has of you is what nature gave her. Go ahead continue in your denial." He pulled out a sealed envelope and flashed it in front of her. "Keep lying to yourself. Because even if you couldn't see us in her, there are ways you could've found out. I never needed this but you do."

He thrust the envelope at her. It fell on the floor between them. The words "Eastern Maryland Diagnostics" were in the top left corner. Marilyn's eyes bulged out and she took a small step back.

"You better pick it up or I will suggest that one of the social column writers does," Cam searched the room for the first available writer.

He caught Adrianna's worried gaze. She headed toward him. He nodded to Chase who made his way to Luciana and Bron. When he turned back, Marilyn had not moved and the envelope was still in the floor between them.

"Pick. It. Up," he said to Marilyn, just as Adrianna reached him.

Marilyn bent and picked up the envelope. She held it in front of her and Adrianna's gaze flew to his. "Open it." Cam barked low at her.

"Cam…this isn't the time…" Adrianna said.

"The hell it isn't. I want her to open it," he insisted, but Marilyn shook her head. "Either you open it, or I'll find someone that will. Tomorrow, it will be all over *page six* how my parents are addicts that used me to fund their addictions, while keeping my daughter from me."

His mother glared at him but tore the flap of the envelope. She pulled out the paper and began to read. Cam turned his back on her, grabbed Adrianna's hand and walked away.

"When did you get the results?" Adrianna asked while they walked.

"Three days ago," he answered, bracing himself for a fight.

She was silent for a while before she said, "You didn't tell me."

He squeezed her hand tighter and turned towards her and pointed at his heart. "It wasn't anything I didn't already know. I never needed that paper to tell me Bron's mine."

***

Adrianna stood there in the middle of the room, staring at Cam. She was dumbfounded and couldn't think of what to say that wouldn't cause her to disgrace herself by openly bawling in front of all the people who came to see his work. She blinked away the tears gathering and bit the inside of her cheek to keep her eyes dry. Her heart squeezed with all the emotions that were currently balled into a knot in her throat.

His complete acceptance that Bronwyn was his child without needing proof or doubts hit her with a deluge of so many emotions. It was a gradient that went from happy to giddy, followed by delirious. Because she didn't dare do anything else, she tugged at his hand and brought him to her. She inched closer and pressed her lips to his, whispering what she'd longed to say. "I love you."

His body went rigid and she almost smiled at the shock, then the light that shone in his eyes as the meaning of her words seemed to surge within him.

"You do?" he asked, sounding so incredulous it almost broke her.

Deep down, he was still that insecure boy that didn't think he was loved.

"I never stopped," Adrianna answered, her fingers trailing his face.

The smile began in his eyes before his lips curved and stretched into a contagious grin. His arms went around her and he whispered in her ear, "I love you, too. I need you to let me show you how much."

She swatted him in the stomach lightly. "What am I going to do with you?"

He tucked an errant lock of her hair behind her ear. "You're already doing it…But there is one more thing…"

"Mom! Daddy!" Bronwyn called out from behind him.

Cam laughed. "Her timing is impeccable."

Before she could say anything, Barron approached them. "I couldn't help but hear this beautiful little angel call you Daddy, Cam. I think our interview has just taken a different turn. Seems like you've got more than painting going on?"

Adrianna tensed. This wasn't something she and Cam had discussed yet, but they couldn't hide from anymore.

Cam looked at his daughter then back at Barron. "As you know, I keep parts of my life very private, Barron. But this is the one thing I want the whole world to know about me. This is my daughter. Her name is Bronwyn."

18

Adrianna's hands shook and her fingers twirled around the tip of her ponytail. Her throat grew dryer the closer they got to the door. Chase and Luciana had offered to take Bron to Chelsea Piers for bowling and laser tag, so her parents could talk. She and Cam were alone for the evening and the time for the truth had finally come. She owed him that. He'd been amazing to Bron. He had been patient, which was not a word she ever would have associated with Cam. But he had given her time, had accepted Bron without questions and with love.

Love flourished in her heart. He told the press about their child, which was the equivalent of shouting it from the roof. The way he'd said Bron was his daughter with so much pride still made it hard for her to breathe. The ride home next to him, pressed to his side, had been pure torture. His scent, musk with spicy tones, hung around her like a curtain. Heat pooled in her belly and between her legs. She pressed them together, trying to alleviate the flutter in her core. The need pulsated through her body and she almost came off the seat when he'd grabbed her hand to help her out of the car.

She wasn't going to last this way. She needed to calm down because tonight she had to tell him the truth. Even if it hurt like hell and he didn't want anything to do with her anymore. It was only fair.

But she couldn't think past his massive shoulders or how good he looked in his gray shirt or how his big hands wrapped around the door knob. The click of the lock reverberated through her whole body.

Her inner muscles clenched and the moan flew out of her mouth.

He whipped around to face her, trapping her in his gaze and she could have sworn the same fire inside her burnt in him.

His fingers reached for her arm and he guided her inside the house. The door slammed shut and in her next breath, she was pressed against it. She wanted to tell him to slow down so they could talk first. But his mouth crashed against hers. His lips moving over hers with hungry intent and hers, having been starved for so long, welcomed the invasion of his tongue, parting. She wanted all of him, his mouth, his hands, his body, the cock nestled between her legs. Thank god for the five-inch heels that had her eye to eye, mouth to mouth, hips to hips with him.

She bucked her hips, getting full contact with his erection and pressing closer for friction. Heat spread over her body and her blood rushed to her head. He groaned against her lips, her knees giving out. His hands steadied her, settling at her hips. But he didn't pull away. Instead, he rubbed himself against her until she gasped. His tongue plunged into her mouth and she spread her legs wider, pushing forward.

"Tell me you want me." He flicked his hips against hers.

There wouldn't be any talking tonight either. The talk could wait. The world could wait. "I want you, Cam," she breathed out.

"I want you too. So much, Adri."

"Then take me. I can't wait anymore."

Her words came out louder than she meant them to, rougher than she wanted them to. She wasn't sorry. Not when he turned those cat eyes on her or when he reached under her dress and tugged at her panties.

"I can smell you, Adri. Is it still the same? Sweet spices and flowers. I need to know it's still you."

He squatted in front of her, sliding her panties down her thighs, past her knees. She leaned her head back, resting it against the door.

Her panties tickled down her freshly waxed legs. She was grateful for the Buff and Glow treatment she'd gotten at the spa but when his lips pressed against her thighs, her head reared forward, and reason flew out the door.

Cam lifted one of her limbs and rested it on his shoulder. His head disappearing under her dress, his mouth paving a wet trail up. He sucked in a gulp of air.

"Fuck fuck fuck, Adri," he said and followed it with a long slow lap of his tongue. "Peaches and glory."

The tickling sensation built, breaking out fresh waves of need in her body. "Again," she panted, helpless to the rush.

His tongue flicked again, a slow brush from the bottom to the top of her swollen petals that made her chest expand. Her hands grasped a chunk of his hair, holding him in place. She pushed her hips forward, urging him. She needed more tongue, more friction, more Cam.

His fingers pressed against her, opening her, and she almost came off the wall, but he held her hips with his forearms at her thighs. His chuckle vibrated against her skin but he wouldn't look at her. She could barely make out the outline of his head, the low light of the foyer bathed over their skin and he was almost anonymous. And that's not what she wanted. She wanted to see him. She needed to witness his undoing of her. She couldn't let it be like the past when she only fantasized about him when she was with others. She didn't want to press her lips together or have to swallow his name.

But he spread her for his mouth and began to lick over her clit in rhythmic and cadenced laps and swirls. The air became trapped in her body and expanded her with each flick. She dropped her hands from his hair, her eyes frantically searching for something to hold on to. Adrianna was trying to brace herself but he wouldn't let her. He slid two fingers inside her and sucked her nubbin into his mouth, strangling a gasp so loud it echoed off the walls.

She shattered, her legs finally giving out, and she slid—more like melted like a rag doll—against the door.

Cam rose, his body gliding up against hers. The smile on his lips triumphant but tight at the corners. His breath a little labored and the massive reason nestled in the apex of her legs.

She wanted to say so much but her words had gone away. He attacked her mouth, his hips rocking against her, unleashing a fresh surge of desire. The craving he'd just satisfied stormed through her once more. She was wet and wanting him, again.

She returned his kiss with hunger and her eager hands fumbled with his belt. She needed him free, in her palm, in the pussy that clenched and released, greedy for his cock.

Her fingers closed around him. He was so hot, so thick, so long she quivered. "Cam, oh, Cam."

Her fingers slid along his length, her mouth watered just thinking that he would be inside her soon. She needed him and couldn't wait.

"You remember what I like?"

"It's going to be torture," he rasped against her mouth.

"I know. But please…"

He didn't make her beg. She got on her tiptoes and he took his cock in his hand and rubbed the head up and down her slit.

Her head fell back, her teeth closed around her bottom lip, and the guttural scream tore out of her mouth. Then his head settled at her neck, and he hoisted her so her legs rested on his hips.

"Adri, my Adri."

He recited her name, his cock slipping in slow, inch by divine inch inside her. He filled her, stretched her, until she almost couldn't stand it. He stopped, letting her adjust to him. The pressure in her chest built. How the hell could he be so calm and patient? She rocked her hips, driving the urgency but he stilled her again.

She mumbled a protest. Something not in any particular language.

His hand wove around her ponytail and he pulled until her whole neck was exposed. He nipped at it, then kissed it.

"Be a good girl and let me take care of you," he bit out so rough her whole body went still and holy shit, if she wasn't wetter than she'd ever been.

She'd always loved those moments when he took control of her, of her body.

He thrusted, sending all his solid, hot dick deep inside her pussy. Her gaze went hazy and she sucked a gulp of air. He retreated and shoved inside again and she gripped his shoulders, digging her nails but she couldn't stop. Not when he began to move fast, pounding into her so hard his balls slapping against her core. The climax ripped through her, rendering her so helpless with barely enough strength to wrap her arms around him and let him plaster her into the wall. He continued pumping into her, as she pulsated until he muffled a groan against her skin and collapsed against her.

19

He smoothed his T-shirt down his body and treaded down the stairs in quick steps. The cold hardwood bit into the soles of his feet, making him miss the warmth of Adri's body from just minutes ago. They'd dragged themselves upstairs and barely made it through the door before he was inside her, surrounded by her warm pussy. She was tighter around him than the baseball glove he'd barely taken off in ten years.

Cameron smiled. He had made her his again, claimed her with every pound of his hips. He hurried along. He needed to get back to her but first he had to check on Bron. Even though Lux had texted them that Bron was okay and would sleep with her aunt, Adri wanted to come down and check. He had a feeling that if Bron asked her to stay, Adri wouldn't come back to his bed tonight. He couldn't risk that, so he came down instead.

He had plans for them tonight. Big, thick, messy and moaning plans.

Chase stepped out of Lux's room and close the door behind him. He put a finger to his lips, spotting Cam. "She's knocked out. I carried her up and Lux laid next her."

"Okay," Cam said. "Thank you." He also sent a million silent prayers to his lucky stars. He turned to head back, his mind already in Adrianna.

"Wait," his brother called out.

Cam shook his head. Whatever Chase had to say would have to wait until the morning because the semi-hard on pressing against his sweatpants was intent on making a beeline for a heavenly cove. Chase probably wanted to tease him and he didn't have time for that. Nothing was getting in the way of him and Adri anymore.

"Cam."

It was the bite in his brother's voice that stopped him at the foot of the stairs. He turned around and Chase came to meet him there.

"I hate to do this right now because I know you're finally getting time alone with Adri, but remember that girl I used to see? The one that worked for the *Associated Press*?"

Cam scratched the back of his head. "Can this wait—"

"She texted me. She had a tip. The two rag papers are running stories about you and Bron."

Cam's heart sledgehammered into his sternum. "What?"

Chase shook his head. "Barron Lyons is not the only one that overheard your story today. The headlines talk about how the Ace of the Emperors has a love child he kept from the media."

"Fuck." This wasn't good. They didn't need a media shit storm when they were trying to get a house, make plans for a life together, and he hated to think of any of this affecting Bron. The New York media was vicious and unrelenting.

"She told me *The Big Apple Post* is pursuing an interview with mother—"

"No, she needs to keep her mouth shut." God only knew what his mother would tell the press about Adri and Bron and he wouldn't fucking allow that. "Chase, I need you to do me a favor. Go to see Marilyn and make sure she doesn't grant them an interview. Please do it now. I'll go talk to Adri. As long as they don't have names, that should buy us some time."

Chase nodded. "We should have some time still. They don't have photos and mother probably took a pill so she is not awake."

"Double check and wait for her to wake up. Tell her I will cut her off without any pity if she talks to anyone. Make sure Walter knows that too. I will stop paying the house bills and make sure they get kicked out onto the street."

"Maybe you should send Adri and Bron back to Baltimore right away, so they're not here for the bullshit tomorrow," Chase said.

Cam's stomach knotted. He didn't want to be away from them. Would Adrianna think he was trying to shake them away? And what about Bron? He should have known shit would just go wrong. It always did when he had two good hours.

But he had to protect them now even if things got a little hairy. "I think you're right. I'll go talk to her. Please head over to the house and make sure no one talks to the press."

Adrianna sighed and sat up on the bed. She had been given specific instructions not to move from the spot, but Cam was taking way too long. Bron was probably wide awake and had a million questions. She pictured poor Cam trying to answer them fast so he could get back to the bed after what he called the seventh-inning stretch.

She smiled. The last two had been—her insides shuddered and her skin sang—greater than her memories. She had not been wrong, the flame scorched. She still needed more, so much more of him.

Which is why you need to get off this bed and go help him. Bron got overstimulated when she stayed way past her bedtime. She stepped off the bed and looked around for her dress. Her legs were a little bit stiff and there was a small discomfort. She hissed, both at the pain but also the desire that sprang in her lower belly, remembering how it felt to have all of Cam sliding through her pussy, filling her to the brink, making her tremble and buck. He'd stretched her so good. *So good.* She couldn't wait for him to do it again.

She spotted the robe in his bathroom and decided to forgo the dress in favor of it. Then, changed her mind. Bron may ask her why she was in her father's robe and though she needed to explain these things to her, it was a long, delicate conversation. *That was so not happening tonight.*

She pulled the dress over her head when the handle clicked and the door opened.

"I know you told me not to move but I thought you may need my help getting her back to bed." She turned around and her next words froze in her mouth.

He was still as mouthwatering as when he'd left, promising to be back soon. With the undershirt clinging to his body and his big arms hanging at his sides. *Discard the dress now.*

But there was something in his face, a light in his eyes that was different.

"What's wrong? Is Bron not feeling well?"

He stepped in the room and closed the door. "Bron's fine. She's sound asleep. She'll stay with Lux tonight."

If their daughter was okay, then nothing could be that bad. She went to him and put her hands around his neck. "I would think that would make you happy. You promised me a whole lot of extra innings and I've been waiting."

She brushed small kisses on his lips. His hands closed around the small of her back.

"Tell me what's wrong, Cam."

He sighed against her mouth. "Someone overheard my talk with my mother and what I told Barron Lyons. It will be on the covers of the main papers tomorrow."

Her stomach clenched but she breathed it out. "You told a reporter. It's only natural he publishes it."

His hands moved to her face. "Yes, but it's not in the context Lyons would put it in, or his paper that's publishing it. It's the city rags. They're a lot like tabloids. They will sensationalize it. Chase told me they're putting out headlines about my love child."

The blood flowed into her limbs and she moved away to sit on the bed. "Oh. And that means—"

"People camped outside, waiting to catch a glimpse of Bron and constant calls for statements," he finished for her. "I don't mean to sound douche-y but because I'm so popular here, this may become a circus. Right now, they don't know who you are and that will give us some time but once they do, they'll want to find out everything."

"I forgot your life could be tabloid fodder. I didn't think about any of that." She stared into her hands. She never shared photos of Bron on her Facebook and there were only a few, but not of her face, on the restaurant's Instagram. "Her photo will be everywhere now."

People would know who her little girl was and would try to get a piece of her. Something tightened in her chest. Jesus.

Cam knelt in front of her. His warm hands on her face again. "I won't let anything happen to her. I think we can buy ourselves some more time if you and Bron head home tomorrow morning. I'll finish tying up loose ends here and join you by the end of the week."

She closed her eyes. "Why aren't things ever simple? Why is it that every time we have something good going, something has to happen?"

"I know it's a lot," Cam said. "I'm sorry. I should have thought things through better. My mother made me so angry and I wasn't going to deny Bron to anyone. I want the whole world to know how proud I am to be her dad. I was impulsive and I just didn't stop to fucking think about how that could affect her or you."

Her heart bent and flooded. How she loved this man. "Cam, don't punish yourself. I happen to think it's beautiful that you love her so much that you don't care who knows it. I'm a little scared of them finding out about her and her face being everywhere but I don't regret that you told everyone. I was so happy about the way you stood up to your mom in Bron's name that I didn't stop to think either."

He kissed her hands one at a time. "I'll have my publicist do some damage control. I'll sit for an interview with whoever I have to. I'll give the vultures what they want so they can leave you two alone."

Something tugged deep inside her. He was willing to do whatever to protect them. "Don't worry about me. I can handle it and I'll keep an eye on Bron. What about you? Will you be okay? I know you're used to this but it's a lot to deal with."

He sighed. "I'll be fine. I've dealt with scandals before and in New

York, scandals come easy. All I had to do was go through a slump or the team lose a couple of games and they'd be all over me."

She caressed his cheek. A stubble was already thickening there. "I'm sorry."

He shook his head. "Don't be. I chose this. But what if Bron doesn't understand? I don't want her to think that I abandoned her like she did last time when she knew we would be separated."

"Don't worry about that. Things are different now. The two of you spent time together. You got her puppies and you're getting a house that she's helping you pick out. We have to make sure to remind her of all the changes you're making to be with her."

"And you, Adri. All those changes were for you too. I've been planning for us this whole time, too."

Her heart beat so fast and so hard, it rattled her body. "How can I love you this much?"

His smile made her breath catch. She'd make it her life's mission to tell him every day. He brushed his lips over hers and rose, rolling her onto her back. Her hands slipped down his body, hooking into his sweatpants and sliding them over his ass. Her body responding because her mind and her heart were just on him.

He pushed her dress over her hips. She firmly planted her feet on the bed and spread. She snuck a hand between their bodies, grabbed his engorged cock and stroked him, up and down. *God, how she needed all of it inside her.*

He pulled her hand off his dick and placed it at her side. She snuck it back to grab his arm, needing every part of her to have contact with his body.

He pushed the head of his cock past her folds and pain vibrated through her core. Her hands tightened at his shoulder, her nails digging hard. She gasped loud.

He froze, his gaze flying to hers. "I'm sorry." He began to pull out.

She couldn't let him do that. "No, hold on. I'm just a little sore. You're just so big."

Heat flashed over his eyes and his hands fisted on the sheets on both sides of her. "Stop talking like that or won't be able to hold still."

She flexed around him and he pushed inside more. She captured his lips with hers, pushing up higher.

"Fuck," he groaned, his tongue swirling against hers, his hand finding her breast.

He squeezed over her dress, his thumb circling her hard nipple. "The next time I'm going to lick, suck and bite this until you come from that alone."

She moaned, growing more wet, pushing up her hips and guiding her pussy toward him. "Fuck me, Cam. I need it."

He pulled out of her, silencing her protest with his lips. "I'll be right back. I swear." He kicked his pants off his legs and rushed into the bathroom.

She ground her teeth and rubbed the tips of her fingers over her clit. She was so ready. Her fingers moved in circle, her gaze on the door willing him back,

He walked out a minute later with a small bottle of lube in his hand. "Adri," his gaze following the movements of her hand.

He sat next to her with his back against the headboard. She watched in awe as he squirted some lube and rubbed it over his rock-hard flesh. He didn't have to say anything else. She climbed on top of him. His hands steadied her as she lowered herself. There was no discomfort this time, only more of that delicious stretching and filling. Her mouth flew open, her palms pressing against his chest.

"Cam," she moaned.

He pushed the dress over her head and flung it over the bed. His hands palmed her breast, his fingers rolling her nipples. She cried out, flexing her hips and rolling them. His hot mouth latched on to her other breast, sucking it hard until she was out of her mind. Her hands shot out and she laid them flat against the headboard on each side of his head. She used it to balance herself and rocked back and forth. She went slow, at first, letting herself fully adjust.

His hands circle her ass and push her closer. His mouth moving to the breast bouncing in front of it. He grunts when his lips close around it. All the sensations crash together, the pressure of his teeth biting on her nipple, the tip of his cock rubbing on her G-spot, the feel of his balls against the bottom of her ass. Her vision blurred and the little specks of gold appeared and everything burst inside her.

"Oh God," she cried out.

His hands tightened around her ass and he pounded up faster and faster. Her arms closed around him. He released one long grunt and stilled. She tilted his head up and devoured his mouth.

20

"You're going to love Diego. He's so sweet and likes to cuddle. Frida just nips on stuff."

Adri smiled, the familiar scene before her alleviating her heavy heart at leaving Cam. Lauren half lay on the couch and Bron half laying on her.

"I can't wait to meet them. Have I told you I missed you like crazy?"

"Not in the past two minutes," Bron said.

"Oh. I'm due then. I love you, I love you, I love you. You can't leave me again. You're the only one that knows how to make my coffee right. I didn't have anyone to vet my outfits. I've probably been looking a mess for the past weeks." Lauren reclined back with a dramatic sigh. "I can't do life without you."

Bron rested against her. "I'm taking you wherever I go from now on."

"That goes for college too. I'm going with you."

"Won't you be old?" Bron asked.

"Nah, your mom will be old. I'll still look this good."

Adrianna mock-gasped. "Hey, you leave me out of this."

"You'll both be old." Bron kissed her cheek and headed to the bedroom. "I'm going to go call Daddy."

The second she was out of the door, Lauren sat up and smiled. "Okay. I got my awesome cuddling time with her. Now, it's your turn."

"You want me to come sit on your lap too?" Adrianna laughed.

"If you want to. As long as you tell me everything. Do. Not. Skimp on the good details. Let me tell you what I already know. She's got two dogs, her daddy is awesome, her aunt and uncle (whom we will talk about after you tell me about you and Cam) are really cool, though I'm still her number one."

Adrianna shook her head and poked at her. "She said nothing about you being her number one."

"Stop stalling on me. And besides, it's written in her face, in all the 'I miss you' kisses I got. Yup, number one. Now get to talking about all the sexiness that went on."

"Well, let's start with the big one. We are together."

Lauren rolled her eyes. "No shit."

"Do you want to hear this whole story or not?"

"Yes." She leaned forward.

"I didn't think I could let him in. Not after everything in our past and Bron. I was so scared that we could hurt her. But he convinced me. He accepted Bron, even without knowing the results of the DNA. He sees himself and his siblings in her. He treats her like a little queen and is so proud of her. You should have seen the way he told that reporter that she's his and how he defended us to his mom."

Lauren's face scrunched up. "Sorry you had to face that witch. I hope Bron doesn't have to be around her much. Our *princesa* shouldn't be subjected to her."

"No, Cam assured me Mr. and Mrs. Blake won't ever be around her."

"God, I love Cam for that." Her facial features relaxed and she sat back again.

"No more than he loves you."

Lauren frowned. "Me? We haven't gotten a chance to talk or anything."

"It's different now. You took his side on the argument to get us to New York and held the fort so I could go." Adrianna paused to glare. "I forgave you for that, by the way."

Lauren shrugged. "My niece needed to get to know her dad and my bestie needed to get laid. And it seems I was right. Because it was all kinds of yummy, sexy, and dirty. Correct?"

Heat flashed over her chest and Adrianna bit her lip. With anyone else, she would have been coy or not answer, but this was Lo. No sense pretending with someone that knew all there was to know about you.

"I knew it. With those shoulders…"

"Yes, those shoulders, that body, that mouth." Adrianna shuddered.

Lauren slow-nodded. "Oh yeah. That's what I needed to hear. Now you're moving in together and it better not be to some God-forsaken place in Bubbafuck, Howard County. I can't be that far from you and *la princesa.*"

"No, I told him it has to be within 30 minutes of the bistro and downtown. But I think if you wanted, he would build you a wing wher-ever we go."

"Wait, what the hell did you tell him about me?"

"Well, your niece didn't stop talking about you the whole time. How cool you were, everything you do with her, the talks, when you go cheer for her during her baseball games, how you get her and Ayla freebies at ice cream spots by batting your lashes at poor, pimply boys. And she asked him to help pick out a gift for you. He asked me about it and I told him about what we've been through together. How you've been there for us."

Lauren did the one thing she never did. Her umber skin glowed into an unusual, yet delightful shade of scarlet. "Adri, why?"

"He needed to know. If I met his ex-girlfriend—"

"Ugh." Lauren waved a hand. "She looks like a vanilla-latte drinking bitch."

Adrianna laughed. "Anyway, if I had to run into her and learn everything about his siblings in the past ten years, Cam needed to know about my number 1-A."

Lauren smiled. "*Loca.* Anyway, so his siblings…"

Adri bit her tongue because she'd been waiting for this. She'd been saving her energy and this was one of the conversations she was looking forward the most on her way back to Maryland.

"Bron has been keeping me up to date. I know Lux is not a witch anymore. She said she is nice and it kills me that she's my favorite blogger and I never knew. I fucking swear by her beauty recommendations. But, I don't want to talk about her right now." Lo's eyes had that sparkle that always signaled fun times.

"You want to know about the other sibling mostly?" Adri schooled her features straight and waited until her friend nodded. She planned to give Lauren a taste of her own medicine. "You mean the one that's now really muscular and bigger than Cam and still has that twinkle of bad boy in his eye but was so sweet to your niece that she now has him at her mercy? That sibling?"

Lauren's hand covered her mouth. "Oh God. Does he look *that* good?"

Adrianna shook her head. "More. He's gotten so handsome. When he came down the stairs, all I could think was that you would swallow your tongue. He still goes around like a player but Cam says it's mostly an act. He's more grounded than he lets on. I didn't get to say goodbye this morning because he went to do some damage control with their mother."

"Poor guy."

"I know. I need to ask Cam how that went."

"Would it have killed you to send me one photo?" Lauren asked.

"Actually, there are tons in Bron's iPad."

"I need to see those."

"He asked about you." Adri smiled but said nothing else, taking in the widening of her friend's eyes, the stiffening of her spine.

Lauren shook her head. "Nope. Nope. Nope. I don't want to know. The past is coming back to haunt me and that's not good for me like it is for you."

"What? You don't want to know? What past? You haven't even seen him."

"Elias came by last night."

"Why?"

Lauren shrugged but there was a guarded look in her eyes. "He said he came to apologize to you and that he saw my photo on the bistro Instagram page and wanted to say hello."

"Oh. How do you feel about that?" She didn't like it. No, that's not true. She hated it. Elias had once been an asshole to Lauren.

Her friend sighed. "I don't know. He seems a little different. Like he's changed. He apologized for being a—"

"Dick, peehole, jerk," Adri finished.

Lauren laughed. "He asked for my number and wants to stay in touch. I gave him a piece of my mind about the email he sent you and he apologized. Said he was only looking out for Cam."

It still felt weird. "Lo…"

She held up a hand. "I know who he is, Adri. I have my eyes wide open and I'm not looking to date anyone."

"Okay." But she would keep an eye on this situation. "So, you really don't want to know what Chase asked?"

"It's weird here now."

Cam didn't lift his head from the papers in front of him but nodded to Lux. He'd just finished talking to Bron but it wasn't the same as having her here. The house was solemn. Even the puppies were quiet. Frida lay by his feet napping.

"Chase is on his way."

Cam looked at her then. She was carrying Diego. Both were sporting the same sad look in their eyes. Everyone was missing Bron.

"Did he say anything?" he asked.

"No, only that he would be here soon. How could we miss her already? I used to love this house but it feels so empty and they've only been gone four hours."

That's why he hadn't want to look at his sister. He would see too much of what he was feeling. Without Adri and Bron, it just didn't feel right.

"Why don't you call her? She's not going to be in school today since they took such an early flight. Adrianna said she would call her friend Ayla's dad and ask if his daughter could come over this afternoon to hang out with Bron."

"Oh, that's nice. I've been texting with her. She said she would call me around lunch time. I have a feeling she wants to check on Frida and Diego." Lux took the chair across from him and eyed the papers. The question danced in her eyes plain as daylight.

"These are interview questions. I agreed to sit down with *Times Big Apple*. That should lay everything to rest. It's happening this evening. I'm hoping to kill all this noise."

"Yeah, and then you can go to Baltimore." There was no mistaking the sadness in her voice or eyes. Lux was rarely expressive when it came to hurt.

It always touched Cam deeply when she was down in any way. "You can come with me."

She stopped petting the puppy in her arms and her eyes widened a bit but then she shook her head. "You guys need your time alone. I don't want to be a drag."

"You wouldn't be. Bron wants you close and Adrianna would be okay with it. And you don't have to live with us, if you don't want to. I can get you a row house in the city. You can run your blog from anywhere."

She was silent for a while but then sighed and said, "I don't want to be here if you're not. It's only a matter of time 'til Chase leaves."

"Where am I going?" Their brother called from the door. He was still wearing the same clothes he'd left with and there were deep circles under his eyes.

"You stayed there this whole time. Why?"

Chase shrugged and dropped himself on the chair next to Lux. "Marilyn wasn't in a good state."

"Has she been drinking or self-medicating?" Cam asked. He hated that Chase was subjected to their mother's company for that long alone. Because they rarely visited their parents, Marilyn was always at her abusive best when she got one of them on her turf.

"I think a mixture. She's anxious over money. Walter's got some woman stashed up. He didn't come home while I was there. Marilyn wouldn't stop screeching. She wants more money. Apparently, your stipend is barely covering her social lunches and designer shoes," he scoffed.

"She's not getting another dime from me." No way in hell was he giving her any more. "Don't either of you give her anything. What she gets from me is enough."

His brother looked away.

"Damn it, Chase."

"It's the easier route. What do you want me to do? I can't listen to her whine for long. As soon as I promised to give her the added amount, she calmed down and went to sleep. I got the fuck out." He buried his face in his hands.

Luciana brought Diego closer. The move made Cam think of Bron.

Fuck.

Marilyn had taken out her encounter last evening on Chase. Cam knew exactly how that disaster went. She hadn't taken her sleeping pills, but boozed it up instead. When Chase showed up, she'd let him have it. His brother would never have left her in a bad state.

"I'm sorry. You went to help me and got the brunt of it."

"Oh, shut up. I faced the dragon for Bron. She told me last night, I can come live with her. I think that kid loves me. And who could blame her?" The teasing smile back in Chase's face but it lacked the usual effect. He had that tired-and-dragged look in his eyes that all three of them knew so well.

"You're not moving in with us." He hated how thick his voice sound. When he joked with his siblings about kicking them out of his house or how they didn't live with him, it came out harder, almost like he meant it. He never did. He never would.

"It's not your choice, Cam. Lux and I got invited last night. Lux doesn't have a life so she can be there permanently. I'll have to get a little apartment to entertain my lady friends from time to time."

"Ew. And for your information, I do have a life. We all know why you want to go back. Like pumping a nine-year-old for information on her aunt isn't reprehensible enough."

Cam laughed. He should be reprimanding his brother for it but he couldn't make himself do it. "We'll talk about this at another time."

"I was a little curious and yes, let's talk about it without Lux's innocent ears around. She still doesn't get the hang of boys and girls."

"Shut up, Chase."

"Anyway, Cam. Marilyn won't be granting any interviews unless you sanction it. Eddha will call one of us if any reporters call the house."

Eddha had been the Blake's maid for over twenty years. She'd always been sweet with them. Cam suspected out of pity because of who their parents were.

Chase stood up and headed for the door. "Wake me up for dinner."

"We are not your parents, Chase." Lux shot over her shoulder.

"Speak for yourself. Cam's the only dad I'll ever admit to having."

They all laughed but it would have been better if it weren't true.

21

The phone was on its fifth ring and Cam should've hung up already. Adrianna was probably asleep by now. She didn't get much shut-eye last night. He'd kept her up until the wee hours of the morning, kissing and fucking. *No regrets there.*

They'd spent some fantasy hours until she'd sprang from the bed at five in the morning and packed hers and Bron's stuff with an agility and efficiency that left him in shock.

They'd texted throughout the day and she had been busy catching up at the bistro and he had meetings with his lawyers, publicist, and virtual assistants. He'd been talked out by three in the afternoon but still had two major interviews scheduled for the evening.

His thumb hovered over the round end-call icon when her sleepy face appeared on the screen. Happiness sprang in his chest but sank into his stomach when he took in her half-closed eyes.

"Shit, I woke you. Go back to sleep. We can talk tomorrow."

She shook her head. "I dozed off waiting for your call. Your daughter was missing you too much. She asked me to lay with her until she fell asleep." She moved the phone around so he could see Bron snuggled against her chest, one foot over Adri's legs, and her mouth in a pout.

It caused a stir in his chest. "I needed that. I miss you two so much. Lux has been moping around. This house is just too damned quiet. Even Frida and Diego…" He shook his head.

"I miss you too, Cam. I was so worried about you and the interviews. Bron and I talked a lot about you before she fell asleep."

He'd just found out Bron was his daughter a little while ago and missing her that much still surprised him. But he had missed Adri since the moment he'd stupidly walked away from her. "Can you do me a favor? Take a selfie of the two of you like that and send it to me. I want to see your face and hers. Then call me back?"

She nodded. "Okay and I'll go to my room so we can talk. Call you back in two minutes."

One minute later, her text message came through with the image of Bron laying half on top of her. He should be with them right now, not here dealing with press bullshit. He was still staring at the image when Adri's name appeared on the screen. He picked up and she was now sitting with her back against an iron headboard.

"You know, I've never been to your bedroom."

She lowered her lashes and gave him one her saucy smiles. "Oh, I was going to tell you. You won a three-hour tour on Friday when you get here."

"Three hours sounds very brief. I want to make sure to give every corner proper attention. That headboard alone looks like two-hours' worth of inspection and structural testing."

Her pupils dilated into huge brown moons. Yeah, he definitely would be fucking her against that wrought iron.

She closed her eyes and breathed out, "I can't wait."

He should get on a plane right now. Fuck everything else.

"How did today go?" Her question yanked him out of his thoughts, crashing him back into reality.

He shrugged. "It was fine. It's over."

Her eyes narrowed like a doctor inspecting a wound. "Try again, Cam."

"What do you want me to say? It's annoying as all fuck out. I spent years playing with the Emperors and only talked to the media when necessary. They're making me pay for it. My publicist keeps bitching about all the strings she has to pull."

She pressed her lips together in a pout. "Thank you. You're doing this for us and I know it's not easy."

He was dying to kiss that pout off her lips. "Don't thank me now. Thank me when you see me. Use that mouth on me, Adri. I'm dying to have all you over me again."

Her lips parted. "Don't start things we can't finish."

"You can finish it and let me watch."

What the fuck. Was he losing his freaking mind? Did he just actually suggest she got herself off on camera for him? His cock hardened with his palm itching to rub against it. He wouldn't be surprised if she swore at him and hung up.

Except her lower lip disappeared between her teeth and a hooded look came over her eyes. Holy shit, he was going to need a cold shower right after he beat off.

"Cam." She shook her head way too slow, like she was reluctant to do so. "It's just not a good idea but…"

"But?"

She brushed the hair back from her face and looked away for a second. She looked at him again and her skin darkened and glowed. "…I want to."

His cock twitched. *Don't ask her, Cam. Don't fucking ask her.* "Want to what?"

Her face darkened even more, if that were possible, but a determined look came over her eyes and she smiled. *Oh shit.*

"I want to put my hands between my legs. I want to imagine my fingers are yours, rubbing me until I come. I want you to watch me come."

Blood barreled down into his dick and he found one of his hands there. His fingers trembled as he lifted them and placed them back on the desk. "You are evil. Do you know how cold the water is in New York all year round?"

She laughed a little. "Yeah, it is."

"I guess letting me watch you shower is also off limits?" *She's going to hang up on you.*

She shook her finger at him. "I'm not taking a cold shower. I have a vibrator for times like these."

The skin tightened around his whole body and he let his head fall back. "Adrianna, I still have to eat dinner with Chase and Luciana. How am I supposed to do that now?"

"Perhaps, we should switch to less sexy topics?"

He nodded. "That would be safe." It wouldn't help his aching cock but maybe it could keep his mind off it. "How's the bistro?"

"Running smooth. Lauren did a great job in my absence. I'm impressed at how Adrianna-like she managed it."

"Tell me how that is."

She smiled and he should have known she was about to tease him. "You know how hands-on and thorough I like to be with *everything*."

"Adrianna."

"Okay. Okay. I'll stop." Her eyes still twinkled and damn him, he loved it when she was this playful.

"Oh. Wait, here's something certain to kill the mood. Elias Saunders. Lauren told me he stopped by last night."

"What did he want?"

"Supposedly, he wanted to apologize to me and see how she was doing." The air quotes, her lips pressed together into a flat line, and that not-amused look he knew so well, all made Cam uneasy.

"Look, he's a friend. I confided in him about Bron and you. I was reeling and he was around. I know he got carried away with that email but I already ripped him a new ass—"

"I'm not mad you told him about Bron. It's only normal. I guess he was trying to protect you. I just don't understand why he came here when you're not around?"

Her tone had more bite than usual when she was mad. "Elias is a good guy. He just takes the lawyer thing too seriously. I told him my lawyers would handle it. Maybe he wanted to make sure they did. I don't think he set out to be an asshole on purpose."

"Okay," she sighed.

"Are you going to tell me what's wrong?"

"I don't like your friend very much."

"You're not the only one," he muttered but she heard him.

"Who else doesn't like him?"

"Chase."

She nodded. "Chase and I don't like him for the same reason, but I know he's your friend. I'll be civil to him, but he better be on his toes."

"Wait, did he do something to you?"

She shook her head. "But it's like he did."

He was about to ask but Chase appeared at the door. "Food's here."

"Go eat. We can talk some more tomorrow. I'll call you during the drive to Bron's school in the morning."

"You're going to bed, then?" Damn, could he sound more pathetic?

"Yeah. I have to be up early and you know I have that thing I need to do before I go to sleep."

He couldn't say anything and she laughed. "Love you, Cam."

"So, what's Adrianna up to tonight?"

Images of her long, feminine fingers with their pretty, pink, manicured nails slipping between her legs, rubbing slow circles against her pink bud washed over him. Cam's stomach dropped and he squeezed the ketchup out of his bacon cheeseburger.

All the self-coaching he had done on the way to the living room flew out of the window. Her lips were probably parting and her hips bucking against her fingers. His dick was once again straining between his pants. *Fuck, fuck, fuck.*

"She's fine." His voice was rougher than he intended.

"You're in a mood. That's my cue to go upstairs." Lux began to stand up but he put a hand to her wrist.

"Don't go. It's been a long day." Yes, he was lying. It's not like he could tell his sister he was about to burst through his pants imagining Adrianna getting herself off.

"This house is just dead without Bron." She sat back down.

"You guys need to get a grip. Even the mutts are depressed." Chase shrugged. "They only perked up when Bron called me earlier."

Cam smiled. His little girl was sweet, caring, and amazing.

"You mean when you were pumping our niece for information?"

"Don't be spiteful or those wrinkles will get bigger, Lux. Anyway, I was asking her how the important people in her life are. That's what you do when you care about someone."

"Yeah, right." Lux rolled her eyes.

That's when it hit Cam. "Lauren. That's why you and Adrianna don't like Elias."

Chase's hand stilled. "We don't like him because he's an asshole."

Lux nodded. "He was always so nice to me and at first I thought he was hot, until one time he came to the house when Cam wasn't there. He was really douche-y to Eddha when I went upstairs to look for something—" Her gaze landed on Diego, who was sniffing circles around the carpet. "Oh, shit."

She picked him up and ran toward the door. Frida took off after her.

"Why did you bring up Twittle-Fuck, Esquire? Just to piss me off?" Chase took a swig of his beer.

"He went to the bistro looking for Adri and Lauren." Cam had expected a reaction out of Chase, but the flash of darkness on his brother's eyes was a bit disconcerting.

He continued. "Adri was not happy about it. She didn't tell me why she doesn't like him. Just that you and she don't like him for the same reason. I'm guessing this all goes back to Lauren. But I never knew Elias had any interest in her. She wasn't exactly his type back then. He was all about law school and Lauren was two years younger. Elias wouldn't have messed with a minor."

Chase didn't look at him. "He wasn't sleeping with her, if that's what you're thinking…"

"I wasn't."

"…but he toyed with her."

"We all did dumb things when we were young. Look at me." Cam pointed at himself.

"And me too. But, there's something about him. He's someone else with you. I am glad you didn't make him your lawyer."

It had been a point of contention in his relationship with his friend. But after the e-mail he'd sent to Adri, Cam no longer felt guilty about it. "It wasn't a business decision. I was advised not to hire friends to handle my business affairs. Then again, I'm full of shit, since I hired you."

Chase shot him a crooked smile. "But I'm brilliant about making you money and you know I would chop off my own arm before I failed you."

"I know. He might have gone because maybe he thought I didn't listen to his advice the other day."

His brother flipped his palm up in question.

"He went to see me when I went to the art show. It was the day I met Bron and saw Adri again. He was giving me sound advice on getting a paternity test and he offered to set it up. I told him no, that I would let my lawyers handle it." Cam finished his burger and pushed the plate aside.

Chase grunted. "That must have been another blow to his mammoth ego."

"He was looking out for my best interests because he said that I'm always stupid around Adri."

His brother nodded. "You are."

"He sent her an email with a paternity test request."

A muscle ticked in Chase's jaw. "That asshole. He's not your fucking lawyer. I don't think he gets that shit. You're never going to hire him."

No, Cam never would. "It bugs me even more after today's visit. It would be normal for a friend to check up on this for another, but…"

"…you had it under control," Chase finished. "There was no need for him to go check and definitely not without telling you. Unless he really was just looking for Lauren."

"Yeah. Are you going to tell me what he did to her? I think I should know, since both you and Adrianna get this death glare when his name comes up."

Chase shoved more fries in his mouth and took his time chewing.

"Did he physically harm her?" No, it couldn't be. Elias would never do anything that would jeopardize his law career. Even back then.

"No. He just played with her feelings then humiliated her."

Cam frowned. "Is that the only reason you don't like him? I keep thinking you never liked him since you first met him."

"I didn't. He hated me first, though."

"Why do you think that?" Cam asked.

"Because he wanted Walter for a father and you for a brother. He could've kept Walter. I would be more than happy to gift wrap that motherfucker and send him to him."

Cam barked out a laugh.

"But Lauren…I guess I'll have to come to Baltimore to make sure that walking queef doesn't try anything with her again." Chase smiled again.

Cam sobered up. "She's Adrianna's best friend and like a second mom to Bron. You better not mess with her."

22

"How long do we have before you get to Bron's school?" Cam's voice came through the speakers and bounced off every corner of the interior of the SUV.

Adrianna took the exit and blew a mouthful of air. The ride had been only slightly better than bumper to bumper. Cam had just called her back five minutes before. She couldn't believe it was the beginning of April and she was blasting the heat in her car.

"I'll be there in the next ten minutes. Why?"

"I wanted to ask you something important." His tone was way too serious.

A pang of unease broke out on the tip of her stomach. *What now?* "Okay," she said in a tentative tone of her own.

"Is Mr. Vibrator making an appearance tonight?"

Adri almost ran the light and slammed on her brakes. Her heart hammered at her throat but no way she was going to let him rattle her like that without payback. "It all depends. Mr. Vibrator is a SatisfyMe 2.0. Although last night I decided it should be called Kam with a K." God, she'd been so tempted to play for him in front of the camera. "Cam with a C should come home so I don't need the SatisfyMe, anymore."

"You're evil."

"I'm keeping it real." She kept her eyes on the traffic light and her bottom lip trapped between her teeth. These conversations were becoming more frequent and she felt like they were back in the summer that changed their lives. They'd teased each other so much back then and spent way too many times between the sheets.

"The real Cam will be there this weekend to retire the SatisfyMe."

"I'll start stretching." The words were barely out of her mouth and they both started laughing. Then an idea occurred to her. "Hey, we didn't talk about birth control but we're safe. I use a method called the ring."

"Okay," he said.

She frowned. "I'm telling you so you know that we have no worries about two nights ago."

"I wasn't worried," he said.

"At all?"

"No. I mean, I didn't think about it. I guess given our history, I should have been, but…"

She kept her eyes on the road. "But?"

"I don't know…for some reason I wasn't. I never can think clearly when I'm horny around you."

She laughed. "Thanks, I think."

"You know what I mean. I take it you don't want any more kids." Was his voice thicker than before?

"I never gave it much thought. Bron and I…we're a well-oiled machine. You know? A new baby would mean starting all over…"

"But not alone. I would be there, with you this time. We would do it together."

Oh, he was really thinking about this. "True. Sooo…are you saying you want another baby?"

"If you'd asked me weeks ago, I would've said fuck no, but Bron and you changed so many things. I don't just want to paint and hide."

It brought a smile to her. "You changed things for us, too. Why don't we talk about it when you get here? By the way, if we have another kid, you'll need to get a minivan."

"A…what?"

"Not a soccer-mom one. Since you're super rich, you can get a designer, state-of-the-art one."

He said nothing.

She continued. "It can be in the Emperors' colors and you can put some shiny rims on it like your Audi."

He still said nothing.

She stirred the pot some more. "Sometimes, I pick Ayla up for school activities and take her and Bron to practices. Her dad, Oliver, is the baseball coach. Maybe you can be his assistant."

She pressed her lips together, counting the seconds of silence.

"His assistant?"

"Yeah," she managed without laughing. "Help him pick up the kids, making sure the helmets are all shiny and taking the smaller kids to the bathroom." She snorted in the end.

"You are *really* evil, Adrianna."

"So you keep telling me. I'm about to go inside the campus. Bron will call you when she gets home or maybe on the way back. I'm trying to get home before I-95 becomes more of a nightmare. Love you."

"Love you, too, Evil Queen. The weekend cannot get here fast enough."

The smile stretched all the muscles in her face. She sat there for a few seconds, savoring the happiness. Things were not perfect, but she and Cam were together and he was coming home in a couple of days. She'd make arrangements to spend some time alone with him while Bron was in school and before she opened the bistro.

Adrianna jumped out of the vehicle and closed the door. Bron's math teacher waved at her and pointed in the direction of the benches near the building entrance. She spotted Bron, Ayla, and Winter. Adri thanked him and headed their way.

"Mom. Guess what?" Bron wrapped her arms around her waist. "Miss Winter is going to have a booth at *Artscape* again and she wants to put one of mine and one of Ayla's paintings in her tent. And she wants to work with us on a project."

Adrianna's chest tightened a little. Her baby's art would be at the biggest art festival in Maryland. Cam was going to be so proud and happy. Her eyes welled.

"Bron, you should have let me talk to your mom first," Winter's gaze was on Adrianna.

She fanned her face with her hand. "I'm more than okay. I'm so proud of you Bron." She hugged her daughter and pressed a kiss to her head. Then turned to Ayla and pulled her into her arms and kissed her cheek. "So proud of you too, Ayla."

Ayla's shoulder curved in and she gave Adrianna a sheepish smile. "Thanks."

Adrianna touched her cheek and so many emotions flooded through her, she had to turn away. Damn Ayla's mother for leaving her. No way in hell would Adrianna ever be separated from Bron. Ayla's mom had just left one day, saying she was going on a business trip. Next time they'd heard from her, she was living in California with a new man.

She looked to Winter and she saw her emotions reflected on her face. The teacher nodded at her and Adrianna sighed.

The girls moved to the side whispering to each other.

"Congratulations," she said to Winter, who much like Ayla, shrank under the compliment. "Stop that. You're now a Maryland gem. Third time at *Artscape*. And thank you for doing that for the girls. We are so going to campaign for this. I'll have a poster made for the bistro. You're going to be sold out."

"I hope so. I'm happy to share this with them. They're always so encouraging."

"We have to celebrate this. I'm thinking of inviting Ayla for a sleepover soon. You, Lauren, and I can have some wine after the bistro closes. Then the two of you can hit the bars."

"You didn't learn from the last time?"

Adrianna laughed. Her hand smacked over her mouth at the images of Winter and Lauren serenading her from the sidewalk outside the bistro at four in the morning. The drunks in the square had joined in. The neighbors were not happy.

She turned away to try to control her laughter. She couldn't do that while looking at Winter. Her gaze almost passed over the man on the other side of the fence. *Almost.* Her heart slammed against her ribs, rattling every bone in her body. It made the blood slush through her veins. Ten years of fear materialized in a face, though far away, clear as day. Walter Blake nodded to her, watching her like she did him.

"Oh God."

"What is it?" Adrianna whipped about to find Winter close. "Who is that man?"

Breathe, just breathe. Don't let him see how scared you are.

She concentrated on willing the air into her body. "Cam's father. Have you seen him before?"

"What? He was around this morning. I assumed he was waiting for someone. Should I call security?"

He'd been there that morning. He was watching Bron. Adrianna's stomach lurched but she grabbed Winter's hand to steady herself. "I need to get home but please promise me if you see him again, you'll call me and never let him near Bron. Please."

Winter frowned but nodded. "Let me drive you and Bron home. I don't think you are okay. You're pale and your hands are so cold."

"I'll be okay. I just need to calm down. I don't want to scare Bron. I'll explain another time. Can you call Lauren and tell her that I'm on my way home? And tell her I saw Walter Blake at the school."

She barely remembered saying goodbye to Ayla. She concentrated on asking Bron about her day, her eyes darting into the rearview mirror. Her breath stuck like a solid block in her lungs. She breathed easier when they'd crossed the tunnel and she took the exit onto Boston Street. She parked her SUV and ushered Bron inside.

Lauren waited at the door. She took one look at Adri and threw her arms around her.

"Why are you hugging her like that?" Bron asked.

Lauren gave her a mock scoff. "Because I missed my bestie. She was gone for weeks and now she left me to go pick you up."

Bron rolled her eyes. "Grow up. I'm going upstairs."

Adrianna couldn't stop shaking. "Wait…"

Lauren stopped her. "Let her. She will be okay there. You have to calm down, go in your office and call Cam. I'll go bring her a snack and settle her. I'll be there to check on you after. Just breathe Adri. He can't do anything to you. He's just being an old, wrinkled dick."

Adrianna took two deep breaths and headed to the office. *Bron was safe. Bron was safe. Bron was safe.*

Now, she just needed to break the news to Cam.

23

Adrianna and Bron did not call him on their way home.

He wished that he could have been a part of their afternoon commute and not here setting things up for his departure. He decided to use the time constructively and meet with his assistant. Marli was the daughter of two of the crew members at Emperor Stadium. Her parents had always been nice to him when he was playing. Cam hired her straight out of college as a favor to them and he'd never been sorry. She was a sweet kid, shockingly efficient, didn't harbor some sort of crush on him, and there was no way Chase could get inside her panties.

In her pink skirt with purple tights underneath, she couldn't look older than fifteen. The one time they'd met, Bron had taken one look at her and declared her a fashion icon. He liked Marli but he needed to get her out of here. He wanted to talk to his daughter at leisure. He'd missed her like crazy all day. How was that possible? He'd never known about her and now he couldn't deal with a few hours of separation well.

"You'll need to handle things here while I'm gone. I'm always a phone call away and I want you to travel to Maryland every two weeks to meet with me. I also need you to check on the sale of the Acacia Falls property. Chase and Lux have no desire to go back and have decided to sell it. It's a money pit right now and I could be throwing that cash into other investments."

Marli scribbled as fast as she kept nodding. The bobbing of her head was pretty much a recording mechanism.

"While you're at it, tell the realtor I need her to look for a beach house an hour or two from Baltimore. I want to have a short getaway place to take Adri and Bron. And remind her that I need some other investment properties in Maryland. Tell her I want in on new developments and row houses."

"Okay, Cam. I'll also make sure your lawyers and Chase get copied on the communication. Do you want it all in your name? Or some in Bron's too?"

He smiled and nodded. "Also, find me a nice row house in the city. Fells Point, Federal Hill overlooking The Inner Harbor, Canton, or Harbor East. I want a place for Lux to run her blog and where she is close to everything."

Marli nodded. "Will do. Is that all on your side?"

"No, I have one more thing. The two-bedroom apartment in the basement. I had it done for whenever one of my teammates stayed over. You know I don't like strangers in my space?"

"We all know, Cam."

He ignored the dryness in her tone. "I was thinking that I need someone to house sit when Lux moves south. I was wondering if you would—"

Her eyes went wide like an anime character's. "I'll do it," she gasped.

Cam chuckled. "You won't have to pay for anything, just your own food. I'll just need you to go through the house, sort my mail and make sure I see what I need to see. You can work from the office. I can have the furniture removed from the apartment if you want and you can bring your own stuff."

"Are you serious? I live in a small, Bronx apartment where my parents had everything covered in thick clear plastic. My room only has my clothes, the white bedroom set they bought when I was five, and Janelle Monáe posters. There are Hello Kitty stickers all over my dresser. I'll keep your expensive furniture." Her energy jumped on her every word but she still managed to roll her eyes in the end.

"About guests, even your girlfriends—"

"I'm only dating Tessa now and she is too afraid of you to come into the house. I will make sure the guests come in through the separate entrance." She pushed her glasses up. The sparkly unicorn horn design glinted against the light. "You can trust me, Cam."

"I know. That's why I'm offering it to you. I think that settles it. You got anything for me?"

"Now that you mentioned it." She rummaged through her purse and pulled out a thick folder. She opened it to reveal a wad of papers with color-coordinated tables. "I have a list we need to go through."

Fuck. "What the hell is that?"

Her eyes narrowed in that you-know-damned-well kind of way. "I think you know. We have to know who's in charge of all your ventures and what to do with all your stuff here."

Cam loved that she wasn't a pushover but shook his head anyway. This wasn't happening. She nodded, her smile sweet as apple pie with two scoops of caramel gelato but her eyes shone with her the strength of the bulldozer she could be.

His cell phone rang and she shot him a forbidding look. Then looked at the object and sighed like she'd already lost the battle. "It's Adrianna."

Yep, she'd lost. And he won.

Anticipation rushed through his body and he reached the desk in two steps. "Hey."

"Can you talk?" He barely recognized her voice. It was strained and thick and it pricked at the hairs on his neck.

"What's wrong?"

"Oh, Cam. Something's happened. Your father is here in Maryland."

"What? Walter is there? At the bistro?"

"He was outside Bron's school when I went to pick her up. And Winter says he was there in the morning. Cam… he was watching Bron."

Her voice dropped at the end and along with it his stomach. *What the fuck was wrong with Walter?* Only a lunatic would try to pull something like this. Only, his father wasn't crazy. Walter was a greedy bully out to manipulate him. He was dead set that Cam should continue bank rolling his gambling habit. No more. Walter had bet wrong this time around. No way in hell would he let him terrorize Bron or Adri.

His hand tightened around the phone. "Adri, listen to me. If he comes to the bistro, call the cops and have him arrested. I'm on my way." He shot a look to Marli. "Book me the first flight to Baltimore you can find."

She was going to punch the damned laptop and then throw it out the window. Except it was Adrianna's, not the laptop's fault. She was the one that wasn't thinking straight and entered the amounts five times, every time messing up the digits.

She slammed her hands on to the glass top and blew the air pent up in her chest. Her gaze drifted to the monitor screen and Bron was still painting by the light of the living room window. Thank God she wasn't here to witness the mess of nerves her mother had become. Adri was relieved she'd asked to go upstairs and paint. She was safe, and Adri could keep an eye on her through the monitor.

No one could get into her apartment before passing by the office door. *So, calm down.*

Her gaze was in a ping pong game from the monitor, to her laptop, to the gold clock. It was seven thirty-five. She had not heard from Cam since right before his plane took off an hour and a half ago and had to force herself not to call him to see if the plane had landed. They'd been on the phone until they'd called him to board. He'd been a calming force for her. And now the silence was killing her.

The office was becoming smaller by the second. She couldn't stay in here anymore. She should go upstairs to check if Bron was hungry and then go help out a little in the bistro. No, she couldn't do that.

Lauren had banned her to the office because she had been getting on the staff's nerves. She had to do something.

She went around the desk and headed for the door. Cam appeared at the top of the stairs wearing jeans, a T-shirt and black zip up with a hoodie over his head. His eyes were clouded with worry. Only one other thing in her life was that beautiful and comforting, her daughter. She crossed the room in two steps and threw her arms around him. His closed around her and she let herself settle into the warm feeling. He pulled her head back, looked into her eyes, and everything faded.

His lips touched hers, tender and warm, pressing her against his chest. It wasn't a kiss of desire or a hello kiss. It was a kiss of love. One that let her nerves settle in her belly so she could kiss him back. She'd missed him so much. Her hands bunched on his T-shirt and she pulled him to her, trying to fuse herself into his chest.

He pulled back, his eyes roaming over her face. The frown was there.

She leaned her head into his chest. "I'm so glad you're here." She usually had to weather the storms alone. It felt good to have him there to lean on.

"It's going to be okay. Walter is just trying to force my hand. Where's Bron?"

She pulled back and turned the monitor around so he could see. Their little girl was in front of the easel but she wasn't painting. Her head was tilted to the side and she moved from one side, closer, then back and to the other side.

He smiled. "I do that. She's trying to see if she caught the light from all angles."

Adrianna grabbed his hand, interlacing her fingers through his. "Come on, it's a good moment for her to see you. She has some news for you."

She pulled him toward the door but he didn't move.

"Wait, are you okay?"

She turned to look at him again and the answer was fast. "Yes." *Because you're here.*

He pushed off the desk and let her guide him upstairs. At the door she motioned for him to go in first. He opened the door and she followed behind. Bron was still in front of the easel, examining the paint.

"Mom, I think you're going to like this one," she said without turning.

"I'm sure she will," Cam answered.

Bron whipped around, her mouth turned into a perfect little O and with rounded eyes to match. "Daddy."

She rushed to him and he picked her up from the floor. Adrianna didn't know who was smiling harder.

"I thought you weren't coming 'til the weekend."

"I pushed up my trip. I'm glad I did. I missed you too much."

She kissed his cheek. "Mom, did you know he was coming?"

Adrianna shook her head and chose a modified version of the truth. "Not until like two hours ago."

"And you didn't tell me!"

Adri smiled, "I wanted to see that surprised look in your face when you saw him."

She narrowed her eyes and then looked at her dad. "Next time you call me, and we surprise Mom. Do you want to see what I painted today?"

He nodded. "Show me." And winked at Adri.

2 4

Coming to Baltimore was the best decision he'd ever made. Adrianna was calmer, happy if he went by the smile on her face. When her gaze landed on him, Cam was euphoric, like when he'd struck out the last batter to win the first round of the playoffs. She was quieter than usual and mostly listening and laughing at the way Bron stole his fries.

"These are really good," he said, holding up a fry.

"They're made in house, with organic potatoes. They're chopped and marinated in cold water with basil. Then, we season them with sea-salt and crackled pepper and fry them in duck fat at three hundred and seventy degrees for eight point five minutes," Bronwyn said.

He looked from her smile to Adrianna's pride flushed face. "Wow. How do you know all that? Have you made them before?"

Bron shook her head. "No. I'm not allowed too close to the fryers but I sit on the stool and supervise. I always help out the newbies on the staff by watching the timer and making sure they add the right stuff. They always give me extras—" She clamped her lips shut.

Cam laughed. It was great to be home. *Home*? "What else do you know how to make?" he asked Bron.

"Everything in the bistro. Right, Mom?" She didn't wait for Adri's answer. "She says I need to know all aspects of the business because

173

it's mine too. I bring out the dessert menus and I help Mom with the flower arrangements. She told me yesterday during our flight that we are doing orange and pink Ranu-somethings in the summer."

"Ranunculus. They look like small—"

The knock on the door had her springing to her feet mid-sentence. "It's probably Lo. She's only knocking because you just got here." She went to answer the door.

"When is Aunt Lux coming with Frida and Diego?" Bron asked for the third time in the past hour.

"She'll be here next week. Okay? Now you have to give me all your attention and we can start brainstorming for your *Artscape* solo piece. I'm so proud of you." He kissed her forehead. It was true, his heart was bursting at how talented and dedicated she was.

"Hey, Cam, I have a question for you," Lauren yelled from the door.

Where was Adri? Why was Lauren the one calling him? He stood up from the couch but kept his face neutral.

"Can I finish your fries?" Bron asked.

He nodded and made his way to the door. Lauren and Adri wore matching strained looks.

He sighed. "What the fuck did Walter do this time?"

"He showed up," Adri said.

"I told him to leave but he refuses." Lauren sighed. "He wants to talk to you and won't leave until you see him."

"Fine. Let's get this over with."

Adrianna's hand clamped over his wrist. Cam could barely take the weight she carried but she squared her shoulders back. "Tell him to leave us the hell alone."

They still had a conversation pending and it would have to be tonight. He'd dispatch Walter and come upstairs so she could tell him what the hell his father had on her. He kissed her and followed behind Lauren down the stairs.

On the last step, she turned to him. "She has nothing to be ashamed of and your father is a grade-A asshole for what he's done to her."

He couldn't have agreed more. "It stops today."

She shot him a wry smile over her shoulder and pointed him to the table at the corner of the room. Walter sat there, facing away from the window. He glanced at his watch several times, the vessel glinting against the light of the table candle.

"I'll bring you a beer, unless you need something stronger?" Lauren asked.

"Beer's fine, thanks." He made his way to the table, ignoring the rage and urges to haul Walter by the neck of his shirt and kick him onto the sidewalk.

His father looked up, a happy-to-see you smile creeping up his cheeks. Cam dismissed the fresh wave of heat creeping up his spine. He wasn't going to let anger get the best of him. He was going to listen to Walter, then tell him to get the fuck out.

"Cameron."

"Walter."

His eyes narrowed. "Father," he corrected.

"You know the biggest lesson I learned playing in New York? Don't boast about titles you haven't earned." He took the chair across from him. "Make it quick."

"You have to help me. You cut me off and I had to go to a loan shark. Now, I need to pay him."

Cam shook his head. "That's none of my business. I gave you a stipend for years. I went to bat for the family after you gambled away even our house that one time. I won't do it anymore. Lux and Chase are adults and you kept my daughter from me."

He shrugged a shoulder. "I didn't do that. Not technically. The Hayes girl did."

"Arenas, and because you forced her to."

Walter smiled. "She told you what I know?"

Cam said nothing.

"Oh. She didn't. The apple doesn't fall far from a tree. She's got Fausto's genes. Though she and her mother may just be worse than him."

Cam scoffed. "You can't even ask for things like a normal human being. You need me. I don't need you. Act like it."

"Don't be so sure. If I revealed what I know, you'd be the one begging me for help. Your mother told me you had the kid tested. Congratulations. You're about to learn the sacrifices a parent makes for his child."

His stomach dropped. He couldn't take much more of this.

"Here's your beer, Cam." Lauren called out a few feet away. She approached the table and placed it in front of him.

"I'll have some water," Walter said.

She leaned closer and smiled. "*You* don't want me anywhere near anything you have to eat or drink."

She walked away still smiling, her long ponytail bouncing with every step. Walter's lip curled, making Cam chuckle.

"That girl is another piece of trash. You and your brother should be forever grateful of what your mother and I did to protect the two of you. At least you were smart enough not to bring your tail home." He tapped the table as if to signal he finished talking.

Cam was still stewing over his implications. "First, Adrianna and Lauren are not trash. They never were. You need to leave and never come back. And don't ever show your face anywhere near Bronwyn's school. I will personally have you arrested if I see you again."

"No, you won't. Because I'm your father and I always protected you. You got to do the same for me with the loan shark. You know these people hurt those who don't pay. You got to help your daddy."

Cam stomach rolled this time. Daddy was a word he now loved and would work the rest of his life to always deserve. But the man in front of him would never hear it from his lips. "Leave, Walter. Go find a new cash cow. I'm done with you."

Walter stood up. He was calm like he'd gotten what he came for. "I'll give you until tomorrow to get me what I need. I can't be responsible after that. Talk to Adrianna. I'm sure she'll tell you how important it is to be there for your father."

He walked away. Cam's hand tightened on the beer. He needed answers.

He headed upstairs, waving to Lauren. The living room was empty and the house all quiet except for the whispers coming from Bron's bedroom.

"Is your head hurting tonight?" his daughter asked.

"No, I think I just need some sleep." Adri's voice was soft but heavy.

Fucking Walter.

Cam move to the bedroom door. Adrianna lay on the bed with Bron's face pressed against her chest.

"Your heart's beating really fast, Mom."

Adrianna opened her mouth but said nothing.

"It's because I'm around," he said, finding himself in the center of her worried gaze.

"Oh, you make her heart beat fast because she's in love with you?" Bron asked in that sing-song way children use to tease.

Cam chuckled. "A little, right?"

"A lot," Adri said, staring into his eyes.

A knot settled at his throat. He didn't know how to ease that pain in her eyes. Her gaze shifted to their daughter and her hadn't realized he was holding his breath.

Bron smiled hard, her little hand pressing closer to her mom. Adri pressed a kiss to her forehead. "Hey, how about if you do bedtime with Daddy tonight? That way I can help close downstairs?"

Bron nodded, padding the spot her mother left vacant.

Adri gave him a smile on the way to the door, then stopped and turned to look at Bron again. "By the way, remember this afternoon when I picked you up from school and you and Ayla moved away to talk?"

Bron nodded.

Adrianna's face was serious now. "I don't know what you said to her. Do you know why that is?"

Bron shook her head.

"Because it was private between the two of you. I was curious about what you had to say to her but everyone's privacy has to be respected. I respected yours, so from now on I expect you to respect mine, Daddy's, and everyone else's. I don't want you eavesdropping anymore."

Bron nodded again, her mouth taking the downturn of someone who's been chastised. The sadness in her eyes wrenched at Cam's heart and he wanted to tell her it was okay and not to be sad, but the forbidding look her mother was aiming his way had the words drying in his throat. She could read right through him.

"Good night, *princesa*," she said and headed out the door.

Cam cleared his throat and made his way to the bed. He lay next to Bron, who was still looking down. "You want to talk about it?"

"Mom's really mad at me."

His chest squeezed. *Damn his fucking heart.*

Still, he understood. Adrianna was making sure they didn't have eager little ears during tonight's conversation. "She's not mad. She's just serious."

"What's the difference?"

"When you're mad, your body gets hot and you're angry and upset."

And you want to punch your asshole father for all he's done.

"When you're serious, you just want the other person to know that what you're saying it's important and they should listen."

"Oh, okay," she said.

"So, no more eavesdropping, right?"

She smiled, her eyes twinkling, and nodded.

25

It had taken all his willpower to stay awake. The only thing that kept Cam from falling asleep beside Bron was the need to put whatever secret Adrianna was keeping in the rear view. As soon as Bron sighed her first soft snore, he jumped out of the bed, tucked her in and headed for Adri's office.

He considered putting his head down on the desk until she got back but soft steps tapped up the stairs and he stood up. Their gazes met when she reached the top step. She had a thick folder in her hand and a wary look in her eyes. The sigh that rushed out of her lips tore right through him.

"I put the monitor in Bron's bedroom. She promised she wouldn't eavesdrop, but I swear she looked like Chase when she said it." He was only half joking and trying to coax a smile out of her. It didn't work. "Chase was a learning experience. I hope Bron doesn't get half as good at fibbing as he used to be."

Her lips inched up but didn't bend enough to pass for a smile. "What did Walter want with you?"

He shrugged. "What he always wants, money."

"What did you say?"

"I pretty much told him to go to hell. He's not getting a dime from me."

She winced. "It's not your responsibility to give it to him."

"Exactly," he agreed.

She walked around the desk, stopping to glance at the monitor, and then placed the thick folder on top of the desk. "It's mine. That's why I want you to give him this." She pushed the envelope toward him.

His heart thumped, and he almost laughed at his own dramatic reaction. He gave it a brief glance. "What is that?"

"All the bistro's papers, the deed to the building, and what's left on my bank account," she said.

God, he hated that fucking blank look on her face.

"I'm not giving this to him. That's yours. You worked hard, sweated, and went without for it. Walter has never had to work for a damned thing in his life."

"Whatever I have to give so he can leave my Mom and Bron alone, it's worth it."

"Adri, he's a bully. You would tell Bron not to give in to a bully."

"This is not a fucking infomercial, Cam. He has us. Don't you get it?" Her face stayed blank, even as she swore like she'd already resigned herself.

"I think it's time you told me everything."

"Fine, sit down." She motioned to one of the chairs but took the one behind the desk.

"Come sit next to me."

She shook her head. "It's better if I'm on this side."

It irked him. Not just her words but the drama and everything. "Okay, fine. But please don't stall. Don't drag it out. Just spit it out, Adri."

Her eyes lit up in such a familiar way. He'd seen that light in every explosive fight they'd ever had and his most vivid memory of it had been that afternoon by the falls when she'd banned him from her life and he'd been stupid enough to listen. He wouldn't have a repeat and opened his mouth to try and modify what he said.

"My mother and I shot my father and left him on the side of the road. He called your father and told him the whole story before he died. Your father has a recording of it. When I got pregnant with Bron, he threatened to send the audio to the cops if I went to you. How's that for blurting it out?"

Cold rushed over Cam's stomach, freezing his blood in place. He hadn't known what she would say but this was definitely not what he expected. "Okay, I think you should start at the beginning."

He would have preferred she'd reacted like this was any other fight. That she'd shoot him an I-told-you-so look or yell at him for not letting her tell him at her pace. Instead of all the things he would have rather seen, her face was unreadable again.

"You know my father went to jail and escaped. My mother had warned me like a million times not to let him in the house. *He's an escaped felon, hon, and even though he is your dad, we need to follow the law.* He did something wrong and had to answer for it. But she never told me about the other things, like the beatings she took at his hands or how he'd steal from her. Fausto used me to manipulate her into giving him what he wanted and never pressing charges."

He reached across the desk and tried to take her hand but she moved out of his reach and kept talking. His body shocked at the rejection.

"One day, he came to the house while she was at work. He told me we could be a family again. That he was sorry about all he had done. That all he wanted was a chance. When I didn't let him in, he talked about family being there for each other and how he had not eaten and wasn't well. He said he would be gone after he ate something and before Mom got home. I let him in. He showered, and I made him food but he wouldn't leave. When my mom came home, he was sitting at our table. He sent me out of the room to get her something to drink. When I got back, my mom was crying and Fausto said we were going for a family ride."

She blew out a shaky breath. "Anyway, we got in the car. My mom was in the backseat. I rode shotgun and he drove. In the cupholder between us was a half-drunk bottle of Rebel Yell and his gun.

Cam's breath lodged in his chest but he didn't interrupt her. He swallowed the churning and let her continue.

"First, we stopped by her school. She went inside and came back with a Ziploc bag full of the petty cash. Then, we drove for a couple of hours and went into a convenience store. He told me to go down all the aisles and pick up chips and a drink. And then we got out and drove some more. He said we would go back and I was going inside with him and my mom would drive when we got out. My mom plead with him not to do this, that I was just a kid. But he told her to shut up and that's when I got it. He was planning on robbing the store with me and forcing her to drive the getaway."

"Shit." The word slipped out of Cam's mouth.

"It was a stupid idea. We would've gotten caught. Except, he was still drinking like he always was and had to pee. So, he stopped the car in the middle of nowhere. He must have been half drunk by then because he made us get out of the car, but left the gun in the cupholder. Mom didn't notice but I did. I reached in and grabbed it. By the time he realized it, I was pointing it at him. Mom ran and took it from my hands. He advanced toward her. She told him to stop. He didn't. She shot him on the side of his stomach."

"Fuck, Adri."

She continued like he didn't speak. "He kept screaming that Mom would go to jail and he would tell them she helped him escape. We ran. Mom let him keep his phone and told him that if he called the cops he would end up back in jail because he was a fugitive. We hopped in the car and drove back home. Mom and I talked. On the drive back, she told me everything, the verbal abuse, his threats to take me from her, how he hit her in places people couldn't see…"

Her lips trembled a bit. "How the cops were no help. When she tried to file a restraining order when he'd threatened her at first, they'd said he had to hurt her first. After that, the abuse turned physical but she couldn't go to the police because he threatened to take me. She'd never see me again. Anyway, after we left him, we went to her job first. Mom went in and put the money back. Then we drove home, talked, and decided to keep it a secret. They called us a few weeks later. Fausto died in a hospital from complications from the bullet wound."

Cam was reeling. He wouldn't believe what he was hearing except it was Adrianna telling him and the truth was in her pale skin and spooked eyes. "Jesus, no one can blame you or your mom for doing that."

"He still messed us up. We left him the phone and he used it to call your father. He still has the tape." She came around the desk to stand in front of him. "You see why I have to pay him? My mom can't go to jail because of me."

Heat flooded his face and he took her shoulders in his hands. "Because of you? You didn't do anything. You and your mom were victims."

"It was all my fault. I let him in. She told me like a thousand times, but I had this stupid idea of a family together. He made me believe it was possible and I let him in and ruined everything. I should have called the cops."

He couldn't let her beat herself up like that. Not when he could understand what it was like to want your parents to love you and be together. He would have done the same. No, he probably would have shot Fausto himself. "You were not dumb. You were a kid. You wanted your family together and you didn't know your dad was an asshole. Your mom didn't tell you. That's not dumb. It's normal."

He wrapped his arms around her and this time she let him touch her. Her skin cold and clammy, she burrowed closer.

"Cam, if something should happen, you have to take care of Bron..." Her voice broke and she buried her face in his chest.

26

Cam had spent the last twenty minutes alternating between berating himself and raging against his father. He should've hopped in the shower with Adri. She was taking too long and he was getting antsy. She was level headed but this whole thing with Walter and the secret, he'd never seen her like that. She had always been so sure, so brave about everything. She'd always held her head high in Acacia, despite what people thought about her family. Fausto had really fucked up their lives.

Now, beyond the grave, he continued to do that. Why did he have to call Walter? Why had he been out to screw his ex-wife and daughter up until his last breath? Cam couldn't blame Adri for being so scared. This threatened everything that was sacred in her life. Her mom. Bron. It covered all her bases.

And what kind of asshole, knowing everything Fausto had put them through, blackmailed women who were only trying to defend themselves? Walter was worse than Fausto. He was a leech and roach. Cam wasn't going to let him mess with them anymore. He pulled out his phone and texted Chase.

Walter is here.

Not even a minute later his phone went off. "What the hell is he doing down there?"

Cam sighed, hit the speaker icon, and placed the phone on the bed. The evening, the secrets, Adri's sadness, the asshole he had for a father all weighed heavy in his shoulders. "He's trying to manipulate me into giving him money by blackmailing Adrianna."

"Blackmailing her with what? What did she supposedly do?"

He looked up to find her standing at the door. Her face serious, her eyes somber, but her shoulders didn't droop. She was holding her head high as ever.

"She did what she had to." He extended his hand to her.

She closed the door behind her, locked it, and crossed the room. He leaned back against the pillows and she leaned against him.

"Okay," his brother said. "Tell me what you need me to do."

"Walter has a voicemail recording from over eleven years ago. I need to retrieve and destroy it. Do you think your friends can help with that?"

Adri's soft gasp was the only sound for a while.

"I can ask, but…"

"I know I told you I never wanted you mixed up with them again, but I wouldn't ask if it wasn't—"

"No, it's not that. I think getting that may be easier than you think. Walter is not a genius. He's probably got that in his old laptop and if he's in Maryland, I can go to the brownstone and get it. Lux has helped him with it in the past."

Adrianna sat back to look at him.

"You can trust them," he mouthed. "Okay?"

She hesitated but then nodded after a few seconds.

"Okay, when can you go?"

"I'm texting with Lux. She's on a date but told me to pick her up."

"Call me when you get there. I'll owe you two."

"Oh, please. If she's willing to end the date without me explaining, it wasn't going well to begin with. Will call you when I get to Hades."

"You guys call your parents' house Hades?" Adrianna asked.

He brushed the strands of hair that had fallen over her eyes. "Tells you everything you need to know."

"Won't your mother have something to say about them snooping around?"

Cam shook his head. "She takes Ambien and is probably asleep but if she's awake, Chase will know how to deal with her."

She nodded. "Thank you. I know I laid all this heavy shit on you and you don't have to—"

He placed his fingertips over her lips. "I do have to. You had to solve things on your own for long enough. But now you have me here and we're going to do it together. I'm your man, right?"

"Yes," she said without hesitation.

"Then let me be your man. Trust me to help you solve this."

"I do trust you, Cam."

"Good. Then tell me I'm your man, Adri."

"You're my man, Cam."

He pressed her tight to him.

"I don't like feeling out of control," she whispered against his neck.

"I know but if Chase and Lux can get the computer and we can destroy that message, he will have nothing over you. I also want to talk to my lawyer, just in case."

She stiffened, her breath rushing out. They sat in silence for a few breaths and then her body went limp again. "Okay."

His chest tightened. He couldn't imagine how difficult this was for her. He pressed his lips to her forehead. He had to reassure her, make sure she knew that her and her mom's lives were safe with him. "I'll retain him in you and your mom's names. That would ensure attorney-client privilege."

She pulled back and looked in his eyes. "How do you know all this?"

Cam chuckled at the surprise in her tone. "Keeping Chase alive and out of jail hasn't been easy. It's taught me much about life, the law, and things you don't even want to know about."

"That had to be hard for you. What did he do?"

"Depends on the age. He ran around with gang members, hotwired cars, beat one of Walter's sleazy ass friends who tried to touch Lux to a pulp, joined a fight club, and landed in the hospital a bunch of times doing stunts."

She stared at him open-mouthed. Cam saw an opportunity to distract her until he heard from his siblings. He told her about what he'd been through with his brother. Chase wouldn't mind.

"Holy shit," she said when he finished. Then kissed him. "You're a good brother."

"I would do anything I have to for my family. Whatever I have to do. I hope you believe in that, Adri. Because you're a part of me, too. I would do anything for you."

She smiled, so hard, so wide. She believed him. It was in the soft look in her eyes, in the warm palms that settled at his cheeks, in the slow kiss that twisted everything inside him. He pulled her to straddle his lap, his hands sneaking under her tank to caress her thigh.

She ground her hips against him and his cock stirred. "Adri—"

His phone went off. It was Chase.

"Cam, we're at the house. Marilyn is sleeping but we can't get into Walter's computer. He changed the password."

Of course he did. Nothing could ever be easy. "Shit. What are our options?"

"Well…I can have someone hack into it," Chase said.

"But?" Cam asked.

"It may be easier to just deal with Marilyn, get the password and then I can take it to someone to locate the audio and destroy it and any other version he may have. I'll have him wipe Walter's hard drive clean."

Dealing with Marilyn meant upping her stipend.

Irritation flushed all over his body. He shouldn't have to pay his mother to do the decent thing but then again, the decent thing had never applied to Marilyn and Walter. He wanted to say fuck it, just have Chase destroy the whole thing but with Walter's password, they could do so much more.

He looked at the wrinkle on Adri's face and he couldn't do it. He'd do whatever he had to do to give her peace.

"Do it. Wake her up. Tell her I'll add to her allowance and will put the house in her name again."

Yeah, whatever he had to. After that, he wouldn't have to deal with his mother again.

"Come on, you have to wake up or I'm doing this without you."

Cam woke up to the fluttering of her lips over his. His eyes drifted open and found her face hovering over his, her eyes hazed, and her hair cascading over them. The smile she wore bled into him until he slowly mirrored it.

He pulled her on top of him, his hands roaming up and down her back. They'd fallen asleep after Chase arranged everything. It had taken a while for his siblings to wake up their medicated mother. Walter had nothing on Adri and the smile on her face before she'd fallen asleep was worth every penny he'd paid.

Adrianna nipped at his lower lip. "We need to hurry before she wakes. I was going to wait until after I dropped her off at school but I can't. I want you too much right now."

Need jolted through Cam's body. "Were you really about to start without me?" he managed between kisses.

"Mmhmm," she murmured. "It took you awhile to get up."

His skin ignited with her touch. He was dynamite too close to the flame. Burying his fingers in her hair, he pulled her back and brought himself to a sitting position.

The soft sound that broke from her throat was sexy like nothing Cam ever heard. Leaning forward, he devoured her mouth. He explored, his tongue slowly sliding over hers, provoking soft moans. Her fingers dug into his leg while she followed the movement of his tongue with her hips.

They moved in unison, touching each other where they needed and how they needed. They knew how to make each other tick. Cam reached under her night tank, pulling it over her head and discarding it next to them. He placed kisses on her neck, his hands slid over her breasts and she arched against them. He circled her nipples with his thumbs, trapping them against his index fingers.

He tugged. She whimpered. Taking his face in her hands, she bruised his lips while her hips drew circles over his cock. One of his hands snuck into the waistband of her shorts. Finding her mound, he pressed his thumb against it. His lips took over for his hand at her breast, trapping her hardened nipples between his tongue and the roof of his mouth.

Adrianna threw her head back, pressing her pussy tight against his hand. He bit the hardened nipples until he heard the small gasp and she shattered around his finger. He caught her against him.

With Adrianna coiled tightly around his body, Cam smiled. He began kissing on her neck until she lifted her head. Smiling, she leaned to kiss him. It was different this time. She leisurely kissed over his jaw, down his neck.

"This one's for you," she murmured, her teeth raking over the soft skin. Her hand gliding along his shaft.

Cam lost it then, flipping her back into the bed. She lifted her hips when he reached for the waistband of her pajama shorts. He slid them down her legs and knelt between her legs. He reached for her hips, bringing her close, setting her ass over his thighs, spreading her for his cock. The morning light filtered in, shining a spotlight on the divine sight that was her pussy.

"God, I want to eat you right now. You're so pink and wet."

She squirmed. "Cam."

He planned to make her scream with pleasure again while he lost himself in her luscious pussy. Cam grabbed his dick in his hand and inched it inside her, shuddering when the head grazed her entrance. Every sense clashed together when he eased past her folds into her wet heat. He reveled in the slow shuttering of her eyes and how tight her teeth closed around her bottom lip.

"God. Jesus. Cam."

His heart sped into a gallop. "I love it when you take my cock, when you tighten around it. Do it for me, baby. Let me feel that."

She clenched and release and clenched again and the familiar ache pulsated through every corner of his body.

He took advantage of the almost foot he had on her and pushed her knees to her chest, rolling forward.

"You're so deep." She gasped.

"I know, so good. So. Fucking. Good," he strangled out.

He placed his hands on the bed by her hips and let his hips drive into her in a natural cadence. Her hands hooked behind her knees and she pressed them closer to her, balancing herself and leaving room for him to sneak one hand and rub circles into her clit.

Her mouth flew open and her belly flushed.

His balls tightened, and his cock turned into granite. "You have to come, baby. Come on. Let it go."

He squeezed her clit and she moaned or exhaled. Cam couldn't be sure because everything inside him exploded and numbness descended over him. He collapsed on top of her, needing to have her all around him. Adrianna wrapped her legs around his waist and her arms around his back. She pressed kiss after slow kiss to the side of his face. He couldn't talk or get off her until his breath evened out.

He raised his head to look in her eyes and she smiled at him. "That was okay. I think we can do better."

He pushed himself on his elbows. "Challenge accepted."

But the next thing he heard wasn't her musical moans but the one sound that could effectively kill his wood, no matter how hard it was.

"Mommy? Why is the door closed?"

The door knob rattled, cutting through his raising heartbeat. Cam swore. One second, he was still buried deep inside Adrianna, the next he was at the foot of the bed.

He reached for a shirt, realizing his pants were only half off. Adrianna jumped back into her pajamas shorts.

"Daddy? Is Mom still mad at me?"

Adrianna flipped on the light switch. "I'll go get her in the shower." She headed towards the door, stopping to flash him a disarming smile over her shoulder. "Seventh inning stretch. We'll continue this after I drop her off."

Cam smiled back. "You got yourself a promise."

27

"We want to do a strong girl concept. Like princesses in jeans and combat boots. Ayla is going to paint her grandma, who was in the army. I want to do *Abuela* with a tiara and a cape because vice-principals are heroes too."

Adrianna's gaze flew from her daughter's to Cam's. His smile was still in place and he didn't hesitate to respond. "You're right. Your *abuela* is a hero too. She's always had to be strong for her family."

Adri mouthed her thanks. It meant the world that he didn't think differently of her mom now that he knew the truth. She was so grateful to him for taking away the threat of Walter. She was lighter today and embracing her happiness full on. "*Abuela* is going to do backflips. She's already so proud of you."

Bron nodded. "Can I please go rearrange the flowers on the tables? They're all crooked now."

Adri nodded. "Yes, please. The lunch crowd was crazy today and they kept touching everything and we had to put tables together. And thank you, beautiful." Bron went to the other tables and she dug into her salad, keeping an eye on her. "I'm so hungry. How was the drive from the school?"

"It was good. Miss Winter invited me to come talk to her art class.

Oh, and I met Ayla's dad. You didn't tell me he used to play or that he's Dominican like your mom."

She grinned at him. "He came drafted from the farm system in the Dominican Republic. He and Lauren joke all the time that we're all cousins. But most important, did you agree to become his assistant?"

"Ha ha ha. No, but I am going to come watch them play. What did you do while I was gone?" His hand snuck under the table and caressed her thigh, triggering goosebumps along her skin.

She made it a point to let her lips linger on her fork until his eyes darkened.

"Recuperate," she giggled.

His phone vibrated and he glanced at it. "Chase on his way with Walter's laptop. He should be here within the hour."

"What's in it now?"

"It was wiped clean and back to factory settings. I had them add all the evidence of every single time I had to bail out our family property or the people I had to pay to keep him alive. He stored his cloud password in a folder in his laptop."

Adrianna shook her head. She breathed out the pang of anxiety that hit her upper stomach. A small voice inside her whispered that it was all too easy. How come they had not heard from Walter? What if he had another ace up his sleeve or had already gone to the police?

She placed the fork on the table next to his plate.

"What is it?" Cam asked.

She forced another breath and her lips into a curve. "Nothing. I'm full."

He snorted. "It's a salad, Adrianna. Since when do you get full on a salad, without bread? Are you going to start lying to me now?"

Her skin heated and she shook her head. "It's stupid. Don't make a big deal out of it. And by the way, nice touch talking about a woman's eating habits. You have excellent dating skills."

He tossed her a side smile. "I love your eating habits. You eat like a human being." He turned in the direction of their daughter, spotting her across the room, and then back to Adrianna. He leaned closer and whispered a breath from her lips. "All your appetites match. I love a woman who's hungry across the board."

Butterflies rose and dove and she went slick between her legs. She pressed her hands to his cheeks and pulled him to her. Her phone went off and he groaned.

She was smiling when she answered.

"Adri. It's so good to hear you." The voice rang familiar, but she couldn't place it.

"I'm sorry. Who am I speaking with?"

"You forgot me already," the man cooed. "It's so sad because I can't forget you."

Across from her, Cam flinched. Her phone was loud enough he could hear. It was in his clenched jaw and the mossy shade his eyes had taken.

"Tommy." Even saying his name was bizarre and incomprehensible. The last time she'd seen Tommy was at a funeral for one of their classmates. He'd been high as a kite and asked her a million questions then. She'd brushed him off in the gentlest way she could.

"Ah. You remember. That does my heart good. How's Bron? She must be getting so big."

Cam went dark. *Shit*.

"Was there something you wanted? I kind of have a full restaurant in my hands." She had to get him off the phone before Cam blew a gasket.

"Can I come see you, Adri? We can have some coffee and catch up. I would love to see your bistro. You look beautiful on the website."

What the hell was he talking about? She didn't have time for this. "Tommy, I have to go."

"Come on, Adri. You must be curious about me too."

"Goodbye, Tommy." She hung up and placed the phone back on the table.

Cam didn't move. His gaze glued to her cell phone, his hand fisted on the table. *Oh, shit, shit, shit, hell.*

She placed a palm over his fist. "Cam."

"Since when do you and Tommy do pleasantries?"

She ignored his biting tone, nothing good would come out of indulging it, and chose her words with meticulous care. "We. Don't. I don't know what that's all about."

"What do you mean you don't know what that's all about? It's obvious. He wants to come see you."

"He can want whatever the hell he wants, Cam. I don't care. You shouldn't either."

"I care. He's trying to come see you. He has my daughter's name in his mouth. How does he even know her name?" A vein ticked at his neck. "He's never forgotten you and he wants to come here and try to talk to you."

"And? It's not like he's going to get me anyway. Don't fuck shit up again. We are good, you and I. Don't do anything stupid. Use your head. Tommy has never called me while you're here. Think about it. Your father probably paid him to. Tommy's a deadbeat junkie who would do anything for money these days."

His face didn't change but his shoulders eased. He wouldn't look at her and that set her off even more. When he was jealous, he became an idiot. Then the memory of Sophia and the restaurant incident hit her with force and she winced. She could become an idiot too. It was better if they had a breather. She wasn't in a rush to go through that shit again.

She pushed to her feet. "I'm going upstairs to check on an order I placed."

He stopped her with a hand to the wrist. "Don't go. Let's talk this out." His face was still dark. No, he wasn't ready to talk about this in a way that wouldn't blow the roof of the bistro off.

"No." She yanked her wrist from his hand. "Let's give each other some space. God knows I need to cool down, too."

Adrianna's heels clicked away against the hardwood, driving the distance between them with each step. A few feet away, oblivious to the mood of her parents, Bron sang along with Rihanna's voice over the speakers about wanting someone to stay. The irony was not lost on Cam. He could have laughed.

His chest loosened and he focused on his daughter's voice, his gaze on the wood grain surface of the table. He counted the fiber lines and breathed like he did before he had to pitch a game, shutting out the world and hearing himself. He couldn't be angry or emotional on the mound and most of the time, he was able to use that in his daily life. The biggest lesson he'd learned in his life was not to let the moment color his reactions.

But when it came to Adri, that never seemed to work. He was always giving himself to the first emotion. They were together now. If he continued like this, he was going to fuck things up.

Use your head.

Walter had stopped by last night. The same Walter who told him Tommy was happy with Adri. And Tommy called, today of all days. Why the fuck was he still jealous of Tommy? She had never gotten back with Tommy and he, Cam, was the man she still loved. He was the father of her child. He was the one she'd woken up that morning so hot for she could barely wait until he opened his eyes, the one she'd savaged with her mouth, deep throating and teasing with her tongue, and made come three times before noon. She was his. He was hers.

Why couldn't he put it all together before he let his temper get the best of him? He'd let his father use Tommy—a proven method—to rile him and take him off his game. Now she was pissed off. Because he was a fucking idiot. He'd screwed things up again. Damn him and his dumb jealousy. She was right. He was a fucking dumbass.

He pushed to his feet, making the chair drag back loud. Bron looked up from the arrangement, a hibiscus in hand. Cam forced a smile. "I'll be right back."

"Okay. I'll be here. I don't know why people have to touch the arrangements." She sighed.

He turned around and headed for the stairs, stealing one last look. She was singing again and shifting the flowers around.

He hurried up the steps. Adrianna sat still at her desk, her palms flat on the glass surface.

"I told you we should take a breather." She didn't open her eyes and her voice was forceful and sharp, like a felling ax.

"I came to apologize."

"That could have waited until we were both ready." This time a tinge of annoyance hovered over her words.

"I know. I'm sorry. I just wanted you to know that I realize what an ass I was. I should have known what this was about. I don't know why I got so crazy."

Her eyes drifted open and there was warmth there. "We can't keep doing this, Cam."

His heart punched his chest. Was she going to break up with him again? "Doing what?"

"Being so reactionary to stuff. We can't keep having blowouts over stupid things. I get so scared of going back there to that summer, to the woods. I don't want us to hurt each other like that."

He rushed around the desk, the air trying to fight its way out of his lungs. He wasn't going to let her doubt what they had or back away from it.

He took her face in his hand, looking into her eyes. "We won't. I promise. It was a stupid moment and it's over. We didn't yell or make a horrible scene this time. You walked away and I reflected. It's only going to get better. Let's cut ourselves some slack."

She stared at him, doubt clouding her gaze but then she gave him a brusque nod. "You're right. We did handle it better than we have in the past."

He exhaled and pressed his forehead to hers. "We're going to have spats and it will get dicey at times but we're going to be okay. I promise."

She nodded.

His mouth swooped over hers and he kissed her slow, savoring her, branding his promise into her lips. He teased her with his tongue, coaxing hers with flicks and swirls until her fingers wrapped around his arms and her nails dug in.

"Save that for tonight. I still have to work and Bron is wide awake," she whispered against his lips. "And you need to help her with her homework today."

He pressed another quick kiss, and then a second, and a third.

She gave him a playful push and laughed. "Come on, let's go back downstairs."

She stood up and walked around him, heading for the door.

"Are we okay?" He asked.

"You just had your tongue in my mouth and I'm having a hard time keeping my eyes off the front of your pants. I think it's safe to say so." She walked out of the office.

He followed behind her, eyes on her swaying hips, smile on his lips. They'd worked through it and he had been right. They were getting better, like he'd told her. And he just avoided the dog house. Big time.

At the bottom of the stairs, they found Lauren by the hostess stand. She was arranging the menus.

"You don't have to do that. I was coming down to start getting stuff ready for dinner."

Lauren waved a dismissive hand over her shoulder. "It's fine. I have nothing to do back there, anyway."

"Oh. You need to keep busy because you're nervous about the certification results."

Lauren stood up and wagged her finger but the smile lit up her face. "Nope. Just checked the state site. Passed those with flying colors."

Adrianna clapped her hands and high-fived her. "Yes! We need to celebrate this."

"Congrats, Lauren. We definitely have to celebrate your certification, now that we're free of Walter, and my brother's coming into town…" He let his words lag off.

Lauren's eyes widened, her mouth drifting open a little, but she closed it quickly and cleared her throat. "Oh. Cool."

Behind her, Adrianna's eyes narrowed but then she looked around. "Tell me Bron is not in the kitchen, stuffing herself with those shortbread cookies."

Cam looked around too. The flowers had been rearranged but there was a hibiscus laying on the table by the door.

"Bron's not in the kitchen. I thought she was upstairs with you guys. When I came out, all three of you were gone."

Adrianna's gaze snapped to his. "Did you send her upstairs before you came up?"

Cam shook his head. "I told her I would be right back."

"What? You left her here by herself?" Adrianna didn't wait for his answer. She took off in a run up the stairs.

But he'd just been gone for a few minutes and she was inside the restaurant. "I didn't think I needed to tell you guys. She was working on the arrangements."

"It's okay. She probably snuck by you guys," Lauren said.

No. They would have heard her come up the stairs. Oh God. His stomach twisted into a knot.

Adrianna ran back down the stairs. "She's not up here. She's so grounded. She knows she's not supposed to go outside without permission. And you…" She pointed to Cam. "You don't leave a kid alone."

A lump at his throat, sudden and thick, threatened to strangle him. "I'm sorry. I didn't think she would go anywhere."

"It's fine. Don't dwell. Let's go look for her and you'll get to punish her this time."

28

Walter took my baby.

No matter how hard they looked, they couldn't find Bron. The still-small voice told Adrianna it was him. That Cam's father had been the one to take their daughter.

The thought pounded her head every time she stood still. And she couldn't take it, couldn't breathe thinking of what he could be saying to her. He didn't care for Bron. He wasn't even good to his own children. He'd probably be cruel to the little girl he didn't consider family though she carried his blood.

She kept moving, shaking the thoughts away, not saying anything until she and Cam went inside places or ran into someone. They'd circled the block four times. They'd gone to all the businesses, asking if they'd seen her little girl. They'd headed to the park and the church a block away. They'd made it all the way to the supermarket and the Canton Harbor. There was no sign of Bron anywhere.

The dark taste of fear took over her mouth.

The wrought iron sign of *Mi Tesoro* didn't bring her any comfort. The title, an homage to her baby, was but an empty reminder that she may not find her once she walked through the doors. She stopped walking and just stared at it. She didn't want to cross the street and go in.

Because Bron's not there. Her heart told her so. Lauren would have called her and told her to come home. She couldn't make herself face the possibilities. How the hell had this happened? She should have been downstairs with her, watching her. But no, she'd gotten angry and stormed away.

Cold fingers wrapped around her arm and she jumped out of her skin. Cam was there. His gaze pained. "We should go inside."

Never in her life had she wanted to put her face on his shoulder and cry more than this moment. But she couldn't. She couldn't fall apart. She was a mom and needed to find her daughter. "I think it may be time to call the police. I think this is your father's doing."

It hurt to breathe those words out. So bad she pressed a hand to her chest. His sharp intake of breath, the gasp that came along with it and the paling of his skin was like a knife twisting in her chest. He staggered back a step. God, she wished she could take those words back.

The slow shake of his head was more than Adri could take. She had to look away from him. "I'm sorry. We should've paid him. He would've left us alone."

"He still would've been blackmailing you," Cam's voice was hoarse and barely above a whisper, as if it hurt him.

"But she would've been safe. I don't care what happens to me anymore. I just want her back."

He cleared his throat. "Me too."

She couldn't take his fear or her own. She turned her attention back to the place she didn't want to go in. Through the glass window, she made out Lauren's figure. Her head down, shoulders sagged. A tall man had his hands on her shoulders. *Oh God.*

Adrianna rushed to cross the street. She walked fast with only her best friend in sight. Had someone come with bad news? Shock had her almost jumping back when Cam opened the door for her.

She barged in and Lauren turned around. It was Chase standing with her. His gaze shifted between Adrianna and beyond her to his brother.

"Lauren told me everything. I was asking if you had cameras. Cam, have you talked to Walter?"

Adrianna's stomach dove past her knees. All ten years of fears showed again, like a ghost, to haunt her. "He has her."

"There's a camera in the office. Adri, let's go now," Lauren said, crossing the distance and pulling her towards the stairs.

"I'm going to kill him," Cam said, his tone low and jagged.

Rage spread through her whole body rooting her in place on the first step of the stairs. She whipped about to face him. "I'll kill him myself if he hurts my baby."

"No one's killing anyone. He's going to jail, where kidnappers belong. Now, let's go see that damned camera and be sure who took her." Chase pointed up the stairs.

Adri ripped her gaze from Cam's, turned back around and followed Lauren.

The four of them crammed in the small office. Adrianna pulled up the camera system, concentrating on what she was doing and forcing all the fear out. She pulled the footage and set back the clock to the time right before she headed upstairs. Her breath strangled, watching the way she stormed away. Her heart tripping on one single fact. She'd never turned to look back at her daughter.

Cam did. He turned and looked and said something but Adri never did. What kind of mother didn't even turn? Tears filled her eyes. If she never saw her daughter again, she would never forgive herself.

A couple of minutes passed on the video and her heartbeat picked up as Bron moved from one table to the next. In the next frame, something flashed onto the screen and under one of the tables. Bron dropped the flower she was holding on the table and scooted down to her knees.

"What the hell is that?" Chase asked.

She opened her mouth but then her daughter stood up with a little dog in her arms. She turned toward the front door and mouthed something to a man at the door. They could only see his face partially but someone sucked in a loud gulp of air.

"Walter."

The next frame, Bron headed to the door with the dog in hand and disappeared out of it. The next person out on the restaurant floor was one of the waiters.

Cam's fist slammed against the glass top of her desk. "I'm going to fucking kill him."

The fucking iPhone screen would not unlock. He pressed his thumb into the home button to unlock the screen. It told him to try again. Again. He punched the numbers into the screen. Heat scaled its way almost violently up his chest. Rage threatened to choke him until he could barely breathe. He punched the digits on the screen as if his breathing was tethered to it. As if unlocking this screen would dislodge everything blocking the air path.

Deep down, part of him recognized he was most likely too pissed to hit the right keys but he couldn't stop fingering the screen like a mad man. It didn't help that feet away from him, Adrianna sat in the chair she'd dropped herself in, not moving with her hands pressed to her face.

And it was all his fault. He had been a fucking idiot again. He'd made the dumbest of decisions. He'd walked away from a child, leaving her alone, to make up with Adri.

"How could he have done this? She's his granddaughter. His blood. She's innocent." Lauren's voice carried confusion and the fear they all shared.

"I should've given him the money. The bistro doesn't mean a damned thing…" Adri's voice cracked and along with it a piece of Cam's insides.

"He would've been back, Adri. He's always back. The man's sick and gambling's all that matters to him," Chase said.

He had the money to spare and paying Walter would have been easy and would've sent him away. Until he squandered that too and came back for more. But what did he care? It's not like he didn't have it. Cam had made a gamble of his own. He'd set out to prove a point, to beat his father, but he had never been good at gambling. His father, the more seasoned player, had bested him.

Cam had opened the door for Walter and left Bron vulnerable. His stupid decisions where always coming back to haunt the three of them.

Fucking Walter. Fucking Walter. Or better said, it was fucking Cam. He did this. If he hadn't been a jealous idiot, he wouldn't have had to chase after Adri. He wouldn't have ruined their good moment. His bastard father shouldn't have had the opportunity to use a little dog to lure Bron out.

Never in his life could he have thought this was possible. Walter had always been a deadbeat father. He'd played and lost the family assets, his wife's inheritance, his children's trust funds. He had used his children and he'd blackmailed an abused woman and her daughter for his own motives. Yet, it never occurred to him that his father would be capable of kidnapping Bron to get his way.

He always thought of Walter as a pathetic victim to his addiction. But this was more. He was a criminal. There was only one place for criminals.

Chase took the phone from his hand. "We have to be smart about this, Cam."

"Give me the fucking phone." He tried to snatch the device from his brother's hand.

Chase shook his head, moving out of reach. "We need a plan first. You can't just go crazy on him. We need to get Bron first."

Bron. Jesus, how her name twisted his gut. The pain that broke throughout his chest was almost unbearable. He preferred the anger, the rage, the uncontrolled urge to kill his father.

"I'm going to call him. I'm going to get his location. I'm going to get my daughter. And then, I'm going to make sure he lands in jail. No one's ever going to threaten Bron and get rewarded with money."

Chase sucked in a gasp of air. His eyes clouded for a second and then that hardened look hooded over them. "He took Bron, so it's only fair. That's what we're going to do. But I need you to be ready for this. You have to be cold and not let him get to you."

Cam couldn't promise anything, not with his little girl away. God, what could Walter be telling Bron? Was she crying or scared? The thought sent his hand to press on the desk for support. He couldn't bear if Walter hurt her.

He listened to Chase. A breath, two breaths.

He was ready by the time his brother unlocked his phone and dialed.

Adri shot to her feet and came to stand next to him. He looked into her eyes but couldn't hold her gaze. The fear in there was what he couldn't take. He'd failed her, failed Bron. He had to fix it, quick.

Walter Blake never could resist a ringing phone. That's what Cameron was counting on as he waited for the call to connect. He concentrated on his breath, using his old baseball game techniques to keep himself sane and in control. His blood ran hot and unbridled.

First ring. If he could get his hands on his father, he would choke the shit out of him. Second ring. He was definitely going to strangle him. Third ring. His gaze met Adri's again, lingering on the way she'd stressed her lip into a bitten red mess.

Walter answered in the fourth ring. "Cameron. I've been expecting your call."

Cameron jumped straight to the point. He wasn't going to indulge the bullshit. "I know you have her. Bring her back."

"Of course, son. We are just having a good time, here. She's telling me about her paintings. She reminds me a lot of Luciana at her age."

The words hit him like a boulder to the chest. Cam imagined a ball in his hand and twisted his fingers around it, timing his response like he used to do with his pitches. "Bronwyn is my daughter, your grand-daughter. You actually took her to get some money out of me."

"I just needed you to listen. You have to help me. My life depends on that money. I wouldn't hurt your little girl. I got her Chick-fil-A, like she wanted. But you know that loan shark will hurt me." Walter's voice was so soft and casual, like he was talking about borrowing Cam's shirt without his permission.

"Bron doesn't have anything to do with this. Just give me my daughter back."

"You can come get her anytime. Just tell me you'll give me the money to pay the loan shark."

The fuck-you was half hanging from his tongue but one look at Adrianna's face and the words dried in his mouth. Her eyes were huge, her skin an unnatural shade. She rubbed her arm up and down in an absent way. He sighed.

"I'll give you the money."

29

Walter didn't have to tell them where he had her. There was only one place in Maryland he'd feel comfortable in. Cam was heading back to the place he'd sworn never to set foot in, at eighty-five miles an hour. For once, he didn't complain that his brother was going to get them all killed. The faster they got there the better. He just wanted to get Bron back and wipe Walter from his life.

"If it were me driving even eight miles over the limit, I would have ten state troopers following me like I was OJ in the Bronco," Lauren muttered.

"Maybe they just want an excuse to give you a sobriety test?" Chase laughed when Lauren pelted him with a look. "Just call me when you want to get somewhere fast."

"Are you fucking kidding me, Chase? This is not the time for your fucking flirting."

His brother nodded. "I'm sorry."

A warm hand slid over Cam's and his gaze flew to Adrianna's, who leaned closer to him.

"I think he's trying to lighten the mood." Her eyes were warm like her touch and though there was still strain in them, there was something there that eased him.

"I just can't do that light thing. Not when she's..." His voice trailed off and he hated himself for the flash of emotion in her eyes. He should be making this easier on her. But he was inept in every way today.

"We're going to get her back. "

The phone vibrated in his hand. It was a phone call from Elias. He contemplated answering but this wasn't the time. He couldn't explain things right now. He hit the send-to-voicemail icon and placed the phone back on his lap.

"Maybe he can help," Adri said, looking at his phone.

"Who?" Chase asked.

Cam didn't get a chance to answer.

"Elias, can I call you back?"

Chase reached across and snatched Lauren's phone from her hands.

"What the hell?" She started but Chase shook his head and hung up in one swift motion and then handed it back.

"Don't tell him what's happening. This is a family issue and everyone here is related. I'm Cameron's brother. You're Bron's aunt. We don't need him."

"I get you don't like him, but for Bron we can all set personal taste aside. He's a lawyer and may be able to help out," Lauren said.

"I agree. And you told me your father likes him. Maybe he'll listen to Elias," Adrianna added.

Something in his gut churned and he found himself emulating Chase's shake of the head. "No. Elias is a friend but he'll also feel bound to try to jump in and do things. He'll want to impose his way and we know what we're going to do. Let's keep this here for now."

The car veered toward the exit and Adrianna's body bumped into his. "Chase, for God's sake. We need to make it there alive."

"And you need to watch it down this road. You know the deer jump out of nowhere," Lauren added.

"Stop being a wuss. Don't tell me you've become boring, like Cam? Besides, I dare a deer go against my Range."

Cam concentrated on his plan.

"Remember, when we get there, you grab Bron and take her out of the room. I don't want her to be there when I talk to Walter. This is already hard enough."

She released a shaky breath. "Okay. My mom is already talking to Bill. They know they have to wait—"

"Bill? As in Sheriff Johnson? He's still in the force at one hundred and fifty years old? He was always on my ass." Chase said.

"Because you were a terror back then," Adrianna said. "He's good friends with Mom so I would watch it if I were you."

"Don't you worry about me, Adri. I'll be a Boy Scout."

"Hmm. They'll be at the railroad crossroads two miles from the house and they'll follow us there."

As they approached the railroad crossing, Cam's chest tightened and so did his grip on Adri's hand.

"I see the sheriff's car," Chase said but instead of slowing down, he gunned on the gas.

Soon, for good or bad, this would be over.

Adrianna followed Cam out of the car, and they rushed through the circular driveway. The night air had taken a brisk turn or maybe it was her insides that had frozen and made her shiver. She couldn't wait to have her baby in her arms. Even if Walter pulled something and she ended up in prison, she didn't care anymore.

The thought that kept playing in her head, like an annoying malefic litany, was that her baby was alone with a man that didn't think her mother was worth anything. The same man that had insisted vehemently that Adrianna get an abortion. She may go to jail after all because if he hurt a hair on Bron, if he traumatized her in any way, Adrianna was going to kill him.

She palmed the taser in her pocket. She prayed to God she didn't have to use it on him. Cam turned to her, as if he could sense what she was thinking. "It's going to be okay. It's almost over."

In front of the door, he didn't pause, didn't knock. He didn't have to. He'd told her how he had saved the house so many times from his father's gambling. How he'd had to put it in his name to maintain it. The apprehension grew in her belly. Bron was alone with a man that didn't care enough for his family to keep it safe.

They barged in and the foyer was a blur. They kept walking, halting so abruptly she swayed forward when they found Walter sitting in front of the TV watching the Orioles game. Adrianna's gaze darted to all corners. Her baby is not there. "Cam, she's—"

"Where's my daughter?" Cam asked. No, that wasn't asking. He raged the words like they sprang from deep in the core of his belly.

A fresh wave of shivers rocked Adri's body. She'd never heard that kind of emotion in Cam. Their fights were always heated and angry. There'd never been this kind of cold, murderous feel to him then.

But Walter wasn't ruffled. His face remaining affable until he looked beyond them to Chase. He blanched. "What the hell are you doing here?"

"Answer Cam," Chase bellowed. "Where is Bron?"

Walter sighed. "Cameron, there was no need for you to bring the family thug. You must know I wouldn't harm a child. Least of all, one that carries my blood. This is all so unnecessary."

Chase chuckled. "Now she carries your blood? Because you must not have thought so when you asked Adrianna to abort her and then later on, when you kept her from her father all her life."

"Shut up, boy. You don't know anything. I didn't keep the child from Cam." He pointed to Adrianna. "Daddy killer did that."

Oh my God. Did he tell Bron that she was a killer?

Her stomach plummeted, diving to the floor and almost taking her whole body with it. Nausea rose up her throat and she couldn't talk. She couldn't do anything but press her hand to her stomach.

"You're a piece of shit, Walter. You knew Fausto abused her mother. You knew he intended to make Adrianna rob that store with him. They shot him in self-defense and you held that over their heads this whole time."

Cam's father shrugged. "I would have never used that recording unless I needed it. You wouldn't listen to reason. I told you it wasn't the time for you to show up with a kid at Cam's door."

He spoke directly to her. There was barely any emotion, like he was talking about the weather and not the secret that crippled most of her life. How many years had she lived in fear that he would talk and she would be torn away from Bron? She had so much to say, but nothing mattered at the moment. Only one thing.

"Where is my daughter? And trust me, if you did anything to her, I will kill again. This time on purpose."

Annoyance flickered in Walter's face. "You're all idiots. You honestly thought I would harm a child? Shame on you. Give me the money, Cam, and then all of you can leave."

Cam threw the bag on top of the table and Walter reached for it.

He rummaged through the stacks of cash, his eyes big and thirsty.

"There's a million in there," Cam said with the delicacy of a glob of spit.

Walter's mouth turned agape. "That's—"

"I know," Cam said, his eyes colder than anything Adri had ever seen. "You'll need it."

"I don't know what to say…" Walter began but Cam raised a hand to cut him off.

"Tell me where my daughter is. That's the only thing I want to hear out of your mouth."

"She's in your old room."

Adrianna took off running behind Cam. Faintly, in the background, the front door swung open and Walter yelled, "What the hell is this?"

They kept going, climbing the long stairs two steps at a time, running down the hallway. At the end, Cam pushed the door open and halted. Music blared from inside the room. Ed Sheeran again, asking a girl to give him love. Her heart an inch from her mouth, Adri pushed past him and would have sagged if he hadn't caught her.

Bron was in front of the window using his old easel. She turned around and smiled at them ever so briefly before her eyes clouded. "You're mad at me, aren't you? I told Grandpa you would be and he said you wouldn't be because you would be so happy to see me here. And he bought me Chick-fil-A and the cheesy fries."

Adri was way too happy, way too relieved to be mad. He knew how desperate she and Cam would be to get to her and he'd exploited that. *Fuck you, Walter.*

But he didn't matter. Nothing else did.

She crossed the room and pulled her daughter into her arms. She wasn't ever going to let her out of them.

30

Cam's eyes were still full of the intermittent blue and red lights. His ears still rang with the curses straight from his father's mouth. He could still feel the stiffening of Adri's body and the panic in her mother when Walter threatened to expose them.

In the end, his father was the one locked up in a cell in Acacia Falls. Chase had left the laptop there for him, with the replaced hard drive. It had been Cam's pleasure to tell Walter to let the cops check the device at his own risk.

The sign for Exit fifty-four came into view and he closed his eyes in a silent prayer of thanks. They were almost home. He couldn't wait to go to bed and fall asleep with his arms wrapped around his daughter and Adri. It was no longer enough to hold Bron's hand while she dozed on the ride back. He couldn't see her beautiful little face. It was buried on her mother's chest.

Adrianna contorted her body to cocoon Bron's. She dropped kisses on her head every so often. Lauren kept turning to look back at them. Even Chase was driving at the speed limit and kept meeting his eyes in the rearview mirror. His father had done a number on them.

He couldn't face everyone's weariness anymore, not even his own. He looked out into the street as they navigated their way into the square. Chase let them out in front of the bistro and went to look for parking. Adrianna took her time disentangling from Bron so Cam could carry her upstairs. Lauren used her key to open the door for them.

Her gaze lingered between Adri and Bron but she looked at him. "I'm going to make sure everything is tidy for tomorrow. I can bring you guys dinner."

Adrianna shook her head. "I'll settle her and come help you."

"No, just stay with her. I can handle it."

Adrianna started to protest. "It's not fair to you—"

"Shut up and go be with *La Princesa*. I got this. Just hold her for me." Lauren shot Cam a pointed look and tilted her head upstairs.

If he went up with Bron, Adri would have no choice but to follow. Cam started up the steps, making his way in quick strides. Soon, Adrianna's footsteps tapped their way up behind him.

He stepped back at the top so she could open the door for him. Her place was in darkness since they'd left while it was light out. She moved around quickly, turning on the lights, and he followed all the way to Bron's room. He placed her in the bed and removed her shoes while Adri worked on taking off her zip-up jacket. She also took off the tie from her hair and massaged her fingers into their daughter's head. Bron sighed and turned into her pillow, her knees coming up until she was almost in a ball.

It made Cam smile. She was asleep and unscathed and unaware of the tears that'd dropped close to her on the bed. His heart shriveled at the soft shake in Adri's shoulders and the almost careless way she swiped the wetness away from her eyes. He put a hand on her shoulder, wanting to tell her it was all over. She shook her head, pressed a kiss to Bron's forehead and sprang from the bed. She pulled the covers over their little girl, lingered for a few seconds, then put her jacket and shoes in the closet.

She left the room and went into her bedroom, pulling out her nightgown.

"Talk to me, Adri," he asked.

"I can't. Not now. I'm going to sleep with her tonight."

His stomach iced, sending a chill through his body. He shook it off. It was only normal. She'd gone through a big scare. She needed to be close to Bron. But why did it feel like a lot more than that? There was so much emotion for Bron but she'd barely looked at him since it was all over. Maybe she was blaming him for this. God knows he blamed himself for not giving Walter the money and preventing them from going through this.

"Look, I know this was my fault and I'm sorry I didn't listen to you and just gave the money—"

She held up a hand. "No, you were right about not giving the money. He would've never left you alone. My situation would have always been leverage. I was wrong and you were right about that."

He should have been relieved but there was something, a finality to her words, a fucking *"but"* that didn't gel. It made his skin antsy.

"Then what is it, Adrianna? Why does it feel like there is so much more you're not saying? You won't even look at me." His voice was harsh to his own ears, matching his mood and uncertainty.

She flinched and turned sad eyes on him. "Because there is. This wasn't about Walter. He has an amazing ability to capitalize when we fuck up. And that's because we always fuck up. And it's always mostly my fault. You've only been a dad for less than a month. I've been a mother for almost ten years. I shouldn't lose sight of what's important. I shouldn't react first and think second. I shouldn't be acting like a fucking hormonal teenager who can afford to have outbursts and stomp out of the room after a fight with my boyfriend."

He opened his mouth, sensing where she was going but she plowed on.

"But I do. Because it's you. Because I always lose my senses around you. Because I'm so crazy in love with you and that's getting in the way of me being a responsible mom. A month ago, all I had was her and I feel like now I'm losing sight of that."

He staggered back. "What the fuck are you saying?"

She pressed her lips together. "I can't do this with you. I'm not going to make another big mistake that messes up her life because we can't control our anger or jealousy. It's not healthy. She's the most important person in my life and I can't risk her. Not even for you."

His vision blackened, like the time he'd taken a ball to the head during an inter-league game. The floor seemed to go out from under him. She was breaking up with him. *Because she blames you.* She just didn't want to say it.

Rage and heat sprang up his body. He opened his mouth, intending to tell her to have the guts to accuse him to his face. That she should just acknowledge it and they could begin to work through it. But one look at her and it all suddenly died inside him: the anger, the venom, the hurt.

Her hunched shoulders and tear-stricken face sent ripples of pain through his body. He couldn't add to it. When they were mad, they could get nuclear, like she said, and he wasn't going to do that to her.

Not today, not after what we've been through. Walk away Cam.

He swallowed and breathed. "You know what? It's been a long day and it's not the right time to make decisions." She started to protest but this time he held a hand up. "No, you go shower and snuggle up with her. Just concentrate on her and getting some rest. We'll talk at another time. Maybe when she's in school tomorrow."

"She's not going to school tomorrow." Her chin went up and the finality was back in her voice. There would be no arguing with her.

"Fine. She's probably been through too much. We need to talk to her about what happened anyway. And make an appointment with Doctor Perkins."

She nodded and paused but then turned around and went into the bathroom, shutting the door.

Cam headed to the living room. He needed to blow off some steam or he was going to punch a wall. He dropped himself on the couch and pressed his fists to his knees. He sat there, going over her words and waited until she came out of the bathroom. She didn't come to the living room, heading straight to Bron's room.

He jumped to his feet and pushed away the annoyance that simmered through his body. He needed a drink and a little distance.

He headed downstairs. Lauren was placing a table cloth on a table with Chase hovering over her. His face was too close to hers as he placed the center piece.

"Are you going to help me or get in my way for the rest of the night? I'm trying to go home and sleep. We open tomorrow." Her voice carried a frost that clashed with the half smile on her lips.

"Well, I—" Cam cleared his throat.

Chase turned around to face him. "What are you doing here?"

"I need a drink."

Lauren scoffed. "Don't we all?"

"I think Adrianna is trying to break up with me."

Chase frowned. "Why?"

Cam wanted to laugh at the incredulous expressions of both of them. "She thinks we distract each other and her attention is not on Bron…"

They stared at him in silence until Lauren moved to the little bar area and came back with three beers. She handed them one each and shot Cam a defiant look. "Well, are you going to let her push you away?"

He didn't have to think about the answer. He wasn't going to pretend that he would think about it and give her all the time in the world to change her mind. Because there was only one thing he could say to this.

"Fuck no."

He'd been too long without her and Bron. They were a family and they were going to stay that way. He just needed to convince her, and the only way he could do that was to prove to her that he could stay in control. He wasn't losing faith in them and he wouldn't let his anger or her doubts rob them of their family.

31

"Have you given any thought to what you want to do for Bron's birthday?"

Adrianna shook her head like her mother could see her. It really wasn't a good time for a chat. She was exhausted mentally, physically, in her soul. She hadn't slept much in the last week, afraid even as she held her daughter, to lose her. And the fight with Cam, if you could call their silent war a fight, didn't help at all.

"No. Honestly, I haven't thought about it. So much has happened lately..."

"It's okay, hon. I understand. It's just you always know what you want to do as early as January. Are you sure you are okay?"

Adrianna let her head hang back and stared at her office ceiling. She hated not being on top of her game and this dancing around subjects. "I'm okay, Mom," she repeated for the fourth time in the span of fifteen minutes.

"I'm sorry I keep asking but you don't sound well, *mi hija*." Her mom was breaking out all the nicknames, which meant she was really worried about her.

I need to put her mind at ease.

"Well, I'm scared as hell that someone may take my baby from me and though I've explained that like a thousand times, some people can't even give me a few days to have her home and work through my fears."

Adrianna swallowed the groan. *She'd failed again.* She was trying to tease, and instead came off angry and bitter. Which is the way she felt since this morning when Cam strolled into Bron's bedroom and ordered their daughter to get ready for school.

"Cam was right on taking her to school, Adri. It's time she went back."

She shook her head. "It's too soon. I needed more time."

"But Bron doesn't. It's been a week, *cariño*. She can't miss that much school or she'll fall behind. She was already absent when you all went to New York."

The rational words pricked her skin. "It's not like she wasn't doing anything. I was helping her through her lessons and she was doing her reading."

Where I could see her, touch her, make sure she was safe.

"You're a lot of things I'm proud of, *mi amor*. You're a good woman, a tremendous professional, an amazing mom but you are not a teacher. You can't keep Bron indoors all her life because you're afraid."

"I know."

In her head she did, but explaining it to the heart that trembled at the idea of being apart from her baby was harder, if not impossible. The minute Bron and Cam walked out of the door, her windpipes had begun to close and she'd had to force herself to breathe. She was alone and anxious and she had to get out of the upstairs apartment. Especially after the panic set in when he didn't come home after. Only his text saying that he'd gone somewhere with Chase, let the breath return to her body.

"Adri, you can't protect her from everything. All you can do is prepare her. I tried to shelter you from the ugliness that was your father and me, and you ended up carrying my cross with me..." Her mother's voice broke. Adrianna had only seen her mother cry twice in her life.

The day she'd told her about Fausto and the abuse, and the day Bronwyn was born.

Her mother cleared her throat. "Hasn't Walter robbed you of enough? Are you going to let him take away the man that you love and force you to raise your daughter in fear? Like I raised you." Her voice dropped in the end.

"Mom, you were the best mother I could ever want. You taught me how to be strong, even if I don't seem like it right now. It's just…"

The ringing of the school bell echoed through the phone line. "Drat, I have to go. We have an assembly, but I'll call you later. Adri, promise you'll think about it?"

"I will. Love you, Mom."

"I love you too. Kiss *La Princesa* for me. I'm taking a day off and coming for her birthday next week. We'll figure out what to do for her."

Adrianna hung up the phone and released a long breath. Her mother was right. Cam was right. Everyone was right but she couldn't help the way she felt. And it was affecting everything. She hadn't been out of the building since they came home from Acacia and Bron only got out today because Cam had had enough.

She knows how jumpy and scared you are. She wants to go outside but doesn't dare ask because she doesn't want to upset you, Adri. I'm trying to be sensitive and supportive, but we can't do that to her. She's a kid.

Cam had said it in a calm manner but there was a tinge of frustration. The past few days he'd been so patient, unlike any version of him. He'd tried to talk to her but when she'd shut him down, he had not blown up sky high. He'd even asked her to come with him this morning. She couldn't.

She would've never let Bron out of the car and into the school.

It was all so stupid. Walter was in jail. The District Attorney had spoken to them and said he'd pled guilty for a lesser sentence. He and his lawyer had asked for the laptop and shortly after called to agree to a deal.

He's looking at ten years. Seven, if he agrees to go into rehab.

Cam had been expressionless and had left the house with Chase after. He hadn't returned until later that evening. She'd asked if he wanted to talk but he'd shaken his head, told her he was tired, and gone to bed. She slept with Bron like she had been doing for the past weeks instead of comforting him like she knew he needed.

A pair of heels click-clicked their way up the stairs. Lauren appeared at the door in a baggy jumpsuit with tapered legs. In her hands, lidded cups of coffee. She set one down for Adri and took the chair across from her.

"Your eyes look super small, which means you're tired but everything else is flawless," Adri said to her friend.

"You know drama always makes me put in the extra effort."

Adri chuckled. "Oh? Drama?"

Lauren shrugged. "I didn't want to tell you before because you've been going through stuff…but it's time we all get back to normal. And that includes our girl cuddling. I'm glad you got your ass out of the apartment. I can handle the bistro but ain't nobody got time for these fucking ledger books."

Adrianna laughed. It's what she loved about her best friend. She never beat around the bush. "Thank you for that. Now, tell me about your drama."

If she dealt with Lauren's she could put off her own. Plus, it would distract her from worrying about Bron.

"I went to dinner with Elias in the evening but spent the rest of the night with Chase."

Adri's mouth dropped. "Okay…this is better than what I imagined."

Lauren pushed her open palm in front of her. "Not like that. He dropped off Cam last night and called me. He sounded funny, so I went out to meet him in Fells Point. We walked all night, went to the Sagamore for drinks and chatted at the pool lounge. He was upset about his father. He said Walter will be doing ten years."

"He pled guilty."

"Yeah, we talked about that. He was conflicted. I felt so bad about it. Like I needed to do more."

Adri narrowed her eyes but then smiled. "And how did you comfort him?"

"Not the way you think, Adrianna. God, you need to make up with Cam so you can put that filthy mind to use."

Her mind conjured images of that morning before it all went to hell, when she had used her mind, mouth, and body to good use on him. Her heart squeezed so tight. "Lauren, don't start…"

"Chase told me they're all having a really hard time dealing with this. Lux is coming down this weekend and their mother is beside herself."

A rush of guilt filled her chest and Adri pressed her fingers in small circles around it. "Cam said his mother tends to go nuclear when she doesn't get her way. She's all about appearances so I can't imagine what she's doing with all the media surrounding this."

"Thank God those vultures are not showing up here."

She frowned. "I guess I didn't think about that."

Lauren's gaze softened. "You've been having a hard time. Cam granted interviews and his publicist has been dealing with the media. You know that whole privacy in these difficult moments thing. Plus, we've been watching out for reporters. But he needs you."

"Why do you say that?" she asked.

Lauren shrugged. "Chase says what's stressing him the most is that he doesn't have you. That he feels like he's losing you."

Cam was handling things on his own. Bron was walking on eggshells not to upset her. She'd really fucked up this time. She needed to fix it soon.

Cam maneuvered Adrianna's SUV into Canton Square. Beside him in the passenger seat, Bron pointed across the street. "There's Mom. She's waiting for us."

Cam didn't have to look at his daughter to know she was smiling. His gaze was already in the direction where she pointed. Adrianna was beautiful in her skinny jeans and flower blouse. Her hair in that bun was sexy as hell. But even from across the square, Cam noticed the wringing of her hands and the strain on her face.

How would he ever undo the damage Walter had done?

His lawyers assured them that, without the recording, they had no legal worries. But it was the emotional wounds his father inflicted that failed to heal.

He circled the square and forced himself to keep his eyes on the road and not on her. "She's going to be so happy to see you. Remember to tell her how much you missed her."

"I will. I can't wait to give her the flowers we got her."

Cam smiled, his gaze drifting to the rear view, which reflected the enormous arrangement he and Bron picked out after school. "Your mom was really brave today. I hope she likes them."

"She will. And she'll probably cry." Bron placed her hand on his arm. "Daddy, you're going to ask her about my birthday, right?"

He could have chuckled. It had only been five minutes since he'd last reassured her. "I will and I'm going to keep my promise."

"And you'll convince her, right?"

Jesus, don't promise her that. Adrianna was going to freak and probably kick him and all his shit out on the street. He put the car on park and glanced into his daughter's angel eyes. As always, his common sense and other thoughts vanished.

"I'll convince her."

You're so fucked, Cameron. His time was running out.

He'd managed to stall Adrianna from talking about going their separate ways by telling her they both needed time and shouldn't make decisions in haste. He'd also used Dr. Perkins' words about not disturbing Bron's world any more than it already had been. He wasn't sorry. He would do whatever it took to stay by their side.

He'd stayed out with Chase all day because he didn't want to face her after he'd put his foot down on Bron going back to school. Now he was about to push her buttons even more by asking, no, telling her, that their daughter wanted to celebrate her birthday in a very public place full of people. It made him want to drive away again.

He sighed, got out of the car and walked around to let Bron out. He grabbed the flowers from the backseat. His little girl had already skipped her way to her mother.

"I missed you."

"I know, Mom," Bron said, making Cam chuckle.

"She's not lacking for confidence, that's for sure."

Her gaze landed on him and on the flowers in his arms. "I always miss her when she's gone."

He searched for bitterness or anger in her tone but found none. "These are for you."

"We picked them out together," their little girl said.

"They're beautiful. Thank you." Adrianna's lips curved into a shy smile and then she kissed Bron's forehead. "And thank you, Cam."

He handed her the flowers and she buried her nose in them. No kiss for him but what was he expecting?

He opened the door and they went inside. "I can take those upstairs for you." He pointed to the flowers.

She shook her head. "I'm going to put them on the mantle behind the counter. They're so beautiful, they need to be seen."

Or you don't want them in your space as much as you don't want me there. The thought came fast and cutting.

Bron sat on a table by the window, the same one they'd been sitting at on the day everything changed. Adrianna sat closer to her this time. Her hand was on their daughter's shoulder as she listened. Bron was animated and smiling, telling her mom about her day and how they started working on their *Artscape* project.

"That sounds amazing," Adri said.

Cam watched them, only half-listening, and feeling fully ignored. He wasn't wrong about sending Bron to school but maybe he'd been heavy handed. He should have sat with Adri and explained things better, but she didn't seem to want to talk to him for the past week.

"I'll work on it some more when I go upstairs," Bron said.

"Good. I'm getting things ready here for the dinner crowd, so maybe—"

"Can I help? I can fix the arrangements and put out the dinner candles. I promise I won't go anywhere." The little girl's voice trailed off and she looked down at her shoes.

Adrianna's shoulders tensed and her smile wavered. The waves of memories washing over her face. But she squared her shoulders back and blew a mouthful of air. "I need your help. Badly."

Bron's smile was big and devastating. "We can do it together."

Adri smiled back. "Yeah, but go on to the back and start collecting the candles and chocolates for the tables. I need to talk to your dad first."

Cam's pulse quickened. She needed to talk to him? That didn't sound good.

"Okay, Mom. Daddy wants to talk to you about something too."

She leaned in to whisper in Cam's ear. "Remember what we talked about."

Oh, for fuck's sake.

Adri turned a narrow-eyed look on him. "What's that all about?"

This was going to suck no matter what. She was probably going to tell him to move to the house he'd purchased or go to a hotel. What's another thing to piss her off?

"Bron wants to go to that *Thrills & Spine Chillz* park for her birthday. She wants Ayla there, some of her other school friends, Miss Winter, and the whole family. In that order."

Her mouth fell open and she shook her head. "Um. The amusement park?" she squeaked, then stopped, pressed her hands to the table, and closed her eyes.

His chest hurt for her, for how hard she was struggling. But she was about to dump him and he needed to brace himself.

After a few breaths, she opened her eyes and said, "Okay."

"Okay?"

She nodded way too hard. "Yeah. It's her birthday. It's about her and her wishes. I haven't planned anything. I've been off my game so it's good she knows what she wants."

Cam could only stare at her.

Adrianna gave him a tiny smile. "I know you're probably thinking I'm crazy. At times I do too. I had some time to clean, and do the books, and organize my office, and go through inventory." She pressed her hand to her head. "It helps me think."

Cam resisted the urge to smile. "I know."

Her lips curved again into a bigger smile. "Anyway, I had time to think and with the help of my mom, I realized that I'm overprotecting Bron. I'm so afraid of losing her..." She sighed. "I can't keep her locked up in here, no matter how much I want to. So, thank you."

He could only blink.

"Thank you, Cam, for doing what needed to be done. I'm not going to say I liked it this morning or that I didn't curse you for the first couple of hours, but you did what was right. What her neurotic mom couldn't seem to do in that moment. You put her first. That's what a good father does."

Cam's throat swelled. He was so taken aback by her words. He'd been preparing all day for her to tell him it was definitely over. He didn't expect this… "Adri…"

He couldn't think of anything to say.

"I'm happy you're in her life."

Her life. Bron's life. Fuck his life.

"And mine."

His heart slammed against his ribs and he coughed out a breath. *Huh*? "I thought you blamed me for everything that happened."

She shook her head. "I never blamed you, Cam. I blamed the way we affect each other when we fight. I mostly blamed myself. I'm the more experienced parent. I should have known better."

"I thought that was bullshit you were saying to let me off the hook."

"Seriously?" She rolled her eyes. She moved to the chair Bron left vacant.

"I was wrong. We shouldn't go our own way. Thank you for showing me we can handle things better and we can be pissed off without going nuclear."

She touched her palms to his face. "I love you, Cam. I need you."

She touched her lips to his, a little tentative, her taste exploding in his mouth. He'd missed her mouth, her body, her smiles, her touch for so many days. Yet, he couldn't do a thing. He was dumbfounded. She'd frozen him in place.

"I thought you were going to tell me to leave."

She smiled. "And let you take the other half of my heart? I don't think so. Bron's the left side and you're the right. I can't live without either of you."

This time he smiled so hard his face hurt and pulled her into his lap. His lips crushed hers but he made sure his hands stayed on her upper back. She hmmmed into his mouth and pressed herself closer.

"Not again."

They broke away laughing.

She pressed another brief kiss to his mouth and moved across the room to help their daughter, her hips swaying away.

"We'll continue this later," she shot above her shoulder.

He wasn't sure what tightened more, his groin or his heart. Yeah, they would continue that late into the night. "You got yourself a deal, better yet, a promise."

She turned her head over her shoulder, her lashes lowered and her lips parted and held his gaze for a second. The little smirk before she turned away said it all. She was going to hold him to that promise.

The End

WANT MORE CAM & ADRI?

If you can't get enough of Adri, Cam, and the adorable Bron, check out my FREE Christmas short story, *All I Ever Wanted*. It's the epilogue to The Summer I Loved You. And you can get it right now! I hope you enjoy it.

You can also see more of this adorable trio by reading the next book in series, The Winter of My Love. Flip over to the next page to read an excerpt.

WANT MORE CAM & ADRI?

Thank you so much for reading The Summer I Loved You. I hope you enjoyed every minute of it. I would love to know your thoughts and would love it. If you can find it in your heart to leave a review.

JL

ACKNOWLEDGMENTS

Thanks to Deranged Doctor Designs for the amazing cover. You found Adri and Cam! Thank you to my lovely editor Nina S. Gooden and my proofreader Katie Testa. Also, thank you to my pot coach Kimberly Kessler.

My critique partners Shadow Leitner, and Laralyn Doran, Robin Lynn and a very special *thank you* to Audrey Couloumbis and Cate Tayler for being my rocks through this book. My Alpha reader Angil for being the cheerleader I always need.

Thank you to my group of supportive friends John, Vivian, Crystal, Maria, Felia, Marisol, Kakazi, Vera, Nancy, The Lake House Writers, The Domingo crowd, and my LPHIDs.

Thank you to, my amazing family. Papi, Mami, my stepmom, my brothers and sister, uncles, aunts, nieces and nephews, and my sweet Trinity. I wouldn't be here without any of them.

Thank you to everyone who supports me, reads my books, and indulges my muse.

ABOUT THE AUTHOR

J. L. Lora is a Dominican-American author. Her stories explore the dark side of good characters, people living in the gray areas of life while playing the cards life has dealt them. She loves strong heroines and their equally powerful Men. She currently lives in Maryland, pursuing her dream of writing compelling, sexy, can't-put-down stories about empowered, badass alpha heroines and take-your-breath-away alpha heroes. You can find her and or chat her up on Social Media.

Sign up for her newsletter and learn more about new releases, events, news, freebies and much more at **www.JLLora.com**.

You can also join *The Gray Area*, JL's private reader group on Facebook.

facebook.com/AuthorJLLora

twitter.com/jtothelove

instagram.com/jllora

bookbub.com/profile/j-l-lora

BOOKS BY J. L. LORA

The Trinity

BOSS

MADE

STEEL

A Love for All Seasons Series

THE SUMMER I LOVED YOU

THE WINTER OF MY LOVE

THE LONGEST DAY — *Novella*

THE AUTUMN YOU BECAME MINE

THE SPRING OF MY HEART (TBA)

Sometimes Love Happens Standalone Series

SOME NIGHTS

SOME MORNINGS

SOME DAYS

WHEN YOU BREAK GIRL CODE

Free Short Stories

ALL I EVER WANTED — The Summer I Loved You - *Epilogue*

En Español

Ella es La Jefa

Hecha Y Derecha